She fought the slithering fear. He wouldn't hurt her; she just had to reason with him through the daze of alcohol. She pushed against his chest to gain distance and chose her words carefully. "I'm sorry if you misinterpreted my friendship gestures. But I care for— no, I love Edward. Very much. Please, please go and be happy for us. We'll put this incident behind us. Forget it ever happened." She would keep this intrusion their secret. She owed him that much.

He paused as if contemplating her plea. She gained hope that he had accepted her explanation. He would leave peacefully.

Instead, the spurned suitor pulled her tighter. "You'll be with me, or nobody." He covered her mouth with hard, demanding lips.

Survival instinct kicked in. She brought up a knee, hard, to his tender maleness, and wrested away to scream—

"Tess. Wake up."

The authoritative male voice pierced her mind and she struggled to rise from the frightening scene. She finally broke through the filmy veil of unconsciousness. Her body trembled with remnants of fear and horror. She shot up in the bed and cried out, her words searing the quiet.

"My husband didn't kill me!"

D1276119

Praise for Sandra L. Young . . .

"…Sandra L. Young walks us back in time to a murder/suicide mystery in 1913 that will keep the reader as spellbound as the lovely vintage clothing the author so adroitly describes. Well-written and woven with enough sexual tension to strum any romantic's heartstrings. I give Divine Vintage 5 stars…"

~Catherine Lanigan, International best-selling author

~*~

"A captivating story that had me hooked from the first page and kept me guessing until the last. An excellent debut novel."

~Rachael Richey, author of The Nighthawk Series

~*~

"…A distinctive new voice who innately captures the music and wonder of falling in love. Divine Vintage is the delightful story of two people drawn together by their corporeal connection with a pair of lovers tragically separated a century ago…"

~Elizabeth Hein, author

Divine Vintage

by

Sandra L. Young

Shay – Enjoy the Divine Vintage adventure!

Sandra L. Young

This is a work of fiction. Names, characters, places, and incidents are either the product of the author's imagination or are used fictitiously, and any resemblance to actual persons living or dead, business establishments, events, or locales, is entirely coincidental.

Divine Vintage

COPYRIGHT © 2022 by Sandra L. Young

All rights reserved. No part of this book may be used or reproduced in any manner whatsoever without written permission of the author or The Wild Rose Press, Inc. except in the case of brief quotations embodied in critical articles or reviews.
Contact Information: info@thewildrosepress.com

Cover Art by *Diana Carlile*

The Wild Rose Press, Inc.
PO Box 708
Adams Basin, NY 14410-0708
Visit us at www.thewildrosepress.com

Publishing History
First Edition, 2022
Trade Paperback ISBN 978-1-5092-3823-1
Digital ISBN 978-1-5092-3824-8

Published in the United States of America

Acknowledgments

Tess and Trey have waited several years for their story to be told. My gratitude to Editor Kaycee Johns for falling for them, too. As I continue along this writing journey, I keep learning and improving and very much appreciate other writers and my supportive friends and family members. This includes members of the Women's Fiction Writers Association and the WFWA critique group, and enthusiastic early supporters and readers such as Catherine Lanigan, Ann, Cheri, Christine and Tom, Dori, Jeane, Kim, Sheila, Susie, Susan G., and Pat.

Also, to Kristen, my sensitivity reader, for the homeless issue. Both of us have worked with scores of dedicated individuals and agencies to improve the lives of those most at-risk.

Much love to my parents, who raised me in the Illinois farmlands.

And to my biggest fan and sweetheart, Rick Swanson—thanks for indulging my writing passion and LARGE vintage clothing collection! Readers who would like to see the garments that inspired the descriptions in this book can find them on my web site: SandraYoungAuthor.com.

Chapter One
May 2013

Tess Burton swept a handful of frothy fabric up to the mid-morning light that streamed through the shop's bay window. The flapper gown was perfect, with no moth holes or stains.

Cradling the dress in both hands, she walked toward her new assistant. "I let my heart rule and pushed my price limit when I bought this yesterday."

Attending auctions and estate sales was a perk of her new adventure. On this sunny Tuesday in early May, they were prepping to offer Divine Vintage's finds to Michigan City, Indiana.

Tess' smile faded in recalling the responsibilities attached to a new business: a decades-old building, a very-part-time employee, and a bank loan. Her fingers tightened on the dress. She'd taken a massive risk in opening the shop. If Divine Vintage failed, she'd lose her dream career along with her inheritance. She could end up a bag lady at twenty-eight, wandering the streets with a knockoff knapsack.

She tried to shove back the insecurities as she reached the glass case that served as a central display and checkout counter. *Don't panic. Focus on the positives.* "You sure can't beat shopping in the name of business," she said. Though she'd have to avoid future splurges.

One hand on a stack of beaded sweaters, Marcy Alexander paused. She straightened to a height of six feet, her slim yet curvy frame topped by a mass of curling auburn hair. "Imagine a 1920s debutante floating down a staircase in such a showstopper. That dress is worth every cent."

"I totally agree. I can't resist a garment when its history speaks to me."

Without a warning, Tess found herself submerged into a vision of the beaded aqua gown swishing around the calves of the first proud owner. An elusive tune played in her ears, followed by a burst of laughter. Her breathing sped up, as if she were dancing a fox trot with a dashing partner. As she and the man twirled toward the center of the dance floor, an exotic fragrance wafted from the fabric of the dress.

Tess clutched the dress to her chest and spun in a wide circle. The sounds and scent faded.

She stopped and blinked—and the world came back into focus. Yes, she really was standing in the middle of her new shop. Ten minutes before their initial opening.

Marcy clapped her hands, jangling the stacked bracelets on her wrists. "You're the belle of the ball." She grinned and resumed folding a sweater.

To calm the lingering sense of dizziness, Tess dipped her head and hid her relief. Marcy's artistic leanings left her unbothered by her boss's sometimes quirky behavior. Others might label her a nutjob.

She'd never shared how her imagination soared when she handled the most appealing vintage items. Trying on a wedding gown that dripped with lace, she'd experience the radiant confidence of a 1950s bride.

Steaming a chiffon prom dress called up a nervous, perspiring teen with a beehive hairdo. These were never fleeting images, but deeper, heart-tugging responses. She experienced an unexplainable empathy where, for a few pulsing seconds, she almost *became* these women.

Yet this latest incident had been more vivid. More real. Probably intensified by her nerves, Tess thought. The fox trot music flitted through her ears as she hung the dress so that it faced the entry door, as if to immediately draw the customers' attention.

Satisfied with the arrangement, she stepped back to take one last critical view of the shop from a newcomer's angle. Over weeks of cleaning, stocking, and decorating, she and Marcy had transformed the former candy store into a cozy boutique. She'd painted the walls herself, rolling on pale lavender with sage green accents. White wicker shelving units and hanging racks featured clothing grouped by type and era. Everything from aprons to earrings was for sale, including dozens of dresses: evening gowns, daywear, cocktail shifts, and mod minis.

Her brow wrinkled as she returned to the counter for her cup of low-fat cappuccino. "I should've brought champagne today. I was so caught up in going over details in my poor, frazzled brain, I hardly slept last night."

"We'll share a formal toast at the grand opening in a few weeks," Marcy soothed in a Zen voice. "For now, here's to a hot new business and a super-hot team."

"Team is the key word," Tess said, knowing she couldn't have handled all the demands without Marcy at her side. "The shop looks fantastic due to your flair. I'm very thankful."

She took a quick sip of coffee, hid the drink behind the counter, and re-checked her watch. She'd survived the anxiety-producing flurry of planning and hard work; the opening hour finally had arrived. She flattened her palm over her nervous stomach and glided to the door in her full-skirted '50s dress.

After one deep breath, she turned the deadbolt, flipped the sign to "open," and savored the moment. *My shop. My sweat. My tears. Even a drop of blood when I jabbed my thumb tacking on that loose button.* She grabbed a scarf and waved it in the air. "I now proclaim the opening of Divine Vintage."

"Woo hoo!" Marcy hooted support.

She draped the scarf on a mannequin and headed back toward the counter, a bit let down at the lack of true fanfare. "I hope the press releases and social media posts will coax a few people in today. Though Tuesdays probably won't—"

The door swung open with a merry chime from the attached bell. An elderly woman entered, with a man young enough to be her adult grandson. All rational thought evaporated into a fog between her ears.

The guy was downright gorgeous. Her former boyfriend—emphasis on "former"—was fine looking, but this one notched it up a full step. Heat flushed her cheeks as she met dark brown eyes, plush as 1930s velvet, under thick, honey-toned hair that lay obedient against his head, except for a cowlick near the right temple.

He caught and held her stare. Embarrassed, she dragged her eyes to his female companion. Tess gauged her as late seventies with coiffed white hair and a tailored suit. Though she was barely five feet herself, the woman who approached the counter at a spry clip was half a head shorter. Her much-taller companion followed.

"Welcome. You're our very first visitors," Tess managed a cheery greeting. "How can we help you at Divine Vintage?"

The woman laid a stack of flyers on the counter. "I'm Esther DeLeon, and I congratulate you on your lovely shop. I live in Carver House, and I thought your clientele would be especially interested in our upcoming special event." She spoke in a cultured tone, reminding Tess of ladies who lunch. "We're holding an anniversary tea and style show on Sunday to celebrate the centennial of the home. The proceeds will benefit one of our favorite causes, the local homeless shelter."

She glanced up at the man beside her. "Trey is my cousin's son. He insisted on driving me to deliver flyers after I sprained my wrist. I attempted to wrench out a stray tree that rooted in my prize hydrangeas." She lifted her other arm, revealing a bulky bandage.

"You know you should have called me to pull out the sapling." The voice matched his look—warm and sugar-coated. "I'll run past your place before or after work, anytime you need help." He patted her uninjured hand.

Gorgeous, paired with kind, thoughtful, and respectful of his elders. Now there's a keeper. Tess warned herself to remain professional, but the heat returned to her face as he stretched the hand toward her.

"Trey Dunmore, Boy Scout extraordinaire, at your service."

She joined in the laughter. "I didn't realize I'd moved to Green Gables. I'm—" She extended her hand

and stumbled, realizing she'd forgotten Marcy's presence. "Tess. Tess Burton. And…" Her mind blanked again as his hand enveloped hers. A whisper of indefinable sound echoed in her head. A spark—bordering on painful—shot up her arm and spread across her shoulders, raising the hairs on her neck.

Her eyes widened as his narrowed. She pulled her tingling fingers back and attempted to capture her thoughts. *Introductions. Open mouth. Speak.* She concentrated to form simple words. "This is my assistant, Marcy Alexander. We're happy to share your flyers."

"Good to meet you both." Seconds ticked before Trey Dunmore's searching expression cleared and he stretched his palm toward Marcy.

As they shared polite hellos, Tess breathed deep to calm her heart rate. She'd never experienced such a strong reaction with a person. Or a piece of clothing. Yet she couldn't dwell on the interaction; she couldn't afford to appear scattered and unprofessional. First impressions counted, especially in a new town.

The house was a safe topic. "Carver House. I enjoy seeing the grand old place when I walk past on one of my routes to the shop." She'd identified it by the historical marker on the wrought iron fencing. The rosy brick home dominated a corner lot, with mature trees and lush, flowering gardens. Though she kept a good pace on her walks, her steps always slowed as she daydreamed about living in such a mansion.

With the homeowner before her, she could only stammer, "The architecture's amazing, with the wrap-around porch and the turret. I can only imagine the lively history inside the walls."

Marcy nodded. "I grew up here, and that's my favorite house in town. Those stained-glass windows are to die for."

Esther DeLeon's brows drew together. She focused on the stack of flyers and aligned the edges with manicured fingernails. "Unfortunately, the early history was clouded by a sad tragedy. But we've risen above that." She raised her eyes, and her voice strengthened. "I couldn't let the century anniversary pass unnoticed. The mansion has been a private home within my family, and people always want to peek inside. I decided to celebrate and welcome visitors while also supporting charity."

A sad tragedy? Had an accident occurred during construction? Before Tess could ask, Trey jumped in. "Esther restored the beauty, inside and out. You might recognize the style as Queen Anne. Our ancestors apparently preferred Victorian romanticism." He grinned. "Sorry for the clinical tangent. A hazard of the trade."

"You're an architect?"

He craned his neck to examine the original tin ceiling tiles. "At a firm in New Buffalo. You've done a fine job repurposing this great old building."

Her gaze followed, delighted at the affirmation. She'd been adamant about salvaging the feature.

"With any old building you have to stay on top of the upkeep," he added. "Hopefully, you had a good inspector if you bought rather than renting. Hidden problems can cost a boatload of money."

Her pleasure withered. Did another know-it-all jerk lurk behind his attractive exterior? "I did my research, as always." She tried not to glare. "The owner didn't want to rent it anymore, so yes, I *own* the building. The inspector was highly recommended, and of course I'll keep up the maintenance."

He shrugged. "Just sayin'."

Her teeth gnashed, barely missing her tongue. She'd had her fill of defending her actions and plans with her ex. The silence grew awkward as Esther leaned closer to stare at her over rimless trifocals. Tess squirmed under the probing gaze and smoothed a hand over her hair. Was the older woman upset that she'd stood up for herself?

"Forgive me for staring, my dear." Esther's expression lightened. "Would you consider modeling for our style show? You'd be a perfect fit for the trousseau gown. I hadn't thought to include it due to the small size, but what a treat to add a special dress dating back to the centennial."

"Sometimes being small is an advantage. Except when it comes to high shelves." Tess was glad to move past the minor friction with Trey. "That sounds like a perfect afternoon to me. Will all the models be wearing vintage clothing?"

"Yes. The garments are from former inhabitants of Carver House. Our ancestors stored some of their pretty dresses in the attic. The oldest are quite tiny." Her voice rose with enthusiasm. "Thankfully, the century-old wedding tuxedo fits Trey like it was made for him."

His mouth turned down, but the look was tinged with humor. "Esther caught me at a weak moment."

The older woman didn't even spare him a glance as she patted his arm. "You're family, dear."

Conversely, Marcy watched him with animated interest. Tess imagined her assistant swallowing a contented sigh. Then she mentally kicked herself to straighten up and behave. The guy was attractive— despite his comments about her building—but the encounter had tilted her precarious balance on this all-important day.

Esther drew her attention again. "I do hope you're free to join us on Sunday."

Tess smiled at her with true anticipation. "I'm always up for a vintage adventure. I'd be honored." She picked up a flyer to scan the details. "Should I stop in sooner to ensure the fit?"

"I'm certain the dress will work." She appeared almost girlish in her glee. "Come by around noon. I'll orient you and provide a quick tour."

"Wonderful. I can't wait." The delightful lady evoked memories of her beloved grandmother. And what a treat it would be to see the inside of her home. No doubt the previous inhabitants had owned some impressive garments. Maybe one day the family would sell the pieces. Tess would appreciate a chance to purchase them.

While Esther beamed, Trey's expression remained cryptic. His gaze lingered on Tess, and another flush of heat traveled through her body, spreading slowly, unnervingly, downward. She held his eyes for another loaded moment, experiencing a flash of déjà vu. *Another time; another place.*

She pushed aside the strange, fleeting thought, and the reminder of their earlier charged handshake. The hum in her body had to result from potent opening day emotions. Plus, she'd attempted to boost her energy earlier with pastry and caffeine. After this distressing encounter, she might have to give in to a second eclair.

But first, she had to fulfill her role as a gracious business owner. She'd faltered a little with her snippy tone about the building. "Thank you for visiting today, Mrs. DeLeon. I'll see you this weekend." *Both of you...*

"Please, call me Esther." The lady halted to grasp her hand. "You are doing me a great favor, but now we need to distribute more flyers. Trey is such the workaholic I must make the most of the time he's taking from his busy schedule."

He rolled his eyes and mocked a servant-like stance as he held the door. Esther lifted an eyebrow at him and addressed Tess. "I promise to visit again, when I have time to browse." She stepped outside, her pouf of hair shining in the sunlight.

Trey flashed another sexy grin. "You've made her day. Thank you, ladies."

Tess smiled back, though her lips quivered. He headed out the door, and she watched them walk down the sidewalk. She wondered how he'd act toward her on Sunday. He'd likely be surrounded by pining women and they'd barely speak.

Probably for the best. Her previous failed relationship had damaged her confidence and soured her on romance. She glanced up at Marcy. "How about you handle it out here for a while, and I'll check for web orders. Wasn't that a fun way to kick off our opening day?"

"Fun?" As she snorted out a laugh, the diamond stud in her nose sparked light. "Trey Dunmore's the yummiest eye candy I've seen in a looong time. To my utter dismay, he only had eyes for you."

"You noticed I wasn't thrilled with his comments about the building. What you saw as interest was pure politeness. A man who'd escort an injured older lady to a vintage shop must have been a Boy Scout for real." Tess turned, intent on retreating to her tiny office.

"You make him sound boring, but your reaction seemed pretty intense in the moment."

"What do you mean?" She whirled to see Marcy's teasing smirk and smiled back. "Very funny. Yes, he's a tad intriguing. But my real interest was sparked by Carver House's 'sad tragedy.' Esther's comment was vague and mysterious."

"I think there's talk of a murder in the house's history." Marcy's eyes danced with excitement. "Ooh, maybe you'll see a ghost."

Despite her assistant's hopeful expression, she chose her words with caution. No need to tempt the universe. "Personally, I'd rather not run into any ghosts. Although my grandmother told me spirits are always here with us. She was kind of…attuned that way."

"Are you saying she was psychic?"

Though she recognized a potential kindred spirit, from habit, she wiggled around a direct answer. "Not that I know of, but she was comfortable with the concept of communicating with the deceased. My parents were straight and narrow farm folks and weren't happy with Gram sharing those far-out ideas." She hesitated. "I thought we'd have more time to sneak in some discussions. She was gone way too soon."

"She sounds really special."

As Tess gazed at the window display, her eyes filmed with tears. How she wished her grandmother could have been here to share this special day. "Gram was an incredible, creative person, and she gave me the greatest gift ever. I could ditch my stressful bank marketing career to embrace our love of vintage clothing. I uprooted and remade my life, thanks to her. I know she'd approve of this gamble."

The shop also provided a lifeline to regain a positive outlook after the draining relationship with Brett, but she wouldn't grant him any headspace today. "Anyway, I'm excited about modeling a beautiful dress and spreading the news about Divine Vintage."

"What a burden that hunky cousin Trey will be modeling, too." Marcy's curls bounced as she angled her hand downward for an enthusiastic high five. Tess reached to meet her palm and mirrored her wide smile.

They pulled apart as the bell tinkled to admit the mail carrier. "Happy opening day. Looks like you gals are having a much better time than I am," he said, with a wink and a flourish of envelopes.

Chapter Two

On Saturday afternoon, Trey rolled the push lawnmower into his garage before trotting into the lakeside house he'd designed two years earlier. The clean Craftsman lines and efficient, open layout met all his needs. He'd achieved that aim by being hands-on with the process.

Before starting the mowing, he'd opened the windows to draw in the breeze. Now he wished he'd turned on the air as sweat trickled beneath his T-shirt. Not that he had a big yard, but he had pushed through at a jog today. A counselor probably would tell him he was trying to outrun his thoughts.

The effort had tanked. He'd envisioned Tess Burton throughout the mindless task. The glossy dark hair that would wrap around his fingers like silk. Translucent skin heightened by a sweet blush he hoped he'd put there. And those mesmerizing, wide-set eyes. Hazel? Was that really a color?

To his dismay, four days later, his imagination continued to rev. "Static," he mumbled, recalling the sizzle of energy that had jumped up his arm when their hands clasped. "Nothing more." Yet he'd watched her eyes widen with surprise.

Weirdly, neither of them acknowledged it. They dropped hands and moved on. He'd offered a shake to her assistant, as a kind of test. No sizzle there.

Trey entered the house and pulled off his damp shirt, tossing it into the washer. He grabbed a beer from the fridge, thinking while Tess tilted toward beauty, Marcy was attractive, too. More on the "darn cute" scale with fine curves and legs like a Vegas showgirl. But Tess' petite package drew him. She seemed smart, confident, a little fiery maybe. He'd picked up on the heat when he'd commented about the building she *owned*. His lip curled remembering her pointed establishment of the fact.

He took a long pull of the beer, catching the time on the overhead clock. In twenty-four hours, he'd be modeling in the show with her. No doubt his mother and Esther would have matchmaking on their minds. When they'd left the shop, Esther had paused before entering the neighboring jewelry store. "How delightful. Such a pretty girl." She'd flashed an over-innocent smile.

Trey hadn't had to ask which one she meant. Esther had spent the months since his break-up keeping an eye on his nonexistent love life. She and his mom figured he'd had time to regroup and move on. They didn't realize the complicated relationship—and the way she'd ended it—had left him flailing. Resembling a fish who breaks the line but takes the hook with him. Tess Burton might be appealing, but Trey wasn't about to dive into such murky waters again.

Chapter Three

Tess hummed a little tune on Sunday and swung her arms with the rhythm as she walked the few blocks to Carver House. She enjoyed the glimpses into other people's lives as they planted flowers, mowed lawns, and chatted or read on front porches. Some offered friendly smiles—though a couple of folks shot surprised glances as she strutted by. She waved, used to such reactions when she donned vintage attire. She'd worn a rose-patterned 1960s dress, one that energized her with a partygoing aura. Meeting Esther's guests could translate to building a solid customer base, and she needed to put her best foot forward. In this case, a red patent leather heel.

A handful of cars and bicyclists passed her, driving down the tree-lined avenue at an unhurried pace. While Michigan City wasn't a bustling metropolis, Tess looked forward to getting to know the town and her neighbors. After a while, she'd likely run into somebody she knew most every time she headed out. There was comfort in the thought. Instead of an anonymous concrete and steel cityscape, she was surrounded by historic homes with abundant trees and gardens, offering shade and enticing scents. A perfect middle ground between a big city and the Illinois farmstead where she'd grown up. Hopefully, she and her business would flourish here.

Despite her initial doubts and jitters, shoppers had flowed into Divine Vintage over the past five days. All had complimented the merchandise and ambience; yet none carried the impact of their inaugural visitors.

She still couldn't wrap her head around the jolting handshake with Trey Dunmore. She'd denied her interest to Marcy, but the connection only added to his intrigue. He slipped into her thoughts several times a day, despite his mixed messages and her best intentions. The images knocked her off-guard as she entered numbers in the bookkeeping program or brainstormed marketing ideas. She'd start daydreaming and analyzing, only to find herself staring at the same figures a half hour later.

Trey Dunmore was a puzzle. She preferred clear answers and logic.

And she'd be seeing him very soon. Her heartbeat accelerated as she spotted Carver House from a block away. With three brick stories, the majestic home dwarfed the neighbors, embracing tall, un-shuttered windows, scrolling white trim, and a jutting turret. She drew nearer to admire the white rail porch stretched across the front. Wicker furniture provided an inviting welcome on this sun-splashed day. The scent of lilacs floated on the air. Tess sniffed the sweetness and relished the warm spring afternoon. She wondered if the bushes had greeted passersby for the past century.

She moved up the wooden steps and rapped the brass knocker. After a few seconds, the door opened to reveal an attractive lady with a smooth cap of white-blonde hair and a wide smile.

"You must be Tess. Esther was right, you'll look precious in the gown. Your dress, by the way, is adorable." She stood aside to let her enter and offered a soft hand to shake. "I'm Clarice. Esther's cousin, and Trey's mother. We're so pleased you could join us. The show will be absolutely fabulous."

Trey's mother. *But where is your son? Did he mention meeting me?*

She bit back the revealing questions. "I love your emerald-green dress, too. The fifties were a fun era for fashion."

"Yes, they were. I was born at the end of the decade though, so I discovered my fashion sense in the boring seventies. Such a shame. Please, come inside."

Tess followed her clicking heels through a trail of perfume. They passed through a wood-paneled hall to enter a large parlor. She took in coffered ceilings, long windows topped by shimmering stained glass panels, and an oriental rug atop cherry wood floors. The picture of understated wealth and elegance.

"Lovely, isn't it?" Clarice asked. "We're fortunate the house has stayed in the family. Though I prefer a maintenance-free condo."

"I grew up in an 1880s Victorian," Tess said. "I appreciate the history in such a luxurious setting." A side table bore a trio of silver-rimmed photos, and she recognized Esther with another woman, bearing a marked resemblance. A young couple faced the camera with an angelic blond child. Trey Dunmore flashed a devil-may-care grin from the hull of a sailboat.

Her pulse kicked at seeing his image, and she moved closer. The table was covered by a swath of black velvet, with fringe dancing from a gust of air conditioning. She bent toward the photos and rested her fingertips on the shawl. A shiver skimmed through her system. Somehow, she knew cloth had also draped a coffin.

Her pleasure at viewing Trey's photo vanished under a sweep of indefinable sadness. The sensation radiated from her chest, pressing against her heart. She caught her breath in short gasps and tried not to hyperventilate. Her previous reactions to clothing resembled mellow daydreams. This was a heightened, chilling…submersion.

"Are you cold, dear? I don't like air conditioning, but occasionally I have to give in and turn it on."

Tess startled and jerked her fingers away from the shawl. Her eyes met Esther's. She hadn't even noticed her entering. She shook her head as the strange heaviness left her body. "I'm fine. Thank you." She hoped she sounded normal. She turned away from the table to collect herself. "I was admiring your pictures, and I see you also have several lovely, decorative pieces. Some look familiar. I guess I might've seen something similar in a museum."

"Perhaps you did," Clarice said. "Many of them are original to the house. Esther has been a wonderful caretaker."

The older woman moved toward them. "I was always drawn by the place, and I was the only third-generation relative who wanted to live here. I was fortunate to be able to move in several years ago after my husband passed. With my dear housekeeper's assistance."

Her reaction to the shawl hovered in her mind as Tess posed a careful question. "At the shop, you mentioned a tragedy connected to the early history?"

Esther frowned.

She offered a hurried apology. "I'm sorry. I shouldn't ask."

"Of course, you're interested." Esther held up a hand, her expression still troubled. "The story, unfortunately, is a painful one. The mansion was built by Edward Carver for his young bride, Phoebe. She was very beautiful. He was said to be completely enamored. They moved in after their wedding for a few days to prepare for an extended Paris honeymoon. The night before they left, apparently, they argued. Edward strangled Phoebe before turning a gun on himself."

Tess had been captivated by the romance until the slap of the shocking final sentence. Another quiver skimmed through the center of her body, and she wrapped her arms around her waist. "That is tragic."

"Yes. And a terrible scandal. The house was shut up for years before Teddy, one of Edward's cousins, determined he was destined to live in such luxury and moved in his small brood. Teddy was my grandfather. My mother grew up here, and I have only positive memories. Including my Sweet Sixteen party in the ballroom we'll be using today."

Her lips tugged up. "People sometimes ask if I've seen ghosts here. Occasionally I've had an odd feeling we're not alone but nothing I can pin to Edward and Phoebe." She raised her chin. "You've come by early to try on one of her trousseau gowns. The dress was among the exceptional wardrobe she planned to take on their honeymoon."

Clarice whisked a dark-purple garment off the settee. "Sadly, their trunks were shuffled off, fully packed, to the attic. But today, we'll only have happy thoughts as you wear this."

Tess attempted to calm her own whirling thoughts. What a horrible way to die. The poor young woman never had the chance to raise children, or to spend her years in a happy marriage. Instead, she met a violent end at the hands of a man who had stood before witnesses declaring his devotion. *And what would her trousseau dress relay today?* After the earlier sensations, she was reluctant to handle it.

"You can change in the first of the second-floor bedrooms, to the left." Clarice said. "Pardon us. We have several details to wrap up before our guests arrive."

She extended the dress toward Tess. "You saw the staircase when we entered."

"Yes." She forced her hands to close around the garment. Nervous anticipation infused her body, and she knew the emotion came from the dress. The sensation peaked and gentled into a sort of calm acceptance—unsettling, yet not alarming. Thank goodness.

"I'll see you soon," she told her hosts.

Clarice and Esther exited through the opposite doorway. She stood alone in the room and registered the luxurious satin against her fingers, akin to dipping them in heavy cream. She shook out the gown to admire the delicate lace at the neckline, which echoed from the elbow to the wrist. The simple design flowed to a long, slim skirt. She understood why Phoebe had intended to wear the delectable concoction in Paris. With a matching hat, she would have exhibited fashion sense and sophistication. She crossed the floor and skipped up the wide stairs, anxious to try it on.

As she neared the middle steps, the front door

opened and closed. She stopped and glanced down, to stare into Trey Dunmore's dark eyes as he stood framed in the entryway. He was more handsome than she remembered in a fog-gray cutaway coat with tails and matching trousers. Yet today he looked subdued. *Because he was wearing a murderer's tuxedo?*

Neither spoke for a few charged seconds as their eyes locked. The satin warmed in her hands as her heartbeat thudded in her throat. She opened her lips to break the silence, but Clarice's voice filtered in.

"Trey, since you've finally arrived, I could use your help. Please."

The corner of his mouth tugged up. "Duty calls. See you soon, Tess." He shifted and walked out of the room.

She savored the sound of her name on his tongue. Yet he'd said nothing of consequence. Had she again imagined a heightened intensity between them?

She reminded her fluttering heart she was here to further her business and continued on her way to the bedroom. She found it decorated with yards of rose-strewn chintz, hanging at the windows and draping the bed. When she removed her dress and spread it on the mattress, the pattern blended like a chameleon.

Tess raised her arms to slide the century-old satin over her body and the form-molding corset she'd put on at home. The fabric cascaded to the floor, cool and rich. She fumbled to close the tiny metal hooks on the left side, then dug out the slippers she'd carried in her purse. She put them on and moved toward the full-length mirror. Her reflection appeared soft and glowing.

A knock sounded at the door, and her pulse jumped again anticipating Trey's return. "Come in."

Clarice entered, her mouth rounding in an "O" of delight. "You are such a vision. Could I snap a photo of you and Trey before the others arrive?"

Not waiting for agreement, she hurried out of the room to lead up the next flight of stairs. "You two will be the hit of the show. We're expecting quite a crowd. But the ballroom has plenty of room. Esther mentioned her Sweet Sixteen was held here; I also enjoyed that family tradition. Though I doubt Esther snuck away to smoke a cigarette with her boyfriend, like I did." She smiled over her shoulder. "My first and last."

"I imagine she rebelled in her own way. She's got a lot of spirit." Tess lagged behind in the tight, heavy skirt as they swept past numerous paintings and sepia-toned photographs.

"That she does. Otherwise, she'd never have taken on this massive old place." At the third level, Clarice entered a set of French doors.

She followed into a sea of tables draped in snowy cloths, twinkling lights, and cascading floral arrangements. The finery dimmed as they drew near the man standing beside a grand piano.

"Trey, isn't Tess gorgeous in Phoebe's gown?" Clarice asked.

"Yes, Mother, she is." His eyes compelled as his lips slid into a grin. "Hello, Tess. Or should I say Phoebe?"

Her cheeks warmed. "Hello, Trey. We might not want to invoke her or Edward today. Esther told me their story earlier."

"Clarice," a voice beckoned from the hallway. "I need you for a moment."

"The caterer." Clarice shot an exasperated glance

toward the back of the room. "Get to know each other. I'll be right back. *Don't take off*."

"My mother, the whirling dervish." His fondness was apparent as her green dress faded from the room.

"She's charming. So is Esther."

"Yes. She's my favorite relation." He raised one honey-toned brow. "You are now aware of our tainted history?"

"Just the bare details. I never expected such a sad, distressing tale."

"I'm sorry if it upset you. I've never thought much about it. I've always connected the house with Esther. At least until she browbeat me into wearing this tuxedo."

"You were sweet to help her out." Tess ran a hand along the piano, picking up a scent of lemony polish. "Did you grow up in the area?"

"I spent my early years on the east coast." He leaned on the gleaming instrument, narrowing the space between them. "Mom moved back here after she and Dad divorced. Three years ago, she learned about an opening at an architecture firm in New Buffalo, across the border in Michigan. While the decision to move was a good one, she'll also tell you I let work consume me."

Before she could question the leading statement, he asked, "How about you? Are you a homegrown girl? If so, I should have relocated years ago."

He was tilting toward flirtation, Tess thought, pleased. "I grew up in a similar area in northern Illinois. I moved here a couple months ago to open Divine Vintage."

"How'd you come to settle here?" He seemed genuinely interested.

"I attended a work-related conference in the area last year. I picked up a brochure for the Uptown Arts District and decided to come back for a weekend visit with a friend." She raised her voice over the increased noise as the caterers plunked down silverware. "We drove down Franklin Street and saw a cozy corner building with a bay window and a For Sale notice. I already had the shop in mind; it seemed to be a sign."

Tess also had a very strong sense at that moment of her grandmother smiling down at her. She knew she'd found the perfect location and smiled at the memory. "We drove to the lakefront, and I felt such…tranquility. When I looked to the west, there was the hazy outline of downtown Chicago skyscrapers. I felt I could have the best of both worlds."

He held her gaze as he played a few trilling high notes on the keyboard. "Sounds like you belong here."

It took them a moment to realize his mother had returned. Tess saw her assessing smile. She probably was used to women falling all over her good-looking offspring.

Clarice raised her phone. "Move a little closer together. Pretend you're Edward and Phoebe. Before the wedding."

He smirked but obeyed, holding out his left hand. He bent it at the elbow, encouraging Tess to lay her right arm upon it. As their fingers touched, a hum skimmed through her ears. A crackling spark shot through her arm to her fingers. She pulled her hand back to see a brief, unreadable expression pass over his face. His arm dropped to his side. "Sorry. Static."

Was it? The charge had mirrored the one between them in the shop. She nodded mutely and faced the camera. He didn't attempt to touch her again.

"Come on, smile you two," his mother urged. "You'd make a gorgeous Edwardian fashion spread. Move together, please, so I can get a good full-length."

Trey shifted nearer.

"Wonderful. Now take her arm."

He grasped her elbow, and the flash exploded in two quick bursts of illumination. Clarice stepped away with a floating "thanks."

Tess blinked as the ballroom dimmed, cocooning them in a hazy dream. She turned to him and couldn't help staring. One could lose herself in those soft brown eyes surrounded by thick lashes any female would envy. With her eyes fixed on his face, his image wavered and blurred in a bewildering transposition of features: a broadening of the nose and softening of the chin; longer sideburns dipping below his ears. She inhaled the scent of Bay Rum cologne as her equilibrium swam.

He turned her toward him and captured her lower arms. She registered the warmth of his hands penetrating the lace. "You would absolutely adore Paris. That gown is comely, but the House of Worth would dress you as a princess. I shall give you furs, jewels, a beautiful home—anything you could ever want. You know how strongly I feel about you." His voice was husky with emotion. "Please, just say yes."

He'd been building to the declaration for weeks. Dropping hints that she had coyly smiled away or pretended to misunderstand. She certainly hadn't expected a proposal today, when they had made a furtive temporary escape from her parents' annual May Day party.

The lips were smiling, but his dark eyes compelled her to comply with his urgent proposal. His hands gripped her arms, perhaps more tightly than intended. "Will you have me wait for an answer, pacing the floors, while you weigh your options? Dearest," he leaned in, and his breath caressed her ear. "I am yours, and only yours, forever."

She closed her eyes, reopening them to his ardent gaze. Of course, she would make the right decision, to link with the promise of adoration and security. Her whispered reply shook them both. "Yes…"

A shattering of glass drove through her consciousness. Tess blinked back into the sunlit ballroom.

"Will someone grab a broom?" Clarice called from across the room.

Trey's lips parted, but he hesitated. He gazed at Tess with a puzzled expression before responding to his mother. "I'll get it. Excuse me, Tess." He moved from her so quickly she swayed toward the piano.

She lifted her hands to cup her warm cheeks, feeling dizzy and disoriented. She peered around the room at the wait staff filling water glasses. Hopefully, no one had noticed her momentary drifting away. Though Trey had seemed to gather something was off. He'd certainly made a fast escape.

What exactly had she imagined? She'd never envisioned *herself* in the clothing before. The interludes had been vague, more impressions than visions. Tess took a moment to regroup mentally and physically and took careful steps toward Clarice to gather further instructions. *You need sleep*, she told herself. Tonight, she'd get more than five hours. Even if it meant swallowing a sleeping pill.

She was directed to wait in a mid-sized room across the hall, where she joined the growing flock of amateur models. Their voices pitched high with excitement as they waited to parade in the ballroom.

As the sole male, Trey drew several interested glances when he entered. Yet he maintained distance, consulting his phone in a corner. Tess moved through the chattering group, exclaiming at a depression-era, cape-sleeved dress. A pouffy formal exuded its own bouncy personality as she helped smooth layers of net. This was what she expected from clothing with a rich history. Feelings, certainly, but not voices. Not distinctive faces.

She couldn't disregard the scene she'd imagined in the ballroom, but she couldn't allow it to shadow the style show. She'd analyze the details later. She moved on to appreciate a royal blue cocktail dress with bulky shoulder pads—a style straight out of the '80s. The petite wearer told her the dress was Esther's.

She skirted around Trey, though she felt his eyes on her as she examined the well-maintained clothing. *Does he realize I'm avoiding him?* she wondered. *Did he sense something odd happened up there*? No way she would ask him.

Too soon, the minutes slid by and the other models were summoned for their moments of glory. He moved from the corner to her side. They'd been instructed to enter together.

"Nervous?" he asked softly.

Of modeling, or of you?

"A little." She caught their reflection in a full-length mirror. In the period clothing, with her upswept hairdo, they were the epitome of Edwardian fashion. Tess started to comment on the style but found herself clutching his arm as his features again wavered and changed.

"Save this one for the captain's table. The gown will remain my favorite as I'll remember you saying 'yes.' Making me the happiest man alive." He lifted a finger to her chin. "I promise to make you happy, my darling." His lashes swept down over jubilant dark eyes as he lowered his lips to hers.

"They're ready for you." Clarice's flushed face poked through the doorway.

Tess released Trey's arm, cursing the nerves that must be driving these weird episodes. A wave of unsteadiness swept her, and she debated whether she should sit down. Yet she didn't want to make a scene and hold up the show. He stared at her for a few seconds and indicated she should proceed him.

"Our time to shine." She forced a smile to reassure him and followed Clarice out of the room. *You'll be fine*, she told herself as his footsteps echoed behind her. In a few minutes she could relax, prop her feet up, and enjoy one of the mimosas she'd seen on the tables.

She concentrated on climbing the stairs toward the ballroom entrance, lifting the gown so she wouldn't trip. Feminine laughter and Esther's amplified voice became clearer as they reached the now-crowded room. The tiny lights sparkled like a shower of diamonds, and the heady floral scent filled her nostrils. Glancing at the expectant, smiling faces, Tess experienced a floating sensation, as if she were wading underwater, blurring sound and details.

Only nerves, she pep-talked. *You can do this.*

Trey paused inside the French doors and extended his arm. His face expressed stiff reluctance. She drew a deep breath and placed her arm on his. They began the slow stroll down the center runway.

Esther narrated from the front of the room. "Ladies and gentlemen. A final treat. The groom's wedding tuxedo and an extravagant satin trousseau gown from our early family history in this graceful mansion. One hundred years later, you sit in their ballroom and welcome Edward and Phoebe Carver in a happy moment as they enter their new home."

Head high, Tess maintained a brave smile, and they promenaded to the end of the aisle. Trey's rigid arm muscles mirrored her own tension, and she grasped his hand beneath hers. They pivoted to face the avid eyes and applauding hands. She blinked twice, hard, as the faces dissolved into a graying mass. Her lips parted in silent protest as her knees buckled.

Chapter Four

Feeling like a prize steer being paraded before an auction, Trey's smile grew more wooden as he and Tess strolled among the tables. He'd mingle for a half hour to satisfy his mother and Esther, then race home to catch the ballgame. His musings jerked to a halt when he felt Tess' full weight lurch against his side. He glanced down to see if she'd stumbled and froze in disbelief. She hadn't broken a heel; she'd collapsed.

His heart pounded as he wrapped his arms around her and observed her colorless face. *Crap.* He lifted her into his arms, and his eyes cut to Esther. If they'd hidden this secret ending from him, he'd share some choice words later.

She didn't appear to be faking. A gasp rippled through the room. Esther murmured breathlessly at the mic, "Oh, my. This is not part of the program. Trey, please take Miss Burton to the master suite." She paused to look around the crowd. "I know this sounds terribly trite, but is there a doctor or nurse in the house?"

A tall, lanky woman stood up from a back table. "I'm a nurse."

Trey headed toward her, Tess' head lolling in his arms. "Follow me," he barked and led the way through the doors. His emotions flared with concern at her labored breathing.

His mother trailed behind. "What's wrong with her? Did she say she didn't feel well? That tight waist might be stifling her."

"Mother. Hush."

His words halted further conversation. She might be right, but he was too rattled to talk. Cradling the slim body to his chest, he headed to the largest bedroom on the second floor. Inside, he bent to lay Tess in the carved wooden bed, then stepped aside as the nurse joined them.

With efficient movements, she took a pulse. "Forty. Quite low." She reached around to unhook the band of lace at the top of the dress. "Can someone get me a wet cloth?"

His own pulse raced as he ran to the attached bathroom and sloshed a washcloth under the faucet. What in the world was wrong with her? She had seemed jumpy and distant after the shock of static passed between them in the ballroom.

Hell, he'd be lying if he didn't admit to his own discomfort at the unnerving reminder of their handshake at her shop. He'd reacted by keeping his distance while they'd waited in the bedroom. He wished now he'd talked to her more. If she'd told him she wasn't feeling well, he might have helped head off this extreme reaction.

He re-entered the bedroom and handed the damp towel to the nurse. He stood back and patted his mother's arm to reassure her. Yet he was as worried as she looked. They watched the woman sponge Tess' forehead. She moaned at the cool intrusion but didn't wake, her face still colorless against the pillow.

****

She shivered in her thin nightshift in the chill air, propped with pillows in the elaborate, carved walnut bed. Waiting for him. Her husband. They had married yesterday, with much pomp and circumstance at the Episcopal Church, applauded by dozens of their peers. After a sumptuous candlelight feast, they had retired here to Carver House, where he had triumphantly carried her over the threshold. She had been nervous, alone with him for the first time in this commanding bed. But the extra bottle of champagne had helped her relax. She had found him to be a gentle, slow, and generous lover.

She fingered the lace edging her virtuous white gown, thinking of the two additional nights they'd spend together before their departure on a glorious, long honeymoon. Her lips curved. Edward had released the small staff after they had settled in, to give them the utmost privacy. They could spend all day in bed if they desired, as their bags already were packed to sail to Paris on the SS France.

Despite the tragedy of the Titanic during the previous spring, he had assured her the liner would be safe and luxurious, with décor reflecting the palace of Versailles. He promised fittings at the House of Worth and tours of the French countryside, sipping leisurely coffees and wines at little cafes. They would make the rounds of the wondrous museums and attractions and visit specialty shops to bring home treasures for their new home.

Yes, she definitely had made the right choice in accepting this marriage. The door opened, and she smiled an invitation.

Her pleasure fluttered into confusion. "What are

you doing here? Get out of our bedchamber! Is this a rude joke?" She grasped the covers up to her neck as her heart pounded in her chest. The unwelcome visitor closed the door and advanced with an unsteady gait. The familiar, attractive features were almost unrecognizable, slack under red-rimmed eyes. Her nose wrinkled at the stink of stale liquor. She realized with shock that he still wore a tuxedo from the wedding, now rumpled, the shirt collar unbuttoned and askew.

"Phoebe, we both know you made a mistake by marrying Edward." He reached toward her as he spoke in a rapid, slurred tone. "Let's not compound it further. Get dressed, and I'll take you away. We never have to return here again. Come, make haste." He grabbed the bedcover and tugged, loosening her fierce grip.

She shrank back, unable to believe her ears. Had he lost his mind? Her mind whirled. Edward must not see him here. "You've been drinking. Go home. Please. After sleep, you'll think differently." She must convince him to leave, immediately. She strove for a convincing tone. "You know I am committed to Edward. I daresay he'll not forgive this trespass."

He clutched her arm so tightly she winced at the pain. "Trespass. Are you telling me you didn't invite my glances and encourage my flirtation? I could tell you really wanted me—someone who could bring gaiety into your life. Not stodgy Edward. I may not have his fortune, or his fine reputation, but I will care for all your needs."

He hauled her from the bed before she could protest. She slammed against his body, forcing the breath from her lungs. She gasped for air and twisted to avoid the sour stench of whiskey. "Let me go. Don't do something you'll regret forever."

"Then don't hide from the truth." His tone had gentled. "Look at me, dearest. Tell me you want to be with me, then dress and pack a small bag."

She fought the slithering fear. He wouldn't hurt her; she just had to reason with him through the daze of alcohol. She pushed against his chest to gain distance and chose her words carefully. "I'm sorry if you misinterpreted my friendship gestures. But I care for— no, I love Edward. Very much. Please, please go and be happy for us. We'll put this incident behind us. Forget it ever happened." She would keep this intrusion their secret. She owed him that much.

He paused as if contemplating her plea. She gained hope that he had accepted her explanation. He would leave peacefully.

Instead, the spurned suitor pulled her tighter. "You'll be with me, or nobody." He covered her mouth with hard, demanding lips.

Survival instinct kicked in. She brought up a knee, hard, to his tender maleness, and wrested away to scream—

"Tess. Tess. Wake up."

The authoritative male voice pierced her mind, and Tess struggled to rise from the frightening scene. She finally broke through the filmy veil of unconsciousness. Her body trembled with remnants of fear and horror. She shot up in the bed and cried out, her words searing the quiet room: "My husband didn't kill me!"

Chapter Five

Tess' lids closed, and her body slumped. Just as she'd experienced a sensation of sinking below water at the style show, she now floated up through the inky darkness toward the surface.

"What the hell?"

Trey Dunmore. Even in her woozy state, she identified his voice and lifted toward it. She opened her eyes and latched onto his hazy image, but the handsome features melded again into a familiar yet unknown man. Waves of panic rippled through her. She moaned and attempted to rise out of the fog cushioning her brain. With concentrated effort, she blinked a few times and pushed out the breath she hadn't been aware of holding. Three frowning faces loomed above her.

She shrank back. Her heart clanged against her ribs, as it did when she awakened from a disturbing dream. She was lying on a bed, surrounded by semi-strangers. "Wh—what's happening?" Her voice was a bare whisper.

A tall woman with cropped hair encircled her wrist with cool fingers. "You fainted, dear. My name is Jean, and I'm a nurse. Do you mind if I take your pulse again?"

Tess nodded. The woman's grasp was professional and efficient, and the demeanor helped calm her jittering system.

"She appears to be coming back to normal." Jean laid her wrist back on the comforter and looked toward Trey and Clarice. Their arched brows mirrored apprehension. "After you get out of this restrictive clothing, you should consider going to urgent care. And schedule a checkup with your doctor."

Clarice leaned forward, her hands clasped tight. "What she said to us. Where did that come from?"

"I'm not a counselor. Possibly just the drama of the day. Have you read or watched any murder mysteries lately?"

"No. Really, I'll be fine." Tess registered the sharp prod of a bobby pin in her loosening updo. She wanted to swing her legs over the edge and trot away from the crazy situation, but she didn't dare try to stand. "I'm so sorry, and embarrassed. I've never fainted in my life."

She closed her eyes to avoid their probing gazes, and her mind began to whirl again, shifting through a collage of vivid images. She dragged her lids open. The least she could do was offer gratitude for their support. "Thank you all for your help."

Clarice took her hand, her usual spark subdued. "Lie here for a bit. I'll be right back. I want to reassure our guests and Esther."

Tess caught her pointed glance at Trey. She struggled to sit up in the heavy dress as Clarice ushered the nurse from the room. He slipped through a second doorway in the room and returned with a glass of water. He held it out without a word. She drank, the simple action helping to distract and calm her.

She avoided his gaze. She couldn't offer a plausible explanation for what had happened. She'd entertained fanciful scenes in her mind plenty of times, but none had shaken or frightened her. What had possessed her to dream up such a scenario? Without any answers, she finished drinking and attempted to move past the awkwardness. "I must have scared everyone silly."

He regarded her with caution. "To say you surprised us is a huge understatement. I imagine a few of the guests believe my mother planned this dramatic showstopper." He glanced toward the doorway. "Are you really all right now?"

"More or less." Was he worried about being alone with her? Her spirits sank lower, but she couldn't fault him. She doubted her own stability. It didn't help that she had no knowledge of what had occurred after she fainted, including how long she'd been out. "What exactly happened after I went down for the count?"

The corner of his mouth finally lifted. "My racquetball reflexes kicked in, and I caught you. Esther asked for medical help. Mom and I led Jean here to the bedroom. You were out of it, but fidgety. We were going to call an ambulance. Then you sat up." He stared over her head.

"And…" she prodded.

He rubbed a hand over his jaw. "You said your husband didn't kill you."

His words unleashed the torrent of images. This time, Tess focused inward in an attempt to process them. She jolted onto a scene of a woman who seemed to be fighting for her life. She tried to shake the searing picture out of her mind, but it remained, taunting her.

"Just a dream," she whispered. Her trembling fingers loosened on the glass, and water streamed out, dampening the bedspread. With a gasp, she scooted away to protect the gown.

He grabbed the glass before it rolled off the bed, frowned, and backed away. "I'll get a towel."

Tess gathered the skirt close as her thoughts tumbled to the other strange occurrences during the day. She realized the dark-haired woman in the images resembled her. The handsome man bore a strong likeness to Trey.

A familial likeness. Had Esther's tale about the murder triggered her imagination to place her in the clothing with a Trey look-alike? And how had she been so sure the encounter had turned deadly? Apparently, she'd said as much when she awakened.

He returned and blotted up the water. She watched his hands, considering her next words. What she was about to say sounded crazy and would bolster his decision to maintain distance. Yet it was the right thing to do. The *only* thing she could do.

"I'm not sure I should tell you this, but…" She wavered as he straightened, eyes lasered on hers. "Today I've been having flashes, you might say. Of people, who I think are Phoebe and Edward."

His fingers tensed around the towel. A few droplets fell to the floor. "What exactly do you mean?"

"Kind of like…we've slipped away. And they're here instead." She rushed on before losing her nerve. "I know it sounds crazy, but have you felt anything…peculiar…today?"

He stared at her for another long moment. Tess lifted her chin. He tossed the towel aside and sat at the end of the bed. She lay in nervous anticipation as the antique clock on the table ticked into the silence.

"To be honest, yes. I've noticed some 'peculiar'

38

moments." His tone was low and grudging. "I can't put my finger on it, but a couple of times I spaced out. I hoped you hadn't noticed."

She nodded, encouraged to continue, with caution. "This sounds so out there, but I swear when we were up by the piano, and then looking in the mirror together, that I heard you speaking as Edward. I was listening as Phoebe. You—Edward—asked her to marry him, and she said yes. He really adored her."

"Or he coveted her so much his jealousy drove him to strangle her." His voice darkened as he drummed his fingers against his tuxedo-clad knee. "A century-old murder provides some pretty intense drama. With us role-playing in these clothes and the nerves about modeling in front of a crowd, let's chalk it up to a bizarre situation and move on from there."

"No." Her voice rose. "There's more. When I was out, I *was* Phoebe, here in this bed, waiting for Edward. She was happy. She was in love with him." She halted, trying to remember the details of her impressions. "The door opened; another man came into the room. He was drunk, and he wanted her to leave Edward and run with him to Paris. When she told him they were just friends and she was in love with her husband, he accused her of leading him on."

She pushed past Trey's disbelieving expression. "He went berserk and tried to kiss her. She kneed him in the groin and broke away. She was absolutely terrified. I don't think Edward killed Phoebe. It can't be coincidence I announced that to all of you when I wasn't even aware of what I was saying."

"Goodness gracious."

Esther and Clarice stood framed in the doorway,

resembling a quaint vintage postcard. "Oh, my dear." The mistress of the house came forward. "Are you sure of what you saw?"

"I saw and I felt it. Very clearly." Though the air conditioning hadn't kicked on, a chill moved over her skin. Her teeth began to chatter. Her body seemed to be in overdrive, every response exaggerated. Trey bent to drape the bedcover over her—gallant despite his disbelief.

"But what happened to Edward? And to the other man?" Clarice's voice was strained as she moved next to Esther, carrying the faint scent of her perfume.

Trey looked between the women and crossed his arms over his chest. "Ladies. Please don't get worked up. Nothing personal, Tess, but this is probably a result of a graphic imagination and too much excitement. Having grown up with my dear mother, I'm somewhat familiar with such things." He attempted a smile to take the sting from the words.

Esther shook her head, rippling the ruffles on her hostess gown. "No, I truly believe it's more than that. There's a diary. Phoebe's diary. I read it a few years ago. While I no longer recall details, it mentions other gentlemen and even hints of flirtations. She apparently was quite a desirable young woman, and Edward wasn't the only fellow vying to win her affection."

She placed a hand on his arm. "I realize it sounds far-fetched to you, but I've found in my travels through life that some persons have gifts we can't comprehend. I believe Tess witnessed this scene. After all, you were wearing their clothes, in the same room where the murder occurred. All this could heighten sensory perceptions. Before you disagree, look at this photo."

She stepped away to open the dresser drawer and returned with a small, framed print. A young couple shared secret smiles—as if they'd been chided to remain solemn but couldn't contain their joy. Esther held the picture low over the bed so everyone could see the man's dark eyes mirroring Trey's and the similar straight nose. His jaw was softer, and he sported a trimmed mustache. The woman was slender and beautiful, with dark hair and large eyes. A veil floated around the oval face, above a lacy white collar.

Tess didn't interrupt. The photo made the case.

"This likely was from their wedding day," Esther said. "I found it in Edward's trunk when I recovered his tuxedo. I registered the resemblance to you then, but looking at Tess, the similarities are astonishing."

He dropped his eyes and began to pace the room. "What does this mean? What the heck are we supposed to do with it?"

Tess answered from her heart. "We need to finish the story and find the truth. Edward did not kill his wife, and I bet he didn't commit suicide, either. We need to clear his name."

"Who would believe us? Who would we tell?" He stopped beside the bed, his tone rising. "I don't even believe in this. We're just caught up in the emotion of the day. You need to rest, and—"

"You don't *want* to believe." She refused to give in to his agitation. She pushed to sit up, leaning against the headboard. "I think you felt it, too. You owe it to your family, to Esther, to *Edward*, to clear his name. I know I'm a stranger to you, but I really feel compelled to find out what happened. We can set them free." Tears filled her eyes as she reached out to grip his hands. She was surprised at the conviction she felt to pursue the way-out conversation.

"How do you propose to do that?" His cynicism remained, even as he allowed her to hold his hands.

"I think we have to finish the story. Maybe we could spend more time here in this room, in this house, and open ourselves to the possibilities."

"Open my mind to a murderer." His expression challenged her. The others stood silent, letting them play out the stakes.

"I did. And I'm still here and semi-sane." Her voice softened. "I don't think we can be harmed by this. Think of it as reliving old memories." She released her grip and sank into the pillows with a groan. "I can't believe what I'm saying."

Esther moved forward. "I think you're on to something, Tess. I certainly wouldn't want either of you to put yourself at risk. But if we could know the truth that Edward didn't kill Phoebe and he didn't commit suicide, what a difference in this family's history. Sad to say, I've always considered him a monster. If he is innocent, at least future generations will know the truth."

Clarice nodded. "In good conscience, how could we pass up the opportunity? If one of us was unjustly accused, wouldn't we hope someone would care enough to make a little effort?"

All eyes turned to Trey, who still looked unhappy. "A little effort. I'm guessing that's a major understatement. You ladies sure know how to pressure a guy." He shoved a hand through his hair. "I can't believe this is even plausible. But if it was, just when, and *how*, would we do this?"

Tess was determined to cement a direction before he changed his mind. "Could we read the diary for more background information?"

"An excellent idea," Esther said. "Though I think you should wait a few days, till we're sure you've got your strength back. In the meantime, let's get you into your own clothes, and Trey will see you home." She smiled warmly. "Dear Tess, thank you so much for modeling, and for your courage today. I think we all should keep this conversation in confidence as we proceed."

After the others agreed, she and a still-subdued Clarice left the room.

Trey's shoulders drooped as if he'd been bested in a real battle. "I think I'm going to have to drink heavily tonight. But first, I'll take you home."

They didn't talk further as he escorted her back to the room where she'd changed clothes. Alone inside, her bravado dissolved, and she acknowledged the vision had drained her, physically and emotionally. If she tried to process her feelings, she might dissolve into a puddle. She was a little lightheaded, but there was nowhere to sit as the other models had shed their outfits on the bed and the chair. She couldn't leave them in a wrinkling mass. She hung the garments in the closet, the familiar action soothing and restoring her. She felt relatively normal as she changed into her own dress and headed down the stairs.

A handful of women in summery dresses lingered in the parlor, buzzing about the fainting episode. Forcing a smile, Tess explained the corset had been laced too tightly and she hadn't eaten all day in order to fit into the tiny gown. She diverted them by sharing brochures for the shop, pointing out the discount coupon and inviting them to visit. The women chirped their intent to do so before Esther graciously ushered them toward the door.

As their clicking heels receded, Tess realized Trey was absent. He'd probably taken the opportunity to make a fast escape, and she wouldn't blame him a bit. Her heart sank as she prepared to say her goodbyes.

Yet apparently, he was too much of a gentleman to avoid assisting her home. He strolled in from the opposite doorway, wearing shorts, a polo shirt, and a poker face. *If only he didn't look so yummy…*

She tried to mirror his casual expression. She couldn't deny her interest in getting to know him but, after today's stress, she should let the poor guy off the hook. "I appreciate your kindness. But really, I can walk home."

"In those shoes?" He pointed to the cherry-red stilettos. "They're definitely sexy, but you could trip and break your neck." His boyish grin flashed again. "Mom and Esther would never forgive me."

She smiled back with relief as his mother entered and handed her a plastic food container.

"I gathered a few sandwiches and treats for you," Clarice said. "I imagine you want to get home and relax so hands off, Trey. You can always come back and clean up the leftovers."

"Thank you. For the food, and for your understanding." Tess hugged her, feeling bonded after the day's events.

"Please get some rest," the older woman said. "I imagine you're already stressed with a new business. We don't want to add to your burdens."

"Actually, this has been an exciting diversion. I do need relief from budgets and mortgage payments."

Esther entered the room as she spoke. "I predict you'll see a flurry of new patrons. You made quite an impression."

"A good one, I hope."

They exchanged a hug, as well, and Trey led her out of the house. He strode down the block and halted next to a gleaming black convertible. Her brows lifted. This was a radical difference from the basic compact cars she'd driven for years. Either he was doing well as an architect, or he lived the high life without her aversion to debt. She'd always leaned on the frugal side from her farming background.

He held the door, and she slid inside, rubbing her palm over the red leather armrest.

"Top down?" He put on a pair of aviator sunglasses.

"Absolutely." After the wild day at the mansion, she didn't care about a wilting hairdo. He revved the engine, and the blocks flew by quickly, painted with genteel images of smaller historical homes, maple and oak trees, and blooming May gardens.

For once, she didn't appreciate the serene view. She couldn't shake the edgy tension and the questions bombarding her mind. Instead of fading, the images continued to haunt her. The unknown man in the room had been obsessed, unhinged, and she wanted to block it all out. But she didn't even have the energy to distract herself with conversation. Trey didn't try to engage her as he looked straight ahead, the wind ruffling his hair. They should have been enjoying a breezy flirtation, yet they couldn't even bring themselves to talk. Her shoulders slumped and she turned to look out the window, feigning interest in the scenery.

At the red brick Victorian apartment house, he opened her door but didn't offer a hand to help her maneuver out of the low car. Tess wondered if he was skittish about touching her. Her spirits drooped as she murmured her thanks, expecting him to run right back to the driver's seat.

"After you." He shut the door and held out a hand, indicating to lead the way into the building.

They didn't speak as he escorted her up the sidewalk and inside, mounting the creaking inner stairs to the second floor. She decided to avoid further discussion about the scene in the bedroom. *Keep it real, and maybe he won't think you're a total nutcase.*

On the landing she paused, key in hand. "I appreciate you driving me home in your hot car." She smiled to lighten the moment, but when she met his eyes, a tingle of heat radiated from her center, traveling down to her toes and up to the tips of her ears.

His eyes reflected the same melting heat, yet he maintained a careful distance. She knew he was interested, too, but the intense day had put him off. Tess couldn't bring herself to insert the key and end their interaction.

He propped a hand against the door frame. "I hope you feel better. This was a crazy afternoon. Must've taken a toll."

The sharp edges of the key bit into her hand. "For you, too."

"I can't quite go there again." He stepped back. "You take it easy tonight and get some sleep."

An almost palpable force tried to draw her toward

him. She resisted and planted her feet. She'd had enough embarrassment for one day without throwing herself at an unwilling target. Tears brimmed in her eyes. She turned toward the door, praying to get inside before they spilled over.

He stretched out his hand. The fingers curved around her cheek, trailing warmth. He pulled away and jogged down the stairs. Confused and breathless, she watched him descend.

Chapter Six

As Trey ran down the stairs of the apartment building, he cursed himself for touching her. He had wanted to, no doubt about it. His churning body reminded him of the fact even now. Yet he was so unnerved by the extraordinary day, he needed to establish distance. Not that he didn't believe "things" could exist beyond his physical comprehension. He wasn't that much of a tight-ass, and he'd read his share of sci-fi. But such mystical hoohah had never intruded into his own orderly world.

He'd prefer it never did again.

He reached his car and swung into the driver's seat. He pushed the button to start the engine and dropped his chin to his chest. "Admit it, bud. You were bowled over the first time you saw her."

Aware that talking to himself could draw unwanted attention, he continued the conversation internally. *If checking out some freaky stuff gets you closer to her, you know damn well you'll do it.*

He barely checked for traffic before pulling out and roaring down the empty street. As the familiar scenery flew by, his stomach rumbled. Trey stopped for a red light and realized he was starving. With all the drama, he'd forgotten about the caterer's leftovers. Still, he preferred to be alone. Esther and his mom would analyze the incident for hours. He just wasn't up for it.

Since his cooking skill extended to frying eggs, heating something from a can, or nuking a frozen meal, he'd better forage for food.

He pulled into the closest drive-through and placed an order for two loaded burgers and a large fry. He tapped his fingers on the steering wheel while waiting to pay, thinking he hadn't lied to the others today. But he hadn't told every detail.

He'd experienced a shock of recognition when their eyes locked after he arrived at the mansion. The feeling shifted far beyond their encounter in the store and rocked him beyond his comfort level. He'd been relieved when his mother called for assistance and he could skid out of the room.

In the ballroom, he tried to pass off the skim of electricity when they touched. He hadn't forgotten the spark when they'd met, but this second, charged moment simmered with an undercurrent he reluctantly categorized as longing. Tinged with a memory of inexplicable sorrow.

He'd been blinded by the flash while posing for the picture. The world had gone hazy for a few moments. He had wondered if he might pass out himself. Then the glass had shattered, and he'd shaken it off and hightailed to help clean up.

Trey considered himself an intelligent, level-headed man, and he was beyond concerned to entertain such fanciful reactions. He'd stood back as they waited to model, amused by Tess' delight as she exclaimed over the outfits. He'd overridden the desire to look deep into those compelling eyes, to seek a logical explanation.

Logic, hell. No hint of reasoning could explain her

fainting episode and the impassioned story she'd blurted out. Unless she was mentally unstable. No, he didn't want to go there. Though he would stay watchful and wary. He wouldn't jeopardize Esther and his mother's safety.

A girl's face swam into his peripheral vision, and he jumped. Now he felt like a fool—which only heightened his exasperation. A teenager leaned through the restaurant window. She repeated his total with an annoying smirk, as if she'd stated the number more than once. He dug into his pocket for his credit card.

He inched the car toward the next window, inhaling fumes from the rusty red pickup ahead, and returned to his troubled thoughts. If Tess wasn't disturbed, could she be a con artist, pulling something over on his family? Pursuing deception was worse than being delusional.

The pickup lurched off with a belch of exhaust. Trey coughed and drove forward to take the food. Muttering thanks, he gunned the engine and headed for home. He dug into the fries as he steered with his knee, relishing the first taste of salt and grease. He reached for his drink and cursed under his breath. He'd forgotten to order one.

He had to get a grip. He could handle challenges, fire-tested by spiraling construction timelines and cost overruns. Though he wasn't as great with emotional stressors. He preferred to compartmentalize people and issues that threatened his balance.

He unwrapped a burger, acknowledging there was no way to box off this situation, or Tess Burton. He preferred whip-smart, attractive women who presented a challenge—mentally and physically. Why did this one have to be so frickin' *complicated?*

****

Tess spent hours on Sunday night, rehashing and analyzing details of the wrenching day. Though she'd been confident about pursuing the visions, she still didn't know how to classify the experience. Some heightened burst of psychic energy? She finally fell into an exhausted sleep after a glass of wine and a bubble bath, tucked under a starburst quilt stitched by her grandmother.

As dawn crept in, she woke to find Gram perched beside her. She wasn't scared or even surprised to see the shimmery form. A luminescent wave blurred around the slim body. Her hair formed a cottony cloud around the beloved face.

Before she could speak, the apparition leaned closer. The lips didn't move, but a familiar Midwestern drawl floated into the room. "Open yourself, sweetheart." A gentle smile warmed the features, lighting the hazel eyes she'd inherited.

She clutched the second pillow to her chest. "To what, Gram?"

Her grandmother's expression shifted toward sadness. The light around her dimmed as she kissed her fingertips and drifted away like the morning mist over a pond.

Tess reached out her hand. "Please don't go. I don't understand."

****

She tugged her eyes half open, registering a brush of warmth on her face. Tess sat up and peered around the dim room. She'd been dreaming. Gram was still gone from her life. She lay down and tugged the quilt under her chin, thinking how very real her grandmother had seemed, as if she'd crossed a boundary between dream and reality. And what was with the message?

Open yourself.

To the visions? she wondered. To Trey? To emotions she would rather hide and deny?

Heightened emotions and drama were always discouraged on the farm. As an only child, living miles from the nearest small town, she had conformed to her parents' expectations. Be polite, work hard and without complaint, maintain good grades, help with the chores. She added her own incentives to excel in extra-curriculars like choir and playing the flute, acting in plays, and competing in tennis. She was the top female singles player for two years at college.

She'd never revealed her guilt that she didn't have the interest to stay and pursue her heritage. Since she wasn't cut out for the farm, she strived to justify her parents' love by trying to be the perfect daughter. She didn't act out or talk back. She always did her homework and studied for tests. Her small group of close friends mirrored the same sweet innocence.

She never felt the need to prove herself to her adoring grandmother. Gram had lived a mile down the gravel road, having been widowed while in her forties. With strength and stoicism, she grieved quietly and raised her two sons—both teenagers at the time—alone.

Open yourself.

All right, so she would admit she had some control issues. Didn't every only child? Tess frowned as light crept under the window shade. She also would admit to building up invisible fences to help protect her from being hurt. When she'd finally scaled them to get close to Brett, his manipulative attempts to control had wreaked havoc with her self-esteem.

She'd certainly had no choice in opening herself to the visions at Carver House. She didn't seem to have much say in opening herself to Edward Carver's handsome relative, either. The attraction with Trey was immediate and strong, bolting past her reconstructed defenses.

Tess' heart dipped. She probably wouldn't hear from him again. Of course, he'd been unnerved by her blurted admissions after she came to in the bed. Who wouldn't be? In hindsight, she should have kept the details to herself instead of spewing them out. Perhaps she'd been dreaming, like this morning, fueled by nerves and lack of sleep.

Yet Esther and Clarice had encouraged her rambling story. They'd seemed to believe her. Maybe they were the ones who were right. Whatever happened—or didn't happen—with Trey, she hoped Esther would let her read the diary. She could at least explore the situation herself and make an informed decision about the episode.

Open yourself.

Wait, was this what her grandmother meant? Was she supposed to bare her cautious soul and expose a family ability to connect with spirits?

She let the idea dance around her mind and recognized her emotional reactions to some vintage garments had hinted of a greater capacity, reaching beyond the physical realm.

Tess pushed out of her cozy nest of covers and resolved to remain "open" to all possibilities. She didn't have to go off the deep end, but she could be receptive to new experiences, and new people. She slid her feet to the cool floor and halted. Who was she kidding? With one misstep, she'd creep back toward self-protection to avoid further public embarrassment, rejection, and loss.

Chapter Seven

On Tuesday afternoon, Marcy rejoined Tess at the store, begging for details about the fashion show. "Did Trey look drop-dead in the tux?" she asked, flashing a knowing grin as they talked in the back office.

"He was the only male model, so he stood out in the crowd." Tess trailed her finger along the sagging hem of a skirt awaiting repair. She couldn't avoid smiling back. "You know very well he'd have stood out if there were fifty other men in the room."

Marcy leaned against the wall in her usual eclectic gear, a striped tunic over black leggings with orange high-top tennis shoes. "Anything else major happen? Wish I could've gotten off work at the deli and gone myself."

Tess realized her assistant might hear gossip about her fainting episode. As a car horn sounded on the street, she glanced out the window, considering her options. She'd sworn confidentiality to Clarice and Esther, but they'd aimed to protect her as much as themselves. If she began researching Phoebe and Edward's tale, she could use an outside ally. As a recent transplant in town, she didn't have other friends or even acquaintances.

Her grandmother's dream directive continued to hover in her mind. She made her decision to dish. "You might want to sit. The story's pretty outlandish."

Marcy took a chair and lifted an eyebrow. "If you can't tell, I'm pretty open-minded. Here, have a cookie first. I baked them at the deli this morning." She retrieved a box from her boho bag and opened it.

Tess thanked her and enjoyed a bite of the rich chocolate, trying to decide where to start. She preferred not to share her heightened reaction to the coffin drape-shawl in the parlor, or her interactions with Trey. She hadn't yet come to terms with those incidents herself. She'd stick to describing the brief initial visions, followed by her fainting spell.

Without one hint of skepticism, Marcy listened and asked only a few questions. Her quick acceptance exceeded Tess' expectations, and she finished her cookie and moved on to share what she envisioned while lying in the bedroom. "Imagine the expressions on their faces when I come to, insisting, 'My husband didn't kill me.' "

Her assistant re-crossed her mile-long legs. "You blew their minds. Poof." She flung her hands into the air. "I imagine 'em all standing around with their mouths hanging open. What was the actual reaction?"

"Mixed. I took a big risk and told them what I'd seen. Sounded fantastic even to my own ears. Needless to say, Trey is a *huge* skeptic. While he was polite overall, I'm sure he thinks I'm a whack job. His mother and Esther, bless their hearts, said they believed me."

She tucked a strand of hair behind her ear. "I also told them I wanted to prove Edward's innocence by trying to channel more visions. Trey got so worked up I doubt I'll ever see him again. At least on a romantic basis. No matter what he thinks or decides, I'm committed to finding the truth. Phoebe's diary could provide clues about her relationships with other men."

"I wouldn't count Trey out. He'll calm down and realize you're not whacked. Personally, I think you're brave. Stand by your conviction and your intuition." Marcy unfolded herself from the chair to stand. "Let me know if I can help in any way. Being a psychic sleuth sounds way cool."

"Speaking of conviction, have you looked online lately to apply for illustration jobs? I don't want to lose you. But you're too talented not to pursue your own dreams."

"Right now, my mom needs me. Whether she'll admit it or not." Her upbeat demeanor dimmed a bit. The doorbell tinkled, and she headed to the door. "I'll get this."

Tess cupped her chin and watched her retreat. Marcy continued to live at home to help her mother, a pottery artist, whose hands were crippled by rheumatoid arthritis. She admired the selfless gesture but hoped Marcy wouldn't give up on her own desires.

She got back to work, fulfilling online orders because the income stream was critical. Without them, she'd have a hard time covering all the business costs, not to mention her personal expenses. She'd thought ahead and kept a stash of her inheritance as a buffer, along with some savings, but they wouldn't sustain her if the business began to flounder.

The thought was frightening. "Maintain a tight budget," she repeated her new mantra. "And work your tail off." She was determined to move her existing stock, buying only if a great opportunity arose.

A few minutes past noon, Tess loaded her small, wheeled cart and headed out to mail the packages.

She'd also grab lunch for them at the deli as the locations were within four blocks. She swung off at a brisk pace, enjoying the eighty-degree weather. Maybe she'd head to the beach later to watch the sunset. She deserved a little relaxing downtime.

Traffic was light in the streets, and she exchanged smiles and hellos with half a dozen people who also preferred to walk. She slowed to watch a group of noisy preschoolers seated around a teacher for library story-time. Near them, a rainbow-hued sculpture of the Owl and the Pussycat smiled down. One of several sculptures in Michigan City's growing downtown Artists' District.

Within twenty minutes she was rounding the corner to return to the store. An angry voice sliced through the air, and she sped up. She recognized Gustavo, the owner of a nearby restaurant. He appeared to be arguing with a man sitting on a bench. He poked a thick finger toward the man's chest. "Why don't you get a job instead of loitering around here all day scaring off customers? Lazy sonsabitches. Always looking for handouts."

She'd noticed the man sitting on the bench before. His tanned fists and square jaw were clenched, yet he wasn't responding to the abuse. In fact, she had never seen him speak to anyone, let alone try to panhandle.

The unfair assumption irritated her. She marched past her doorway. "He isn't causing trouble. The bench is in full view of my store." She gestured toward Divine Vintage and glimpsed Marcy stepping out to join her. "I've never seen him or anyone else try to approach people. They have as much right to sit on this bench as you or I."

Gustavo glared at her under thick white brows. "Taxpayers have a right to sit on this bench, or visitors with cold, hard cash to spend helping our town."

In fight mode, she wasn't about to back down from a bully. Marcy moved up to her side, folding her arms over her chest.

He thrust a flyer at them. "After you've been here a while, you'll see and think differently. You sure don't want your neighbors—or your patrons—thinking you're an agitator. I'd advise you to attend this meeting about the problems down here." With a snort, he turned and walked into the next store.

"Aarrgh, what a jerk," she muttered—low enough the restaurant owner wouldn't hear. She didn't desire further confrontation.

"If we weren't in the presence of a gentleman," Marcy said, "I'd call him a less favorable name."

Tess scanned the street, to ensure no one else had heard the argument. She didn't regret standing up for her ideals, but in hindsight she recognized Gustavo was right. It could damage the business if she was branded a troublemaker.

"Damn, girl," a low male voice drawled beside her. "You got some backbone to take that one on. He means business."

She looked down at the bench and saw a slow grin move over the man's face. She shrugged. "He's a bully. I didn't mean to take him on. Or interfere in your business. His nasty comments pushed my buttons."

She met his eyes, the color of faded denim. Fine lines crinkled at the corners, echoed on either side of a generous mouth. His features were attractive but careworn under a couple days growth of whiskers. Sun-bleached, straight hair fell below his ears. The T-shirt and jeans covered a lean but muscled build. She'd peg him to be in his early thirties.

The door opened at the neighboring jewelry store; she tensed for a return engagement with Gustavo. Her pulse settled as his heavy footsteps stamped down the sidewalk. She blew out a breath as they watched him shove through the doorway into the next shop.

She turned back to the man on the bench. "Are you hungry?"

He mimicked her shrug. "As you said, I don't ask for handouts."

Tess hoped she hadn't offended him with the question. "You didn't ask, but I'm offering. After all, I risked your reputation involving you in street fight."

He barked out a laugh as she dug the sack from her cart and pulled out her turkey sandwich and a bottle of water.

"Please take my chips and potato salad," Marcy added, reaching into her own bag.

"Thanks. You two ladies are very kind. I appreciate it." He set the food next to a bulging backpack and stared down at his scuffed boots.

"My name's Tess. This is Marcy, and that's my store, as you may have gathered." She waited until he raised his head to glance in the direction of Divine Vintage. "We need to get back to work, but you have a nice rest of the day. Don't let him get to you."

"That would be giving him way too much power. I've handled worse in my time."

He didn't offer his name, and she didn't push. She gave him a small smile and headed back to the shop.

"Share half my tuna," Marcy said after they were

inside the store. Without waiting for a response, she split the sandwich between them. "The guy's right. You do have balls to take on Gustavo. Way to go, tiger."

She couldn't help but gloat. "Thanks for joining us. I got riled when I heard his unjustified accusations." Her expression turned solemn. "I had a friend whose family was homeless after they lost their farm. They camped in the woods until her dad got a job as a hired hand. After she finally told me what was going on, I invited her to sleep over a lot. I never told my parents why. I asked her to live with us, but she was too embarrassed."

"That's tough. I've known people who had to couch surf. Without having a name on a lease, they're considered homeless, too."

Tess rubbed her palm against her temple, where the stress of the encounter had kicked up a tiny ache. "Most of the homeless are regular folks who've hit hard times. Hassling them won't help." She retrieved the now-wrinkled flyer and uttered a low whistle. "He's holding a meeting at his restaurant next week to take action against a planned homeless resource center."

"I guess he'll see us there," Marcy said. "Sometimes you gotta stand up and fight for your beliefs. You've already fired the opening shot."

Chapter Eight

Trey contemplated a blueprint in his multi-windowed office facing Lake Michigan. His cell phone lilted the mellow notes of *"Tea for Two,"* Esther's ringtone. He'd set up a handful with some of his favorite jazz tunes: *"In the Mood"* for his high-energy mother; *"Take the 'A' Train"* for his father—who didn't settle in one place for long. The saxophone jive of *"Take Five"* reflected his laid-back younger brother in Colorado. The songs cued him to the potential urgency of taking a call when he was buried in a project.

Considering the jarring circumstances at her home the past weekend, he didn't hesitate to pick up Esther's summons. Actually, as she was one of his favorite persons on the planet, he tried to avoid sending her to voicemail. "Hello, Esther. Have you recovered from the festivities?" He relaxed into his cushioned leather desk chair.

"Quite nicely, thank you. I wanted to see how *you* were doing since the style show. I keep reliving the events of the day. Especially the conversation with Tess after she came to."

"The scene was pretty intense." The comment was a lame expression for what had transpired, yet he didn't trust himself to say more. He still couldn't quantify how he felt about the happenings. Or about Tess Burton.

Though surprisingly, the outrageous incident hadn't lessened her attraction.

"Tess seemed to have recovered her equilibrium when you two left. You saw her to her door, I presume." She phrased it as a statement rather than a question.

"Yes, ma'am."

He stared through the window at the sunlight glinting off the indigo waves. He wished he was out there on his jet-ski. The lake was unruly today, and he could imagine riding up the crest and slamming down on the other side. Then he remembered he'd worked so many hours over the past few months he hadn't even pulled the machine out of the garage.

Esther sighed. "I suppose I'm going to have to extract every detail from you. I'm sorry, my dear, but this is too important for me to politely ignore. Did the two of you talk about getting together to read the diary? And explore the situation further?"

The situation. She might've been discussing a picnic in the park, rather than a dive into a murky, fantastical undertow. "No, we didn't discuss it." He inhaled deeply, thrust the breath out noisily, and felt guilty at his semi-rude behavior. "I'm sorry. This has been a little too much for me to process. I'm still not sure I can comply with what the three of you want me to do."

"Oh, Trey." Her tone softened. "We don't want to pressure you to do something against your better judgment. But I would ask you to take time to think things through. And to call Tess to discuss it."

He closed his eyes, remembering the soft skin of her cheek against his fingers. He'd had to fight the urge to pull her into his arms. He sensed their interactions could never be casual, even without such craziness. If he agreed to Esther's request, he opened himself to complications and depths he wasn't ready to handle. Physical risks like jet-skiing or downhill racing, oh yeah, he was your man. Emotional risks, not so much anymore.

"I've started reading the diary again." Esther pulled him back to the conversation. "I know you'd both find it fascinating. From a historical perspective, if nothing else." She dangled his love of history as bait. "If you decide not to be involved, I hope you won't fault us for moving forward. Tess said she would like to read the story and assist in trying to clear Edward's name. I'll call her at home tonight. I don't want to disturb her at the store."

"You have her cell number?"

"She jotted it on her brochure before you two left the house."

She was playing him like a bass violin, but he couldn't resist. "And will you share it with me?"

She rolled off the digits and Trey entered them as a new contact in his phone. He wondered what ringtone he might assign to the lovely Tess. The opening bars of *"Unforgettable"* drifted through his mind. Or maybe *"At Last."* The thought shook him, and he pushed out of the chair and paced to the window.

"I assume you'll be calling the number," Esther said.

He pinched the bridge of his nose. "I'll think about it. I can't promise more."

"Fair enough." Having achieved her goal, she said her goodbyes and clicked off.

He sat to face the blueprint again, but his concentration had fled. He decided to run out for a sandwich. As he left the office, his cell sang with *"In the Mood."* He ignored the twinge of guilt and let his mother go to voicemail. He already was vulnerable. He couldn't hold up against both of those persuasive ladies in one morning.

****

Tess hoped to lose herself in mindless television that evening. After a half hour she tuned out the laugh track to revisit the disturbing visions at Carver House. Were they a result of her overactive imagination? Or did she have a strange skill to reach into the past? Perhaps the proof rested on repeating the experience.

"Will I channel you again, Phoebe?" she whispered.

When her cell rang, she jumped with alarm, knocking it off the couch. She shook her head with amusement and retrieved it. She recognized the local area code, but not the number. Spam? Or maybe Esther? She answered with a cautious hello.

"Hi, Tess. Trey Dunmore."

She was surprised at the emotional jolt evoked by his voice. "Hi. How are you?" *Ugh, could she be more boring?*

"Grinding away at work, as usual. Esther called me at the office today to discuss reading the diary. My determined mother followed up."

"I'm sorry if they pushed you. They're excited, I guess." About a crazy, hard-to-fathom experience she couldn't wrap her own head around.

"Yeah. Unfortunately. Listen, I still can't say I believe, but I've decided to humor you all. Despite my better judgment, I'm wondering if you'd be willing to get together and look through Phoebe's pages."

Her mouth dropped open, in surprise mingled with relief. She hid the emotions to reply, "Of course. Why don't you bring the diary over here, and I'll cook dinner. Maybe this weekend?" She braced herself to hear he was booked with a steady girlfriend.

"Saturday night would work for me if you're free. How about I come over around seven? Give you time to get home from the shop."

Tess smiled, glad to hear he was open on a prime date night. "Sounds perfect."

"Is there anything I can bring to help? I can uncork a mean bottle of wine."

"You don't need to bring anything—this time. I'll see you Saturday." She clicked off and danced around the room, amazed at her daring in suggesting a possible "next time."

Happy energy gave her the boost to unpack the last of her boxes, previously pushed aside in favor of opening the shop. Two hours later she peered around the living room, surrounded by her favorite possessions. Framed artwork and photos adorned the walls, and colorful glassware sparkled on every flat surface, creating an eclectic, vintage-chic vibe. She sipped a soda, satisfied at how well everything was clicking in Michigan City. The move truly had proved cathartic.

She flattened the boxes for recycling, drifting back to when she finally told Brett her idea for developing the business. He was a loan officer at a different branch of the bank where she'd worked in marketing, so she'd waited to hone her concept.

"Tess. Honey." He'd used the patronizing tone that

set her teeth on edge. "Starting a business from scratch is hard work. Even seasoned entrepreneurs don't leap into something because they enjoy it as a hobby. You need a savvy business plan to secure a loan, a building, and stock. Don't you agree the market's not stable enough to support something this frivolous?"

"I have a business plan. I'm well aware of the steps to be taken." She'd met his cold stare head-on. "I've worked through all the details, and I really think I can make a go of this. I'm starting to scout locations."

"Well, I guess now you have to commit it all to paper and see if you can move forward. If you're sure you want to take this challenging path."

The snarky tone. The small, sad smile. She'd come close to splashing her wine across the near-perfect features. They'd finished the meal in strained silence.

Tess stomped down another empty box, rankled she hadn't ended the relationship on the spot. She had endured two more months of his manipulation to control and change her direction. She secretly had questioned the very issues he'd raised—but she wasn't about to admit that to him. Now, far away from the situation, she couldn't believe she'd endured his emotional abuse for so long. He was an overall decent guy, so she had justified it as caring, rather than a power play. She'd allowed him to tank her confidence, just when she needed it most.

Yet her determination was paying off, and the successes were helping rebuild her self-esteem. She was thrilled with the store, her apartment, and the nearby Lake Michigan shore. Most importantly, online sales helped maintain a slim profit margin each month, and they were seeing an increase in foot traffic.

She did miss her parents and few close friends, but she called, texted, or skyped with them when she had downtime. Eventually, when things slowed and her parents returned from a cross-country RV tour, she'd go back to visit. In the meantime, she was enjoying Marcy's company.

And Trey Dunmore was coming for dinner Saturday night. She flattened her palm over her heart, trusting the time together would paint a positive impression of a normal, stable young woman. Well, *most* of the time anyway.

Chapter Nine

The scent of fresh tomatoes and herbs filled the apartment as the doorbell jangled on Saturday night. Tess checked her lipstick in the hall mirror with a tingle of expectation. She opened the door, and the tingle increased to a buzz. Trey's yellow golf shirt provided contrast to his tanned forearms, and the jeans molded those long legs oh-so-nicely. He looked just as appealing dressed up or casual.

He stepped inside, balancing a box of high-end chocolates in one hand, a small bound book in the other, and a bottle tucked under his arm. She thanked him and reached for the chocolate and the wine.

"Hmm, ambidextrous," he murmured, following her through the foyer. "I was wondering which hand would intrigue you more."

"I covet both equally," she stopped and quipped over her shoulder. With the sudden halt, their bodies were mere inches apart. Her sense of anticipation soared as he tilted his head and drew in a long, appreciative breath.

"Something smells wonderful. And so do you."

Caught in the warmth of his velvet brown eyes, Tess imagined sliding a hand up his cheek into his hairline, to brush down the springy cowlick. Then drawing his head down toward hers…

Her eyes widened, and she stepped back. "Thanks.

I made linguini, salad, and my grandma's straight-off-the-farm recipe for sauce. She canned it every year to use up the bumper crops of tomatoes."

"I love a fresh marinara. Especially homemade."

His face loomed near hers, as she was wearing high heels. She could smell a hint of spicy aftershave, rising above the sauce. A blush of heat sneaked under her gauzy peasant blouse. "Would you like a glass of wine while the pasta cooks?" She was glad her voice, at least, sounded steady.

"I brought red, if you want me to open it?"

"Please. We can get started while the pasta boils. Not to rush us along, but I'm curious to dive into the diary." She turned, aware her favorite slim-cut jeans showed her rear to best advantage.

In her compact kitchen, they shared the meal along with tidbits about their lives. After Tess described the farmhouse where she'd grown up, he asked, "Is that where you developed a passion for old clothes?" He twirled his linguini onto a spoon in European fashion.

"Old clothes? They're an art form," she said with mock indignation. "Many of the materials and designs are superior to what we have today. My interest started because I was involved in theater in school and the community. I performed onstage and helped with costuming. I fell for the uniqueness of the clothing and eventually decided to pursue my own boutique. Though I admit, I keep my favorite items."

"From what I've heard tonight, you have a really strong concept, especially with your online sales. I appreciate someone who knows what she wants and goes for it."

"Thanks. I appreciate the support, plus any help

you can give in spreading the word around the area." The positive comments racked up another point in his favor, compared to Brett's constant put-downs. Tess was enjoying their interaction, and the underlying current of…potential.

After she prepped the coffeepot, they headed into the living room where she'd lit the candles for ambience. Trey laid the diary on the steamer trunk she used as an accent table. They settled on the couch, staring down at the book.

Tess restrained herself from grabbing it. "Do you want to read it out loud? Don't even tell me you haven't looked at it. My curiosity would be killing me."

"I'm a patient kind of guy. Why don't you jump in and read to me. Not to be crass but skip to the juicy parts. References to Edward or another man." He settled back and rested his arms on his stomach.

She stepped out of her heels and reached for the book, braced for a flash. Her fingers closed around it, but the room and atmosphere remained static. A tad disappointed, she opened the fragile pages. "January 1, 1913," she began.

Dear Diary. During the Christmas holiday festivities, I have entertained the intuition 1913 will be a most memorable year. Thus, I've begun this journal. I am pleased to share my feelings were correct. As they so often are.

Last night Mama, Papa, and I were invited to an intimate New Year's Eve gathering at Thomas and Stella Grant's new home on Washington Street. I gathered many interesting decorating ideas from the impressive house befitting his role as president of our local bank. I'm thankful for their close friendship with our family and his employ of my dear father.

Certainly, my father's position provides us a most comfortable lifestyle, allowing me more freedoms than other young ladies. Yet I also find myself chafing under the strict expectations of 'polite' society. Why must a lady stifle her views in fear of being considered unfeminine? I don't believe I boast in saying I am intelligent, educated, and I daresay, better read than many local gentlemen. When I begin to consider marriage, the man must respect my capabilities.

Speaking of eligible men, Mr. Edward Carver of the prosperous shipping firm was among the attendees last night. He is perhaps five years older than I, at twenty-four or five. Handsome, yet rather stoic and intense, perhaps from carrying such responsibility. His father is no longer living, and he is at the helm of their enterprise. He has recently returned from a visit to the London operations. I had heard chatter of his spurned romantic overture toward a London debutante. The silly girl was angling for a titled gentleman.

Despite the influence of those challenging circumstances, he unbent to immerse in the games and songs. Dare I admit? Mr. Carver also was quite attentive. I felt his eyes on me throughout the evening. He complimented my piano skills and my new dress, a delicious dove gray with teal accents. Better still, we engaged in a conversation about current novels, including Edna Ferber's amusing short story collection.

Edward endeavored to sit next to me as we welcomed the new year. I definitely detected the spark of interest when he clinked his glass against mine. As we bid farewell, he asked if he could call. I smiled prettily and told him he could.

I'll gladly accept the challenge to call forth his lighter spirit. With all of his worldly advantages, Edward Carver certainly should appreciate and enjoy his life.

"Oooh. The game begins. I appreciate her feminist edge." Tess paused to imagine the festive party atmosphere. "I imagine she and other guests wore their best winter finery as they anticipated a prosperous new year. I wish I could see the gown she described."

"They visited a house on Washington Street." Trey, however, considered the architectural aspects. "Not that it would impact the mystery, but I could make a quick search of the records for the Grant family's ownership, and also find Phoebe's family residence."

"I'd love to see those houses if they still exist." *With you.* She hoped he felt the same way. Though he appeared interested, she had never been aggressive about pursuing men. But with Trey Dunmore the attraction was heightened—which also opened her to vulnerability.

She ducked her head back to the journal, where Phoebe shared general information about their family and everyday events. She skimmed through the next two pages before looking up with a grin. "Edward didn't waste any time."

January 2 – Mr. Carver came to our home to inquire if I might wish to go sleighing with him and some friends tomorrow afternoon. The snow provides the perfect blanket of coverage. Of course, I said yes. I do believe he blushed when I accepted.

January 3 – The day dawned cold, crisp, and sunny. Perfect weather for a sleigh ride. I bundled in multiple layers, until I felt I might roll away through the woods as a giant snowball if the sleigh were to overturn.

"She's a witty young woman, not just a pretty face," Trey said. "Though I'm not sure yet if she's more interested in him or his money."

Tess narrowed her eyes at him before continuing to read aloud:

Edward arrived in a sleek, polished red sleigh pulled by a gorgeous bay stud. He was most solicitous, covering me with a mink rug. We were joined by two less-admirable beasts and apparatuses. Nestled in their black sleigh, his cousin, Teddy, and fiancée, RuthAnn, were most welcoming as we joined them in front of Edward's family residence. At the last minute, Edward's stepbrother decided to join us. He sauntered out to plop next to their friend, Nick.

The latter is a handsome, jovial fellow, adding an enjoyable note to any gathering. He kept us laughing through the ride and at a stop to warm ourselves with spiced cider at Duneland Inn. I couldn't resist tossing a snowball as we raced back toward town, which collided with the back of Nick's head. He mocked I had best beware his retaliation."

While Nick is a cut-up, Stepbrother Stephen presents as a spoiled child, used to being handed whatever his heart desires. He is also blond and quite good looking. The pair of them drew many female glances as we passed other sledders and skaters.

"Stephen is 'also' blond? Wow, we've already got two other potential blond men who could present as love interests." Tess stopped and stretched her tight shoulders. "Do you think the Teddy she mentions was

Esther's grandfather?"

"I do. He also was my great-grandfather. The paternal link binding our family to Esther. I have to admit, the history is intriguing." The hiss of the coffeemaker interrupted, and he rose, offering to bring back two cups.

Tess was too keyed up to wait and continued to pore through the pages, raising her voice to provide brief bursts of commentary. "She's seeing all three of these men in group settings and enjoying the attention. Edward brings a sober respectability and assured future, while Nick the jester who tickles her whimsy. As she gets to know Stephen, she discovers an appealing artistic bent in him as he writes poetry and reads the verses to her."

Trey entered and handed her a mug of steaming coffee. "Stephen's a smooth character. I imagine she might have been happy to continue flirting with all of them. But apparently Edward had other plans. Maybe Nick and Stephen did, too."

He resettled on the couch, closing the space between them by a few more inches. She noticed the adjustment, and a small splash of red sauce on the yellow shirt. She didn't know if it would embarrass him to have her point it out, so she didn't. Though she could also suggest he take it off and she'd soak the shirt for him…

She took a big swallow of coffee and singed her tongue, drawing attention from the enticing thoughts. She set down the mug. "Maybe we'll find another blond suitor in the pages. For now, I'd consider these two prime suspects."

"What did the guy in your vision look like?"

"He was a mess. But cleaned up, he'd have been good looking." Tess hesitated. "Honestly, I can't recall specifics. I was overwhelmed by Phoebe's emotions. Her confusion, leading to panic and fear."

"I wonder if we could find photos of them? If we can come up with last names." He stopped and frowned. "I can't quite believe I said that. I'm still a skeptic about the visions, but my subconscious at least must be pondering the possibility."

He shook his head and offered her a dark chocolate from the box. She hid her delight. She'd best not gloat over the revelation when his defensive walls had begun to crack. "Great idea. I can't wait to uncover more details." She savored the rich candy and read on silently.

She paused after a couple of pages of mundane daily life led her to Valentine's Day. "This could be a telling entry."

February 14 – The Sweetheart Ball was quite the gala affair this year. I wore a red velvet gown with the fashionable slim skirt. Unfortunately, a mincing gait is required. I'm embarrassed to admit I stumbled. Stephen was near, dashing in his formal black tails. He caught me handily. I started to thank him, but instead of releasing me, he pulled us through an open doorway into the library.

"You're ravishing tonight," he whispered. "You've shot me with Cupid's arrow." In the darkened room, his breath warmed my cheek.

"Sounds painful." I giggled, having indulged in a bit too much champagne.

"In one or two spots." He tightened his hold.

I placed my hands against his chest, to add

distance. He responded by gliding one of his hands down, toward my waist. I realized perhaps he wasn't jesting. I should have been scandalized, but we often indulge in harmless, playful interludes.

"Stephen, I'm flattered," I told him. "You're such the enchanter. Have you noticed Penny Cooper giving you the eye tonight? Among scores of other eligible ladies?"

"I only have eyes for you," he said, most solemnly. Then he kissed me. I was so surprised I didn't even resist for a few mesmerizing moments. Indeed, the kiss was soft and delicious, and I rather lost my head.

I broke away, ashamed, scolding, "Don't." I scurried back into the main hall as fast as the skirt would allow, plying my fan to cool my blushing cheeks. I sought out Edward, praying he hadn't noticed our absence. He had not, thank goodness. He smiled with welcome, and we swept into a waltz. He is rather accomplished, having recently come from the London scene.

I didn't see Stephen again before we left, near to midnight. Part of me was glad. But another part—oh, naughty girl—scanned the crowd for his face.

My, what complexities. As we arrived in front of the house in his luxurious new coupe, Edward took my hand. He appeared very serious. Though he has begun to relax in my presence, he is often over-earnest. "I've told myself not to rush," he began, "Yet I believe you know how I feel. Phoebe, I hope you are coming to care for me, as well." To my surprise, he kissed me, too, quite nicely.

Is it wrong to wish for traits from both of these fine men? I am so muddled.

Tess plucked another chocolate from the box. "What a dilemma. She's conflicted and has no idea this triangle could tighten into a noose." With a mock shiver, she handed the book to Trey. "You take over."

"Stephen's a suspect, all right. Both those poor guys seem caught in her spell. I'm feeling a little empathy for them."

Did he mean in general, man to man? Or was he flirting, referring to *her* impact on *him*? She hoped for the latter. "I'm still Team Edward." She tucked her knees up under her on the couch as he thumbed through the pages. Her nerves had vanished as they'd shared the enthusiasm for delving into Phoebe's world, but she was very aware of his enticing nearness. He pointed toward the middle of a page, and she leaned to peer at the spot, smelling another spicy hint of aftershave.

"Don't count Nick out yet," he said. "March 17, St. Patrick's Day. She didn't write much, except to relay he got drunk at a gathering."

I'm quite dismayed at Nick, as he succumbed to drink and became boisterous. He should beware, as his reputation could become tarnished. His behavior has been sloppy at the last two gatherings we all attended. I drew Edward aside today to ask if Nick is under pressure in his role as a foreman at Carver Shipping. He says no more than usual. I urged him to provide counsel, friend to friend. But ah, the stubbornness of men. He said if the antics don't interfere with his work, he won't act as a damper. I do wish he'd reconsider.

Trey looked up. "We'll have to see if Edward, or Phoebe, calls Nick on his actions. Or if she shares any direct, suspicious interactions with him. Okay, moving ahead." He skimmed the pages. "Nothing juicy. Details about Edward building Carver House. She's excited to give decorating input. I get a kick out of this, but I won't bog us down tonight."

He read silently for a few more moments, and his face grew animated. "We're in April now, at another party. Michigan City must have had quite the social life. She says she's wearing the new satin aubergine gown."

Tess resisted the urge to hang over his shoulder and read directly. "Could be the one I wore. Aubergine is eggplant. Dark purple."

"She and Edward are out on the balcony getting fresh air. He takes her arms and pulls her close." Trey's voice deepened.

"You'll adore Paris. That gown is truly lovely, but the House of Worth would dress you as a princess. I shall give you furs, jewels, a beautiful home—anything you could ever want. You know how strongly I feel about you. Please, say yes."

Ah, a true proposal, after weeks of hints and cajoling. I'd foreseen the moment and practiced a joyous response. Yet his heated, fervent manner led me to hesitate.

"Well. Will you have me wait, pacing the floors, while you weigh your options?" His lips were smiling, but his dark eyes belied his nerves as he gripped my arms. "Dearest Phoebe, I am yours, and only yours, forever."

"Yes…" Tess whispered the word, drifting on a sizzling internal longing. "Those are the same words you said to me Sunday afternoon by the piano. Or at least, that's what my mind heard." Tears misted her vision. "I told you, he loved her so much."

Chapter Ten

Trey's heart lurched at seeing the distress on her face and the hovering tears. He smoothed back her hair, intending a gesture of comfort. Her chin lifted, and he couldn't resist searching out her lips. Softly, for just a moment.

The touch wasn't enough. He couldn't pull himself back. Their lips locked, parting so tongues could caress. He tugged, and her arms wrapped around his back. Time and space skewed for a few jagged seconds, and Trey lost himself, his mind and body humming with energy. Tess moaned as he slid his mouth to the tender skin at her throat.

A vehicle's horn blared outside the window, startling them apart. They separated to opposite ends of the sofa. He rubbed his forehead, dizzy and keyed up, as if a triple espresso had kicked into his system. He was unnerved by the blinding intensity of the kiss. Enough so he had to ask, "Are you really sure you want to do this?" His voice came out low and hoarse.

"This...?" She regarded him steadily, though her fingers trembled on her knees.

"Open ourselves to their influence." He stood and paced away, ignoring his body's urging to take her mouth again, to drown in the sweetness.

"Do we have a choice?"

"Exactly." He breathed out slowly through his

mouth, to calm his body and mind. "I'm still not a hundred percent believer, but if we plunge ahead, we don't know who—or what—will be in control."

Her eyes drifted to the diary, which now lay between them. "I truly believe nothing will hurt us. I was a vessel for the visions, and you may be, too, when the circumstances are right. We should test the theory."

"I wish I was as sure. You talked about spending time in that bedroom together. Which makes sense as the murder occurred there. But we don't know the true risks."

She didn't respond, just watched him with those liquid eyes. Damn, he was coming off as a coward. "We've got what we need to know so far. I'll head out of here so you can wind down to get some sleep. We'll have to work off the adrenaline from the caffeine and sugar."

And the flare of undeniable heat from the kiss.

Her expression flattened, as if she was re-establishing her own distance. "Of course. I'm glad we gained such great insights tonight. Thanks for being open to reading the diary with me."

He couldn't handle more emotional disruptions, either. He was nervous about touching her again, but his mama had drilled in good manners. He offered his hand to pull her to her feet. "Do you want to keep the diary?" He'd rather not read, or even touch it again.

"This comes from your family. Why don't you finish it and fill me in. I'll catch up when you've finished." Her smile seemed wistful. "You have a greater need for the knowledge. I'm going from the gut." Out of the high heels, she had to tilt her head back to meet his gaze.

"Fine." He had a sudden image of Phoebe's face superimposed over hers. He shook it off. All the more reason to leave. He retrieved the book and followed her to the door. Despite his internal turmoil, he couldn't help admiring the swaying trim hips and the enticing bottom in those close-fitting jeans. She flipped the deadlock and opened the door—gorgeous, yet somehow vulnerable.

He very much wanted to kiss her again, drawn by attraction and the current of want hanging between them. Yet the freaky situation held him back. He stepped out into the safety of the hallway. "Thanks for a great meal. You sleep tight."

"You're welcome. You, too."

Trey kicked himself for mentioning sleep. Sleep led to thoughts of bed and bed led to… He trotted down the stairs, increasing to a run when he hit the sidewalk. He'd had to park a block away due to a nearby house party, and his steps pounded in the dark night. He got in the car, opened the windows, and gunned away from the curb. He leaned back and embraced the rush of cool night air. The chill calmed his pulsing body as he attempted to center his thoughts.

Though he was definitely interested, he hadn't intended to kiss her. Not on the couch, anyway. The tears had kicked all rational thought from his head, and he'd reacted. One taste of her lips, and he'd been lost to sensation, surrounded by a welcome impression of recognition.

Damn it. Tess was a beautiful and alluring woman. He wanted them to share in calling the shots in a relationship, not feel they were dancing to some predestined tune.

He drove the dark roads and pondered the diary passages. He was drawn in despite his misgivings. Yet he didn't know if he'd be able to return to Carver House with her to invite potential visions.

If he didn't, he'd be shutting the door on a relationship with her. She'd never demand he investigate the mystery, but his refusal would hang over them.

Add in his mother and Esther. They'd needle him about clearing their family history and sabotaging a relationship with a fascinating woman. To their dismay, he hadn't even mentioned any females over the past months. He'd shown a pointed lack of interest in commitment. He hadn't been compelled to see any woman beyond a date or two.

Whereas a relationship with Tess Burton had definite long-term potential. He wasn't ready for that, either. His last relationship—the one he'd thought would go the distance—had left him more than a little skittish.

He sighed as he garaged the car and entered the house. He headed straight to the refrigerator. His thoughts along the drive had squelched his earlier passion. He'd forego a cold shower for a bottle of beer on the deck and contemplating the starlit sky. Or maybe two or three beers. Sleep wouldn't come easy tonight.

Chapter Eleven

On Thursday afternoon Tess and Marcy closed early to attend the meeting on the proposed homeless resource center. They walked south down Franklin Street, past scattered sculpture installations. A towering red metal piece featured a spiky halo reminding Tess of Marcy's untamed curls. The amusing image didn't deter her jangling nerves. She feared they might face a nasty scene at Gustavo's restaurant. He was holding the gathering on his turf to establish dominance.

"I hope we aren't the only supporters tonight," she said as they waited to cross the street.

"We've both talked to nearby business owners." Marcy strode forward as the light changed. "A bunch of them agree with us. Nobody's keen on confrontation, but at least you and I can take the stand. We'll earn a reputation as warrior-chicks."

"That's what I'm afraid of. Though I've never been afraid to ruffle feathers if I believe in something."

Inside the eatery, Tess was relieved to see a few friendly faces. Others stared ahead with stony expressions. The owner wasn't in evidence. A hum of conversation buzzed as they sat at an empty table next to the window. When the door opened again, she caught her breath, recognizing Esther, Clarice, and Trey. Clarice saw them and waved. Esther beamed and headed forward.

She read surprise, followed by wariness, on his features and cringed. If he had determined not to see her again, the forced encounter could be awkward. And darn him for looking so attractive, in black slacks and an ice-blue button-down shirt. She busied herself pulling a pen and notepad from her purse as the two ladies swept up.

Esther grasped her hand. "How nice to see you both. Might we join you?"

Marcy moved over on the bench seat, and the older woman joined Clarice there. That left Trey to drop into a chair next to Tess. The other three chatted after Esther made introductions.

He looked around the crowded room. "Are you and Marcy here to support the center, or fight against it?"

His shoulder brushed hers, spurring a skitter of awareness, but she couldn't help glaring. "We wholeheartedly support the efforts to help at-risk people," she said, with a cool edge. "All these folks need is a hand up to help them improve their lives. I don't consider their presence a problem. If the center can help them succeed, we're all for it."

"I'm glad to hear that. A lot of the owners have been influenced by Gustavo. Sure, once in a while there's a problem with someone downtown. But the center will help eliminate that."

He lived and worked over the Michigan border, rather than in the city. Was his interest tied to designing a new center? She was about to ask when a door in the back of the restaurant flew open.

Gustavo pushed through with bravado, his gruff voice booming a welcome as the hubbub trailed away. "Some of us remain open for business tonight. Let's get started." He jabbed a finger toward the crowd. "You all know I've called us together to protest opening a day center for the homeless in the city. That place'll make our problem worse, with homeless guys hanging out at all hours, scaring away our customers and acting out." His steely eyes swept the room. "Some of you have businesses a few blocks down. But don't think this won't impact you, too. You see those bums hanging around already. This place will encourage them to gang up and roam the streets together."

Comments began to bubble. Gustavo held up a palm. "In the essence of *fairness,* I've been encouraged to let the other side have a minute to explain their concept." He stomped away to sit at a table with his supporters.

Trey rose and headed to the center of the room. Tess' lips opened in surprise. She watched a pretty young woman with short, dark hair join him.

"I'm Jenna Delgado, executive director of Supporting the Homeless," she began in a musical low voice. "Our board president, Trey Dunmore, will share the *facts* about the new center."

He stood at ease in front of the crowd. "Thanks, Jenna, and to all of you for coming tonight. As you're aware, the county has a homeless issue. Not just the people you might notice on the streets. I emphasize that these are *people*, male and female. Our nonprofit specifically assists families with children who hit a rough spot. They lose their housing, and some bounce between friends and family. We also help the women who are sleeping in their cars or hiding out somewhere they hope will be safe. The new center will offer help to single men and women, as well as families, to re-stabilize. The goal is to link them into housing, food, clothing, health insurance, and needed medication and treatments. Plus, education, employment, and training."

He scanned the crowd, making brief eye contact with Tess. "Instead of compounding the issue, The Hope Center will help alleviate problems. These families and individuals will regain their pride and self-respect as they work with us to help themselves."

Gustavo leaped up. "Watcha gonna do about the guys who pee in the alleys?"

Tess and Marcy exchanged a disgusted glance at his tactics. Around the room, others nodded their heads and muttered agreement.

Jenna appeared as unruffled and confident as Trey. "We'll offer them bathrooms. Plus, showers, washing machines, and dryers where they can clean up."

A gray-haired woman stood. "Some of these men are a little scary. Are you going to patrol and walk me to my car when it gets dark early in the winter?"

Tess didn't realize she'd risen till she landed on her feet. "If you're tense about leaving your store in the dark, I'd imagine we'd all, as fellow shop owners, be willing to keep an eye out for each other. I usually walk the few blocks from my apartment to Divine Vintage. I've never had any trouble, morning or night. Data shows the homeless don't cause any more crime than other citizens."

The woman stared her down. "I sure hope none of us has any trouble. But we shouldn't encourage more congregating. You're new here, so you don't have the full picture."

Her cheeks flushed with heat. "The services will help those who are in trouble, so that they don't resort to living on the streets." She'd have to carve out time to meet more of the neighboring business owners so they'd realize she wasn't a radical, but an informed and caring citizen.

Trey gave her an approving smile as she sat. "That's exactly the point."

Gustavo stepped up to cut him off. "We need to hear from other vested business owners. George, you have legitimate beefs." A man with a thick beard began to detail a negative encounter.

Dismissed, Trey and Jenna returned to their seats. He turned his chair to face the front, parallel to Tess, and leaned toward her. "Thanks for the support."

As other comments were offered, for and against, the time neared five p.m. Gustavo clapped his hands, regaining the floor. "We're working to get a hearing before the city council. I expect those who shared stories about the problem to be there to tell our government leaders. Feel free to stay for dinner; I'm opening up now."

The crowd shifted, drawing a line between supporters who hunkered down for a meal and those who favored the resource center. Trey ushered their group through the door. They walked half a block from the restaurant before stopping to regroup.

Esther clasped her hands under her chin, her eyes shining. "My dears, you were so brave and convincing tonight. I was very proud of you both."

Marcy stood next to her, tall as Trey in her red flare of a jumpsuit. "How long have you been on the board?"

"Esther linked me in after I returned to the area. She'd served several years and wanted to retire. As usual, I couldn't say no to her." He smiled down at his cousin. "Besides, as an architect I appreciate the cause of housing and homelessness. I've been drawing up a concept of a community of tiny homes. Please don't air that controversial idea in public," he cautioned. "We've got enough grief to deal with in pursuing the resource center. Fortunately, we thought ahead and secured the zoning. That could have been a way to stop the plans."

The restaurant door opened. Jenna Delgado swung toward them in her short-skirted coral suit. She was accompanied by a gentleman who'd made comments supporting the program. She stopped next to Trey and placed her hand on his arm. "Would you be able to join us for dinner? Sean wants to discuss some more financial options as we've hit a little obstacle. We wouldn't drag you away, but it really is an emergency."

"Sure." He looked torn but followed his obligation as board chair. "You've met Esther and my mother," he added, moving through quick introductions.

Tess swallowed her disappointment and offered a polite hello. She'd been hoping he might ask her to dinner, or suggest their small group eat together. Her companions also seemed to register dismay as he walked away with the others.

"Anyone else hungry?" she asked. Though she no longer had an appetite, she tried for a cheery tone. "I'm not cooking tonight."

"I second that," Clarice said, linking arms.

They walked back two blocks to enjoy dinner at a popular Italian restaurant. After ordering, Tess confessed she'd shared details about the visions and the diary with Marcy. The other two nodded assent. They spoke in hushed voices about what went on during the

the Saturday night diary reading.

Clarice sipped her wine. "What's your next step?"

"I'm not sure how far Trey is willing to go with this," Tess said. "He's rattled, and with good reason."

"I'll talk with him. He doesn't usually shirk his responsibility."

Esther touched her arm. "No, let me approach him. You heard him admit he can't say no to me."

Tess toyed with the stem of her glass. "I appreciate how the situation affects your family. But this is Trey's decision. If he's not willing to pursue anything, we need to respect that." As she'd have to respect any decision he'd make to distance himself from her. She'd be hurt, but if they could help right the wrongs from a century ago, she'd buck up and make the sacrifice. Like a true warrior-chick.

Chapter Twelve

Tess still was trying to reconcile herself to not hearing from Trey again when he called the next night. She'd hardly gotten past the surprise when he said, "If you're interested in going, there's a jazz concert in Washington Park Sunday evening to benefit the local homeless efforts."

She pressed her hand to her heart. "To be clear, are you trying to sell me tickets as a board member because you have a quota to meet? Or are you inviting me to go with you?"

He chuckled. "I guess maybe I deserved that. Sorry for seeming to blow hot and cold with you. Yes, I'm inviting you to attend the concert with me, as my date. I hope you can understand where I'm coming from when I tell you I want to see you, but I'm not so keen on dating Phoebe."

Her whole body felt lighter. "Yeah, I get it. Although I'd love to know what happened to her and Edward, I'd rather not have him tagging along, either."

****

Sunday dawned as a balmy, sunny day, and Tess kept busy with chores and a trip to pick up snacks for the outdoor event. She took a leisurely walk around the neighborhood to burn off excess energy in anticipation of seeing Trey, wishing she had a close girlfriend nearby to dish the good news over a cup of coffee.

She wondered if Clarice and Esther were aware of the plans. He probably wasn't telling. She'd sensed they were alike in that way: friendly and fun, but slow in allowing people to get close. He hadn't even brought up any past relationships. With his looks and easygoing personality, she was sure there'd been several. Yet she'd also stayed silent about Brett. Eventually, if they continued to connect, she'd share her story and hope he'd do the same.

A few hours later she was perched on a blanket with him, surrounded by other music lovers waiting to be entertained under the stars. In front of them, towering trees backed the limestone amphitheater. The breeze carried a slight, fishy tang of Lake Michigan, reminder that the water lay beyond the crested dunes.

Tess peered around at the groups of families and friends scattered on the immense green lawn. A young family with two pre-teen girls sat nearby. She applauded their efforts to introduce them to the arts. They had certainly enriched her life. As the musicians warmed up, she asked, "What else can you tell me about the Carver family history?"

He finished a last bite of cheese, then stowed his plate in the picnic basket. "Esther's the expert. I don't know anything about the early days except what she told you about her grandfather, Teddy, moving into the house. The family agreed she could be the caretaker after he passed away decades later. No one else wanted to live there. Her live-in housekeeper, Carol, helps her maintain the place. While her siblings moved out within a few hours' drive of Michigan City, Esther married a local boy and stayed. They're all hoping another generation will move in eventually."

"Hmm, like yourself?"

"Maybe. Not sure that's my style, but you can't beat the architectural features."

She would adore living there, Tess thought. Though stating that might seem too leading on their first real date. "Does Esther have children?"

"She had a son around my mother's age. A great guy. He died a few years ago of a heart attack. Esther was devastated. He also had one son. No one's heard from him in a couple years. He served two stints in the Marines. He was injured and went through recovery at a veterans' hospital. Records show he was discharged. We don't know where he got to."

Tess couldn't imagine dropping out of the lives of her loved ones. "Poor Esther. After losing her son, this must make her doubly sad."

His face reflected a shared sadness. "She doesn't talk about it much. That's partly why I keep in close touch and help her out. She has no relatives nearby except for my mother and me."

The evening's introductions blared over the loudspeaker, ending their conversation. As the opening jazz measures charged the air, he draped a casual arm around her waist. She reveled in his nearness and the superb music.

During a saxophone solo, he murmured, "I used to play sax. Not like this, unfortunately."

She imagined him working to master the challenging instrument. She could see him playing as an adorable youngster and teen, breaking lots of female hearts. Now she was the lucky girl capturing his attention. She burrowed against him as the cooling air chilled her skin.

He stroked a finger across her forearm. "Are you cold?"

"A little. But what a perfect backdrop for such a majestic sunset." Fiery bursts of gold and magenta hovered across the western horizon.

He draped her sweater around her shoulders and resettled her against his warm chest.

"Thank you." She found the courage to take his hand, cozy and comfortable in the gathering dusk. Her eyes closed as she drifted with the evocative, swirling tones.

After the final notes trilled, they took their time packing up, allowing the crowd to disperse. She wondered if Trey would suggest going out for a drink. Or she could—

"Trey." Jenna Delgado walked up the hill in a sundress that molded to her curves, focusing her attention on him alone. "Did you enjoy the concert?"

Tess was annoyed. The woman seemed to have a knack for breaking their stride. She tried to interpret Trey's expression. Part surprise and part…expectation?

"The band was great." His voice was polite and neutral. "You remember Tess from the meeting this week."

Jenna stopped next to him, with a pointed look at the basket and blanket. The two women exchanged bare nods before she spoke, again honing on him. "Thank you for coming. I always appreciate the support of our board members. You are *sooo* dedicated to our cause."

The comment was professional, but her vibe indicated potential history between the two of them—or a desire to create some. Tess reminded herself that he had invited her, not Jenna, to join him tonight. Still, the encounter felt awkward.

"That's the role of the board. I was glad to see other members here, too." He bent to pick up their belongings. "We're heading out now. Guess I'll see you at the next board meeting. Unless they set the council hearing about the resource center. If you hear anything about a date, alert me and the board immediately. We'll need to rally support."

"Marcy and I will be glad to speak if you'd like," Tess said. "We both support the project."

The other woman raised a dark eyebrow. Tess held her gaze. She couldn't tell if Trey had noticed the snarky look or preferred to ignore it.

"We appreciate any help," he said. "I'm confident we'll move forward, but we can't take anything for granted. Gustavo's a tough, crafty old guy, with followers who share his prejudices and want to stay on his good side. We'll talk strategy before the hearing."

The director hesitated. "All right then. Have a good night." She walked away with an exaggerated sway of those lush hips.

She had a good body and a sharp, attractive face, Tess admitted. Maybe she was more his type than her own petite, slender frame. A barrier started to form in her mind, creating a safe emotional distance. She was silent as they made their way to the car, aided by overhead lights spilling pools of illumination onto the expanse of grass.

He stopped to give her a hand as they stepped over parking blocks. "I've got an early work meeting in Illinois tomorrow. What about you?"

"The shop's closed, but there's always lots to do to stay ahead of the game." The offer of a potential drink had evaporated with Jenna's interruption.

He opened the door of his low-slung car and she sat and buckled in, fuming at the derailed possibilities. He made general conversation about the music and the town's summer festivities as he drove several blocks south. She tried to add enthusiasm to her responses, yet it burned on her tongue to ask if he was going to join her in pursuing the visions at Carver House. Fear held her back. If she pushed, he might shelve the idea.

After pulling up in front of her building, he calmed her doubts somewhat by taking her hand as he led up the stairs. They reached the landing, and despite her jumbled emotions, Tess very much wanted to kiss him. She searched out her keys and her pulse jumped as she recalled their hot embrace after reading the diary. Would he try again? After the encounter with Jenna, she wasn't assured enough to be the aggressor. She looked up to find him watching her, his eyes intent on her lips. Her body became fluid. Boneless. Infused by heat. The keys clattered to her feet.

He cupped warm fingers along her throat as his lips grazed hers. She strained toward a heightened intimacy, but he prolonged the dance. His hand curled around her collarbone as his tongue moistened her parted lips. Her knees sagged, and his other hand tightened to support the small of her back.

The third pass of his lips brought a spreading, blind ache. She clutched silky strands of his hair as he finally merged with her mouth. For a few seconds, her consciousness shifted through the fog of desire to another indefinable time and place.

She drifted back slowly, aware of the firm body molded against hers and the urgent demand of his lips.

As she eased away, his eyes flickered open. His pupils were enlarged and unfocused.

"They were here, weren't they?" His shoulders tensed under her hands.

"I think so. I didn't see anything, just drifted away for a moment. Maybe the connection is strengthened when something they owned, like the clothing, is involved."

His brows knit. "Damn it, Tess. I don't like this. Especially the loss of control. I can't help wondering if these emotions are ours, or if they're from a couple who died a century ago. You may be fine with it, but I'm having trouble dealing."

She dropped her head to his chest. Her body and mind were still awash with sensation, and she was afraid to look at him, to reveal too much. "We seem to have two options. We either follow this through, or we part as…friends."

He was silent long enough that she forced herself to meet his solemn gaze. Her heart stuttered.

"I can't do that," he said finally, though his expression didn't lighten. "I can't just walk away."

"Good. I don't want you to."

Her grandmother's floating reminder to *open herself* couldn't be denied. Nor could her response to kissing this man. The engulfing reaction had to be connected to their own responses, not just driven by a flash from the past. The only way they'd know for sure would be to confront the visions head-on.

Trey traced small, tantalizing circles on her back. "Despite my better judgment, I think I'm ready to consider your plan to go back to the mansion. Let me talk to Esther and wrap up reading the diary first. I hadn't been able to convince myself to finish."

She nodded, lulled by his arms encircling her body, and the lazy, caressing hand. What she really wanted to do was repeat the melting kiss, again and again, but the inclination warred with her caution. "We're in this together. I'm as rattled by the situation as you are. You set the agenda and decide how you want to proceed."

"Now that's a complicated answer." He tipped a finger under her chin. "For now, we'll take the safe route. I'll see you inside and head home." He picked up her forgotten key and inserted it into the lock.

Chapter Thirteen

Tuesday morning Tess again struggled with her keys—this time to open the back door of the shop. Her hands were full, with a purse and a lunch bag balanced against an umbrella that threatened to turn inside out. She'd been warned the nearby lake brought heightened weather conditions, and today the side alley resembled a wind tunnel. She had driven rather than walked and was already damp from dashing the few feet from the car to the store.

"Here, let me help." A male voice sounded behind her right ear. A hand grasped the umbrella and angled it to withstand the gusts.

"Thank you." She didn't recognize the voice but took advantage of the opportunity to open the lock and push open the door. She knew she had to turn off the beeping alarm within seconds, but an inner sense of *safety first* drove her to seek the identity of her helper. The man she and Marcy had shared their lunch with was standing in the rain, his hair slicked to his head. Her intuition again told her he wasn't dangerous.

"Come in and dry off," she invited.

He shook his head, but she insisted. "At least for a few minutes till it lets up. The rain is brutal."

He entered, and she hurried to punch in the alarm code. He settled the backpack off his shoulders, finding a spot on the floor away from furniture and clothing items. Tess hung her damp jacket on a hook. She held out her hand to offer him the same courtesy.

He gave her the sodden jeans jacket and stared at the pooling water on the floor. "I appreciate your hospitality, but you know you shouldn't go around inviting some of the other homeless folks in here. A few have mental health and addiction issues that can make them unpredictable."

She crossed her arms over her chest, chilled from the weather. "The new resource center will help people seek treatment. If they can move through the opposition's hoops to get it open. Do you know about the place?"

Water dripped off his hair onto his shirt. "I've heard rumblings. I've seen places like that work in other cities."

"That's great to hear. Would you like to sit?" She indicated the chair behind him. He shook his head at the offer; she didn't take offense. "At least have a cup of hot coffee before you jump back out there. As my Gram would say, 'you'll catch a chill.' "

She pulled off some paper toweling and handed it to him. "Sorry, we don't have anything else in here to dry off with."

He grinned and patted the towels around his head as Tess tried not to stare. He was an attractive guy, and he spoke as if he was educated. With a haircut, a shave, and a suit he wouldn't stand out in a group of local businessmen. She turned to pop a coffee pod into the machine, appreciating the heat and the scent filling the mug. "Not to pry, but where have you been before Michigan City? Have you been here long?"

He leaned against the door, watching her with now-cautious eyes. "I guess you could say I've moved around. Some places have been better than others, and I've worked when I could. I was laid off in April in Chicago and decided to swing down here for a while."

For the services, or another local connection? She sensed that was as much as he would share. She handed over the full mug and reached into her lunch bag to offer him half a brownie. He didn't refuse, just thanked her before taking a large bite.

As she inserted the second pod in the coffeemaker, an idea flitted into her brain. "Since you've seen the benefit of these resource centers, would you speak in support at the public hearing? I'm sure it would carry weight coming from someone who knows what they're talking about. Store owners, residents, and the officials need to hear how the center will help people and lessen the problems, rather than create them."

He remained silent as she added creamer to her cup. She perched on the edge of her desk. "Did you know Gustavo has a lot of folks running scared, and he's trying to derail the project?"

"He's a jerk. I still smile when I think about you standing up to him." But he didn't smile now. He sighed and looked up at the ceiling.

Tess waited, not wanting to push him either way.

He drained his cup. "Look, I can't promise you anything. I'm not sure how long I'm staying around here, for one thing. I prefer to keep a low profile."

"I understand." And she did. The nomadic lifestyle, whether by choice or circumstance, couldn't be easy. "Please think about it. I really believe you could help. In the meantime, is there anything you need?"

She sensed he wanted to say something, but he

stuck to a simple, "Nah, I'm good. But thanks for the coffee and the humanity."

Her heart twisted. Most people probably preferred to avert their eyes and attention from him. "Thanks for helping me with the umbrella. I was starting to feel like Mary Poppins." She watched him gather his soggy jacket and backpack. "What's your name, by the way? If you don't mind telling me."

He hoisted the pack around his broad shoulders. "Jake. I'll see you around, Divine Tess."

Divine Tess. The nickname caught her off guard. She couldn't help smiling, but she felt herself blush, as well. He stepped out into the curtain of rain before she could think to hand him her umbrella. She was pretty sure he'd have refused it, but she had gained some measure of trust. He'd told her his first name.

She worked solo in the shop the rest of the day and was pleased to make good sales when a visiting family bought several items. "I had similar clothing in my closet for years," the older woman said as they paid for the purchases. "I should have kept them and handed them off to my granddaughters."

In the early evening, she left the apartment to walk and found herself taking the scenic route past Carver House. Her steps slowed as she again admired the impressive home. Edward had set the stamp of wealth on the property, inside and out, and the family had maintained the grandeur, including the gardens. Behind the wrought iron fence, an azalea had burst into a profusion of pink blooms.

She stopped to finger one of the flowers, releasing a spicy clove scent. Her glance wandered back to the house. How crazy to think that she and Trey would meet inside here soon to try to channel the original homeowners. She hadn't wavered in her determination, but from an objective standpoint, she understood why he hesitated. She was surprised he'd even agreed to try. And what would he do if they geared themselves up and nothing happened? Ah, well, one step at a time.

Her phone rang, and she experienced a little thrill at seeing his number. Maybe he was in-tune with her vibes already. "Hello there. I'm taking a walk. Just passing the mansion."

"Perfect timing. I talked with Esther, and unless you'd prefer to handle it another way, she'll stay with my mom on Saturday night. Her housekeeper has the weekends off to visit her family. Esther debated about being there. We finally decided it could be better mojo if she doesn't hover and fret about us."

Her pulse kicked double-time. "Wow. Umm, yes. I'd be free after closing up the shop."

"Good. I'm out of the area working with a client for the rest of the week. I'll roll back in that morning. We can decide how long we want to stay at the house. So how was the rest of your day?"

Nervous energy propelled her to resume walking. "Actually, I had another well-timed encounter. I may have convinced one of the homeless men to speak at the hearing about other successful centers." She filled him in on the basics of the experience.

"You know I support the homeless, but you have to be careful in dealing with some of them." His tone had sharpened. "Don't get me wrong, most folks are cool. I hope I don't sound like a hypocrite, but please be safe."

"This guy is stable, and he said the same thing. I do appreciate your concern. Marcy and I have seen and talked with him before. I thought it could be helpful if he'd testify."

"Sure, if he's willing. I'll talk to Jenna about getting some of the shelter's current and past residents there. Think of the impact if these folks are sitting in the audience along with everyone else. Then they stand up and show a different face of homelessness than the stereotype Gustavo and the others are promoting."

She wrinkled her nose at the thought of him talking to Jenna about the idea—or any topic. But, of course, that was the best strategy. "The scenario could convince some skeptics."

"Anyway, I'll connect with you later this week about getting together at Carver House. Enjoy the rest of your evening, Tess."

She echoed the sentiment and clicked off as she neared her building. Her anticipation bubbled. He'd moved the idea into action. In four days, she and Trey would come together again, in hopes of solving a century-old mystery.

She personally refused to worry about the unknowns of opening themselves to more visions. She didn't believe there was potential for physical harm, though she couldn't discount a possible mental risk. They'd need to stay strong—and promise to cut loose if either of them couldn't handle the experience.

Chapter Fourteen

As Trey opened the door to Carver House on Saturday evening, Tess inhaled slowly to calm her system. Would additional visions and revelations make themselves known? Or would they leave in defeat? If they didn't progress, she feared he would decide he'd made enough effort and move on.

The house was still and quiet as they passed through the parlor and dining room. They entered a kitchen the size of her living room. "What a gorgeous stone fireplace," she said. "I'm glad they left it when they remodeled." The counters and appliances were updated to reflect the current stainless steel and marble preference.

He deposited a bag on the center island and extracted two bottles of wine and containers from Northside Deli. "The cherry cabinets also are original but refinished. Now our feast tonight includes chicken salad on croissants, fresh fruit cups, and raspberry chocolate mousse cake. Marcy was working, and she pointed me to things you'd enjoy. We can eat in here if you don't mind." He indicated the stools at the counter and retrieved wine glasses from a cabinet.

She smiled at the thought of her assistant smirking with glee as she advised him. "Can we start with the cake?" She reached for the package showcasing a mound of dark frosting.

"No. Let's delay our indulgence to make it that much more delectable." His eyes crinkled with mischief as he popped a cork and poured.

The man knew how to flirt. Tess envisioned grabbing a napkin and flapping it in front of her face to adjust her temperature. She reached for a glass of wine and took a fast sip, hoping her reactions weren't transparent. Her mind and body re-centered as they helped themselves to the food. They talked and laughed, skirting around the reason for the get-together. She could almost pretend the outing was another fun, getting-to-know-you date. Almost.

A half hour had passed, and she slid the last bite of cake onto her tongue. She appreciated that he'd allowed her to eat more than her share. "Worth every extravagant calorie. I wonder if Marcy baked this? She's got rad culinary and artistic skills."

He smiled over the rim of his glass. "Chocolate's definitely your bliss, isn't it?"

"One of them. The darker and gooier the better." She ran her tongue across her upper lip with a playful intention. He paused, his glass halfway to his open mouth. He shook himself slightly before drinking. She lowered her lashes. Good, she wasn't the only one affected by their banter.

She brushed away the accompanying thought that they could be flirting with danger in the house. As they cleared the counter, she was attacked by another layer of doubt. She really didn't know Trey *that* well, and the situation could become somewhat…intimate. She'd never been one to become casually involved. Whatever that might mean in this situation.

She gathered the courage to ask a burning question.

"Forgive me if I'm being forward, but is there anyone special in your life? I picked up some undercurrents from Jenna the other night." Her heart thumped, waiting to hear the defining answer.

He looked down for a moment then met her eyes. "No, I'm not seeing anyone. Jenna and I toyed with the attraction when we met. We didn't feel it was appropriate as I'm considered her boss as a board member. Especially serving as president."

He was single, but she hadn't imagined their spark. Jealousy pricked at her as he continued. "I was in a pretty demanding relationship for more than a year. That ended six months ago when she met a guy who had a water-front mansion. Not that I'm bitter." He halted and pursed his lips. "To be honest, yeah, it sucked. For a while I thought she might be 'the one.' Then she showed her true colors. I caught them making out at a party. Unfortunately, she made quite a scene."

Tess winced. "Yeow. That's lousy. I know something about seeing the real side of someone you're dating and not liking it. The guy I was with before my move was not only controlling, he often ridiculed my dream of opening this business."

"I hope you dumped him hard."

"Not hard enough," she admitted. "When somebody cuts you down consistently, you lose trust in yourself."

He broke eye contact to stare out the window. "Messing up any relationship can leave you wary."

She grasped the hidden message: *I'm wary.* The conversation was heading a direction neither of them was comfortable pursuing. She stood and turned away under the guise of rinsing the takeout containers.

After a few moments, he spoke over the running water. "On a more positive note, I've been concentrating on major work projects. Our firm's consulting with one of my former colleagues who lives in France."

She turned off the water and walked back with the containers. "Sounds exciting. I can empathize in burying myself in work, and I'd love to hear more about it. But tonight, we're here for a purpose. We'd best get to work."

"Though I'd prefer to keep delaying, how about we read more of the diary?"

"Good idea, to give us a better framework for what we might see."

With a grimace, Trey took the items from her. He tossed the trash into a hidden bin. "You're so upbeat, and I'm cringing here."

She laughed at his pained expression. "Don't worry. I'll protect you."

"That's what I'm afraid of. Losing my man card." He grabbed the second wine bottle. "Let's go then."

They headed to the front of the house, and he motioned her into the library. Tess stood in the center of the room, admiring the ambience. Rows of books filled the floor-to-ceiling shelves surrounding another fireplace. A massive carved desk dominated the opposite wall.

He switched on the gas flames as she ran a finger over the gleaming wood. "Was this Edward's?" A pinching sensation seared her fingers, and she pulled away. "Ouch."

He was at her side in two steps. "What happened?"

"It bit me. No, really, kind of a cross between an

electrical shock and a pinch. You try."

"I'd rather not." He stared at her. With a sigh, he stabbed his index finger onto the desk and quickly withdrew. "Nothing."

She took his hand and pressed it onto the desk. A warm current ran between them. "Do you see anything? I don't."

"Thankfully no, but it feels really warm. Must be the fireplace heating the place up."

Tess didn't argue with his rationalizing. "Let's sit on the couch and read the diary. Why don't you update me on your progress."

They sat together, and he opened the book and sifted through the pages. "You and I left off with Edward's proposal. There are a couple other passages you should hear, beginning with the party to celebrate their engagement announcement."

May 11, 1913 - Edward's mother, Bernice, hosted a delightful party at their home to celebrate our engagement. As the house is quite large, both he and Stephen continue to live there with her and Victor, Stephen's father. Edward had planned to move out when his new home was completed. The widowed Bernice married Victor five years ago, having met him through the company. He and Stephen still work in executive capacities at the Carver Shipping firm. But Edward holds the reins to the dynasty.

About thirty family members and friends joined in the gaiety. We started the festivities with a brunch of eggs benedict, smoked salmon, and other delicacies. We then toasted with fine champagne. After lifting our glasses, the guests clamored for a wedding date. I can't comprehend why I have wavered on the point, but despite Edward's intent suggestions, I'd not yet committed.

"I'm aspiring to August," he told them, "so we may travel to Paris during the better weather for a long honeymoon. Saturday the 16th would make me the happiest man alive. I'd celebrate my quarter-century birthday by marrying my beautiful bride."

As they all peered at me with expectant faces, I knew I had to make the decision. After all, what was I waiting for?

"Of course, we shall choose that date for a double celebration," I agreed. Ignoring propriety for once, Edward swept me up and kissed me as our friends applauded. It really was a most memorable moment.

As the weather had warmed that week, we spilled out into the garden. Edward and I shared another passionate kiss, hidden from the others' eyes, as we sought my errant croquet ball. Between the champagne, his adoring attentions, and the giddy well-wishes of our closest friends and loved ones, I was in a high, reckless mood. I laughed and twirled between the groups, almost dancing in my joy. Though there were splashes of dissonance that in sober hindsight I could have perhaps handled better.

Trey stopped to pick up his wine.

Tess grasped his arm. "You've got me on pins and needles wondering where this is going. I love her accounts of these parties. I can almost see them, even without the visions."

"This next section's important." He drank and resettled his glass. "Introducing another potential suspect."

She gripped her knees as he resumed reading.

"Number three."

"Four if you count Edward." He ignored her reproachful look and read on.

When I entered the house to visit the facilities, I encountered Victor in the dining room holding a bottle of champagne. I said hello and attempted to press on, but he took my arm. "As near-relatives, let us enjoy a private toast." He took a glass from the sideboard, filled and offered it to me. I accepted, not wanting to seem abrupt, though I've never felt entirely comfortable in his presence. There's something disturbing about those smoldering eyes, as I have caught him staring at me on more than one occasion.

I kept my distance as he toasted with his own goblet, "To a most happy marriage."

I thanked him and prepared to step past. My skin crawled when he grasped my forearm, whispering, "Lovely, lovely Phoebe. I most certainly welcome you to the family and anticipate getting to know you better. Consider me your most humble servant for anything you may need...or want. Either before or after you join our illustrious clan."

I smiled at him nervously and attempted to walk on, but his grip tightened. I placed my hand on his chest, desperately seeking a comeback to put him in his place. Yet I didn't want to damage the relationship with Edward's stepfather. I've intuited he could be a dangerous foe if crossed. Thankfully, I heard Stephen's forceful voice behind me.

"Father, Bernice has been looking for you. Please take the bottle of champagne and go find her outside."

Victor released my arm. He bowed low, mocking us, and retreated. Stephen approached with a most serious expression and asked after my wellbeing. In truth I was shaken, yet I assured him I was fine. His next words further rattled my composure.

"I'm pained to admit this, Phoebe, but you should not trust to be alone with my father. He's been known to flaunt convention with women he admires." His lips thinned, and he crossed his arms over his chest. "Actually, you shouldn't trust being alone with me."

I watched in shock as he swung on his heel and retreated outside. Remembering our stunning kiss on Valentine's Day, I stumbled on in my journey. I took my time in the ladies' room, trying to collect my wits before facing Edward. When I stepped back outside, I saw him near the koi pond circled by Victor, Stephen, and Nick. A staid, dark-winged owl surrounded by posturing goldfinches. I decided it best to join the ladies who lounged under the trees chatting about the garden, fashions, and other generalities. When they veered to our wedding, I was able to lose myself and regain my humor. I don't believe there's any profit in telling Edward about these encounters. I will heed Stephen's advice and mind my whereabouts.

Tess considered the entry. "Edward's stepfather put the moves on her, too? Eww."

"I gather Victor was a few years younger than his wife. Stephen was nearer Phoebe's age than Edward's."

As he refilled their glasses, Trey's thigh brushed her knee below the hem of the summery dress. Their fingers trailed together as she accepted the wine. The touch combined with the alcohol sent a sweet hum of awareness through her system and also kicked up an overlying tension. Tess wondered what in the world— or outside it—they might be in for tonight.

On her urging, he read a few more passages. They pictured a vivacious young lady's focus on fashion and social life. Though Phoebe mentioned each of the men, no clues arose.

"Did she write about the wedding and coming here to the house with Edward?" she asked.

"I didn't read every entry, but I flipped to the end. The wedding was a gala affair. She even enclosed a clipping." He opened the back of the book. "As for the wedding night, she seemed satisfied."

Though he appeared to be trying to insert humor, she didn't laugh at the innuendo. She didn't need additional sensual images hanging between them. "After you've finished reading, pass me the diary, and I'll go through from the beginning. Interesting, I haven't noticed any disturbances here tonight since the episode at the desk."

"Me either." He shut the diary. "Esther said she left more of their clothing in the master bedroom. She thought it might be helpful. I suppose you'll want to check it out." He attempted a grin. "I can't say I'm jumping up and down, but I'm a man of my word."

"That you are." She stood and led the way to the second floor.

Despite her brave words and intentions, her chest tightened. She was nervous about the possibility of channeling another vision in the bedroom. She lingered on the stairs to inspect the framed photos she'd glimpsed on the walls. "Are these Carver relatives? I'd love to know more about them." Definitely a delay tactic.

Trey halted mid-step behind her, one level down so their gazes were closely aligned. She guessed he was just as anxious about the evening, as his eyes cut from hers toward the gallery. He pointed to a posed family shot. "This is Teddy with his wife and their children. Including Esther's mother." He indicated the oldest child with a halo of fair hair.

"I see the resemblance between you and Teddy. And Edward." A feeling of intimacy grew in the close quarters of the stairway, intensified by the nearness of his tempting mouth and lean, muscled body. And the large bedroom at the end of the hall.

Tess stepped up a level, with the pretense of peering at additional photos. She asked questions, he answered. As time ticked by, she knew they had to resume the trek, yet her knees wobbled as she crossed the landing.

Inside the master bedroom, a lamp illuminated garments spread on the bedcover. "Edward and Phoebe's night clothes," she said softly.

His strained voice came from behind her left shoulder. "I suppose they are."

She usually would have been intrigued by the vintage wear. Tonight, she was taken aback. The white gown and matching ruffled robe were very fine—and very sheer. She'd brought along much more conservative sleepwear in case they did decide to stay the night in some capacity.

He looked equally wary as he stared at the linen pajamas from a safe distance. "You haven't had any visions tonight. Maybe we need the catalyst."

She edged forward to pick up the gown, trying to open her mind. She waited, expectant, but stayed grounded in the moment. After all the build-up, she was disappointed. "I don't see anything. Maybe we have to be wearing the clothing?"

"If you don't feel comfortable, you certainly don't have to wear that, uh, that…"

"The gown's similar to what I saw Phoebe wearing in my vision here." Tess tilted her head toward the bed. "Why don't you touch the pajamas."

He grabbed the bottoms with his fingertips, holding them away from his body. After a few moments he shook his head. "Nada." He tossed them on the bed.

She giggled at his caution; it helped her adopt a braver demeanor. "We came here with the intent to test our theory—or at least *my* theory—and I don't imagine you'll give it a second chance. I'll change in here."

She stepped inside the adjoining bath before he could see the blush rising to her cheeks. Behind the closed door she slipped into the gown and smoothed her hair. As she tied the robe, she was thankful the ruffled front provided some coverage. She exited to find Trey wearing the pajamas.

"Edward may have been about my height, but his shoulders sure weren't as wide. His wedding tux must've been cut more generously."

She followed the downward focus of his eyes. His wrists were exposed under the too-short sleeves. The fabric pulled tight across his shoulders and at the two buttonholes he'd secured. He shook his head, undid the buttons, and tossed the top on an armchair.

The action gave her an eyeful of sleek, muscled chest. Tess bit the inside of her cheek and flicked her gaze to the floor.

He seemed to feel awkward, as well. He put on the wool robe that had been lying next to the pajamas. "Why don't I camp out in the chair here," he offered, looking somewhere over her head. "I don't know if this 'flash' thing might come on when I'm awake, or if I need to try to zone out and head toward sleep. I'm not feeling anything yet. In regard to visions." He winced and tightened the tie belt.

She folded her arms at her waist, longing for a drink of water. Her throat was incredibly parched. "You take the bed." Her voice came out breathy. She stepped toward the closet, trying to regain control of her body and thoughts. "I've already experienced the visions without any warning. You should be as relaxed as possible to encourage a visit from Edward."

He groaned behind her. She turned to see him rubbing the back of his neck. "We're both adults. I don't mean to come off like a teenager on a sleepover. I'm sure we can share the bed for a while."

Her heart thudded as she weighed her options: be a priss, or match his casual attitude. "Sure, we can," she agreed slowly. "Do you usually fall asleep pretty fast?"

"Yeah, usually. Unless I'm sweating over something. Not that this is a high-pressure situation." He grinned and walked to the bed. He pulled back the spread, tossed the robe onto the armchair, and clambered under the covers.

She watched his torso disappear. The tanned arms popped out in sharp contrast to the white bedcover. She hung her robe in the closet. Then she remembered the sheer fabric. She stood with her back to him for a few seconds. She wouldn't make a big deal about it. She pushed out a calming breath and prepared herself to move to the bed.

He'd lowered his gaze and lifted the covers on the opposite side. Once more the gentleman. "Thanks."

Tess was relieved as she got between the silky sheets. She hugged the extra pillow to her chest, vowing to stay at the edge of the double bed. While undoubtedly not original, the mattress had been used enough that sleepers would roll into the dipped middle. A dangerous position, for sure.

"What happens if we stay through the night and one or both don't make an appearance?"

She peered up at the bronze chandelier. "I really haven't thought that far ahead. But at least we've given our best shot. No matter what happens, I'm going to keep on believing the vision Phoebe showed me. I think it gives Esther and Clarice comfort, too."

He nodded, rippling his hair on the pillow. "Of course, they want to believe. A scandalous murder-suicide isn't a desirable pedigree for a socially-connected family."

"I suppose not," she murmured. Her eyelids were growing heavy. In addition to the effects of the wine, the mattress was soft and enveloping and the sheets must be at least four hundred count—smooth and caressing on her exposed skin. She drifted into sleep, loosening her protective hold on the pillow.

Chapter Fifteen

"Your shoulders are tense," he whispered. "Come, Mrs. Carver, let me help relax them with a massage after such a long, celebratory day." She hung back, nervous to finally be alone with him, he thought. His own nerves were thrumming, as well, and he continued to speak softly, coaxing, *"Please, sweetheart. I promise I won't hurt you. I realize you must be somewhat fearful. We'll take our time."*

He had sworn to himself that he would indeed go slow, gain her trust, give her pleasure. This night was too important to rush, as it would set the tone for their future intimacies.

Though her eyes remained averted, she slid toward him. He shifted to gather her stiff back to his chest. *"You are breathtaking, my darling. I can't believe you're mine."* Adoration bordered on reverence as he brought his hands to her creamy white shoulders beneath the fall of silken hair. He splayed his fingers over her shoulders and neck, smoothing the knots of tension for a few silent minutes. Her skin grew warm and pliant under his hands.

Holding his breath, he moved lower down her back. Her waist was tiny, freed from the constricting corset. He grew bolder. His hands brushed the tops of her rounded buttocks. She drew an audible breath but didn't move away.

He closed his eyes and cupped her close against him, allowing her to feel his straining manhood. Such exquisite torture to move so slowly, but he was not a man to rush intemperately. He lifted his hand to her right shoulder and stroked down her arm—once, twice, three times—before sliding his fingers back up the side of her body.

He continued his exploration over the filmy gown, circling over her flat stomach. He held himself in check as he caressed her breasts with bold fingers. She moaned deep in her throat and turned to him. He slid his hand lower, toward her center. When she gasped his name, he savored the triumph as his lips found hers in a searing kiss...

Trey awoke, tangled in the embrace of a female body. They were pressed together, flesh to flesh. Naked. His mind was fogged, but he recognized the sense of release and languor. Tess' head was snugged beneath his chin. He listened to her even breathing with a hint of panic. Surely, they hadn't reenacted the sensual scene that had flooded his mind. The idea was beyond comprehension.

Wait—had he experienced a vision? Or just a hormone-fueled dream? In any case, he recognized, the *issue* would be better discussed in the cold light of morning. Though he couldn't help being aroused by the images he'd seen, and the body curled into his. He breathed in the citrus scent from her hair and ignored the instinct to stroke her into wakefulness. He didn't dare move away. He squeezed his eyes closed and willed himself into fitful sleep.

One last signature on the sheaf of papers before him and he could, in good conscience, clear aside the final work necessities and return to the second floor. To his wife. Darling Phoebe. He looked forward to greeting her in the wide, soft bed, but being a disciplined man, he would complete the documents that would allow them the freedom to tour France.

He rose and stretched before striding toward the main staircase. The trunks were packed and ready, and the servants had been given the night off. After a round of goodbyes tomorrow they would begin their first leg of the journey, which would end on a Europe-bound liner.

Smiling, he reached the landing and headed toward the master bedroom. His startled attention was pulled by a feminine cry. Was that Phoebe shrieking? Had a mouse or spider invaded? He sprinted down the hallway as a second wail rent the air. The eerie, guttural noise reminded of an animal in pain. A howl of anguish.

He threw open the door to behold a scene beyond his comprehension. Why in the world was he in their bedroom, holding Phoebe in a tight embrace?

Trey lunged upright. His heart raced, and he knifed forward to rest his head on his knees, drawing in deep lungsful of air. What the hell had he seen?

"What is it?" Beside him, Tess struggled to push up out of the mattress. "What's happened?" She stroked his back, calming him as her palm circled over his shoulders and neck. "Did you see something?"

He lifted his head, but it took a few moments before he could answer. "A blond man, in the room with Phoebe. Edward burst in. His take was they were hugging." He rolled his head to crack his neck. "That's all I saw before I woke up."

"Hugging? Believe me, he got violent."

"Sorry, my scene ended there." He regretted his snappy tone, but he felt off-kilter. He regarded Tess, now holding the sheet above her chest. Her hair was tousled, her face lit with interest. Usually if he'd woken up with a gorgeous lady in his bed, he'd follow the motto less talk, more action. But his libido was far from mind. He almost felt he'd been violated, used for someone else's purpose. He didn't care for the sensation one bit.

He realized maybe there was a reason he hadn't seen more details. "I know you don't want to hear this, but if we add the new info to your vision, we still can't rule Edward out as the killer. He could have assumed the worst, and in a jealous rage ended up strangling Phoebe and turning a gun on himself. The other guy could've run out before that and been too scared to go to the police in case they wouldn't believe him."

She frowned. "Anything's possible, I suppose."

"Exactly." He leaned back on the headboard and tried to relax. "When you reason through the details, however the scenario played out, the guy must have relocked an outer door from the inside. As an apparent murder-suicide, and with the house shut tight, the police didn't look for another suspect or witness. They were using fingerprint IDs by then, which could mean Edward's prints were the only ones on the gun."

Tess still looked grim. "You know I don't want to believe those theories, but I agree we have to stay open to all possibilities until we find the truth."

He knew she wasn't deterred. She'd follow the instincts triggered by her initial vision. He had to give her points for trying to keep an open mind. To his dismay, she'd already been proven correct in one theory. Apparently, he also could see into the past. He just hadn't realized how overwhelming the immersion would be. He was struggling to stay manly in his reactions, but he was shaken.

"Did you get a good look at the intruder?" She dragged him back to the conversation.

"You're assuming Phoebe didn't invite him in. We haven't considered that scenario." He'd ticked her off. She glared at him as he thought about the scene. "I only saw the back of a blond male head. I'm no closer to being able to identify the man than you are."

Her face fell. She crumpled the sheet in her hands. "I keep thinking they had so much to live for. If they'd had children, a whole new line could have been added to your family." She swiped at the tears blurring her eyes. "I know you want to be objective and consider all the possibilities, but I'm still convinced Edward did not kill his wife. I really want to find out who did and what happened to that other horrible man."

"Even if the other guy did it, maybe he wasn't horrible. He could've overloaded and unintentionally committed a crime of passion." He scrubbed his hands up his cheeks. "What I don't get is why they aren't telling us who did this? And showing us exactly how it played out?"

They? Crap. Now he was identifying with ghosts.

"I wish I knew. There must be something missing. Hopefully, the details will be revealed to us soon, as we're both seeing visions." She shot him a hopeful glance. "Are you willing to continue looking into it?"

With his body and mind reeling from the nighttime adventure, Trey wasn't ready to commit. "Let me think about it. You may be okay with losing yourself like this, but I'm not sure I want to do it again."

Before she could answer, her attention shifted downward. Her eyes widened and her mouth popped open. "Wait a minute. Are we…naked…under here?"

He lifted the corner of his lip. This wasn't going to be an easy conversation, either. He braced for her protest as the chiming clock in the hall interrupted.

****

Tess grasped the sheet higher and tighter. She didn't want to believe Trey had taken advantage of the situation or drugged her, but they were bare as newborn babies. She'd been so anxious for him she hadn't even registered her state of undress. She closed her eyes and began to recall wisps of a sensual dream. Heat crept over her body, and her throat tightened. "I think I might've had another vision last night. Did you, by chance…?"

His eyes dropped to the sheet covering their bodies. "Yeah. Their wedding night. I woke up first disoriented by that vision. I truly didn't know what had happened. You were lying here next to me, and the nightclothes were gone. I swear to you—scout's honor—I didn't remove them."

She hoped he wasn't playing her. If he had spiked the wine, she wasn't experiencing any side effects. And they appeared to have shared the same vision.

"I didn't want to wake you, because at that point I was too groggy to wrap my head around it. When I fell asleep again, I envisioned the finale."

Realizing the situation had spun in a whole 'nother direction, Tess glanced around the room. She spied her gown on the floor. His pajama bottoms and briefs lay near the chair.

"So. This is awkward." She believed him but couldn't bring herself to analyze what might—or might not—have happened.

Trey tipped up her chin with his index finger. "It doesn't have to be awkward."

Her heart pounded, anticipating the kiss. Instead, he said, "I think we should look at this as a beginning. A new beginning for Edward and Phoebe's reputation, if we follow your line of reasoning. And of possibilities for you and me, should we choose to pursue them."

Her heart fluttered against the sheet. "Go on."

"For me, I really hope that we do. And I can assure you of one thing: when we choose to make love, it will only be the two of us. No ghosts, no visions, but just as earthshattering."

She was definitely interested and very attracted, but it was too soon, and too complicated, for her to consciously commit to sex at this early stage. She gripped the sheet. "You're saying we can make our own history. That could be intriguing." Her train of thought dissolved as she met his rich brown eyes. With the sheet now pooled at his waist, she again admired that strong, tanned chest. Despite her vow to wait, her imagination couldn't help sliding a little lower. Maybe she should revisit her decision—

He shifted closer. "This is unorthodox, for sure, but I'm kind of an old-fashioned guy. I'd like to go backward and court you." He traced a finger along the outside of her arm.

The touch reminded her of Edward's initial restrained caresses. Tess melted a little more, pleased with the idea. She tried to ignore the allure of that smooth chest. "I'd love that. I'm pretty traditional, too. I've never been one to jump in and out of relationships." *Especially sexual ones*.

Suddenly, another alarming thought reared. "Oh my gosh, what time will your mother and Esther return?"

He whirled to glance at the clock ticking by the bed. "Whoa. In about a half hour. Why don't you hit the shower first?"

Again, with the courtesy. Without her asking, he flipped to his other side to give her privacy. *What a sweet, sexy guy*, she thought as she left the warm bed to rush into the bathroom.

****

They were waiting in the parlor when Esther and his mother returned. He watched his mom glide toward him, anxiousness lining her face.

"Thank goodness you two are all right. I was so worried."

"We're fine." Trey stood to hug her. He kissed Esther on the cheek as Tess said her hellos.

His mother took his arm. "Don't keep us waiting. You know patience isn't one of my virtues. What happened last night?"

He was tempted to delay, to tease her, but she'd probably swat him. "Despite my strong skepticism, you'll be thrilled to learn Tess was right. I had a vision, or flash. Whatever you want to call it. I saw another man in the bedroom, but only from behind. I got the impression Edward believed he and Phoebe were embracing."

Looking dismayed, Esther edged closer. "That's a different take on the story. Please sit and fill us in."

He held out his hand, indicating Tess should join him on the couch. He shared the basic, non-spicy details, and she chimed in as he outlined the potential scenarios. "From her more specific vision, Tess still says Edward didn't kill Phoebe. Without additional details, I agree that's possible."

His mother glanced between the two of them. "Thank you both for the willingness to help us clear Edward's name. This has been a horrible, unfair stigma on him and the entire family, as well as on this house."

The weight of their expectations suddenly pressed on him. He couldn't guarantee anything, beyond the weird night they'd just spent. He pushed up and paced to the wall of windows to stare out into the lush side yard. "I've seen things I never in this world imagined possible. But at my core you know I'm a realist." The frustration overtook him, and he spun to face them. "Again, I have to ask, how would we go about clearing his name? We have no proof. Only details we supposedly saw in a dream-like state. Now maybe if one of us was a renowned psychic, they'd believe it."

Esther cupped her chin in her hand. "Maybe we should bring in a psychic. The authorities sometimes work with these people. That could carry more weight."

"I was being sarcastic."

"I know, dear, and your points are valid. But eventually, I do want to invite my brother and your grandmother to come here and learn this information. If nothing else, as a point of family honor. They hopefully will believe your story, as well."

Tess regarded him with a probing expression before turning away. "Esther, didn't you say Phoebe's trousseau trunk is in the attic? I'm wondering if there may be more memories triggered through that connection. I believe the answers are in the visions, and I'm willing to keep trying."

"The flashes occurred when you were wearing items of their clothing. It makes sense, as much as anything does right now."

They were steamrolling past his objections. Typical.

His mother got to her feet and moved toward the staircase. "What a marvelous idea. I can't wait to see her gowns."

Trey held up a hand, knowing he was outnumbered. "Can I at least get some breakfast first? I'm not exactly a champion of this effort, and we'll need our strength for another foray into the past." They'd need to entice him with food to even consider undergoing another vision.

Tess stood to follow the ladies out of the room. When they were alone, she straightened the collar of his shirt. "I bet those two have spoiled you silly through the years. Are you used to getting your way?"

"Actually, I am. Though you all are pushing the agenda this time." Trey rose. She remained in place, mere inches away. So close he got another whiff of the citrus in her hair. "I'm also used to going after what I want. I can be *very* determined. And very persuasive."

Her smile had an irresistible sexy edge. "Lucky for me I prefer a man with strong persuasive skills."

"Trey." With impeccable maternal timing, his mother's voice rang out: "How do you want your eggs today? Scrambled or sunny-side?"

"I think scrambled fits the occasion," he called, placing his hand on Tess' waist.

Chapter Sixteen

After a light breakfast, Tess and the others followed Esther upstairs. The ballroom appeared desolate, emptied of decorations and the tables and chairs rented for the style show. Yet the trio of chandeliers still reflected rainbows of light through the crystal droplets.

Their footsteps echoed toward a corner door. Trey fit an oversized key into the lock, adding extra muscle to wrest it open. The revealed space was dark and spare, with a vapor of natural light filtering from a porthole window. Esther flipped a switch to provide illumination from hanging bulbs.

Discards from past generations lingered among the shadows: the tilting lamp a homeowner planned to fix, a brass headboard with a sagging framework of metal springs, a glinting silver Christmas tree. Plus, boxes and trunks from a variety of eras.

Tess peered around the inky perimeter and hugged her arms to her chest. There was something spooky about an old attic, and especially with the legacy of this particular house. If the door slammed behind them, she'd probably wet her pants.

Esther swung a flashlight in wide arcs. "The trunk's over there. Someday we really should go through all this and decide what is worth keeping."

"Count me out," Clarice said. "Unless someone

hauls everything into the ballroom first."

Trey helped Esther duck deeper under the eaves. Tess hung close to his mother and tried to avoid the shimmering spider webs. Apparently, the housekeeper's duties didn't extend to maintaining the attic. He reappeared hoisting a large, flat-top trunk. He set it down next to them.

Esther pointed with her light. "See the initials. Phoebe Patterson Carver. P.P.C." The letters glimmered with gold paint that hadn't dulled despite years of residing in darkness.

Due to the weight, Trey accepted Tess' offer to help move the trunk. Her left arm strained as they shuffled out to place it in the ballroom, but she didn't gather any ghostly impressions. The ladies followed with metal folding chairs to lay the clothing on as they freed it from century-long captivity. On a collective hushed breath, Trey disengaged the locks and flipped open the lid.

Her eyes widened at the first peek of vintage finery. On top were dainty white garments, a blouse and matching skirt.

Esther touched her arm. "Please do the honors."

She brushed her fingertips over Phoebe's gold initials and bent to touch the blouse, an example of popular "lingerie wear" for that era. She lifted the sheer fabric and held it against her thumping heart.

The full-length mirror offered a pleasing picture of the pristine white ensemble, showing to full advantage against her dark hair and eyes. She tossed a pretty pout and tilted the extravagant hat to a rakish angle. The ostrich plumes arched above her head. She hoped it would be fashionable enough for the streets of Paris.

Her mother tutted beside her, hovering as an anxious hen. "Phoebe, dear. I must say that is too daring for my taste. Although I suppose it is all the rage in Paris. Perhaps by the time you return to Michigan City the fashion will have entrenched here. You should not risk your reputation for fashion."

Such a dear little woman, lacking in imagination and constricted by society's forbidding rules. "Mother, I promise I won't go out in it without my camisole." The feathers shook as she laughed at her aghast expression. Really, her parents had no sense of fun. Life was meant to be lived and enjoyed.

Tess refolded the garment and set it aside, hovering in an aura of melting time and space. She dug down farther to lift out a mound of plush red velvet. The image burst forth vividly as the siren color.

The kiss was unexpected. Full lips stroking across hers. Light, then deepening pressure. Her mouth opened to protest, and his tongue slid inside, provoking a shocking new sensation. She reveled in the charged feeling, the recognition of his desire. But even as her arms returned the embrace, the sober voice of reason reared a chastising head.

"Don't." She broke away from the engaging mouth and scurried back into the main hall as fast as the slim skirt would allow. She prayed the indiscretion wasn't emblazoned on her blushing face, her swollen lips. Entering the ballroom, she nearly collided with her date.

"Edward. Shall we waltz? I believe I can manage it even in this cloying skirt."

"I'd be delighted, my dear." He took her arm and led onto the crowded floor. As usual, he held her at a

distance. She must not be seen as a girl who would invite and accept casual intimacies. The prize awaited the virtuous—a ring and wedded bliss to a man of wealth and notable social standing.

Her face flamed in remembering her wanton behavior in the library. Her body stirred, as well. Living a life of virtue could be quite stifling, but she should have rebuked Stephen more roundly. He might take her reaction as welcoming his intentions.

The idea was compelling... No, she must not.

The waltz ended. Edward peered down at her. "Your face is flushed. Quite becoming against your gown, but perhaps you should sit and recover?"

A voice beside them boomed, "Nonsense, Edward."

Her heart plummeted. Victor stood with an extended arm and an oily smile. "Phoebe is young and healthy. The exercise is good for her. After all, aren't we celebrating the heart at this Valentine's affair?" He gestured to the garlands of cupids festooning the room. "I desire to claim a dance with her now, if I may."

Edward frowned but stepped aside. "If she wishes."

They must not make a scene. She kept her eyes on Edward. "One dance. Then I'll join you for refreshments."

Victor moved between them and placed his hands at her shoulder and waist. He tugged her close and twirled away as the orchestra began. "Loosen up, darling. I won't bite."

His breath tickled her cheek. She tried to draw back, but his grip anchored her.

The velvet dress slipped to the floor.

"Tess." A man spoke her name as a command. Firm hands clutched her shoulders.

She tried to pull away.

"Get a chair."

Not Victor. Trey? The name hovered at the edge of her consciousness as someone settled her onto the cold metal seat.

"Can you tell us what you saw?" A female. Esther.

Tess blinked and locked onto familiar dark brown eyes. A disturbing replica of those she'd seen in the vision.

"I think we should stop." He placed a hand on her forehead, as if gauging her temperature. Esther and his mother watched with serious expressions.

"I'm fine." She gently removed his hand and held onto it. "I imagine you got the same strange, enveloping sensation last night. I'm not hurt. The information is valuable." She squeezed his hand. "I've been chosen to convey Phoebe's messages, and I won't let her down. Her life was snuffed out much too soon. Apparently, she has something to say about it." If they could discover the truth, she doubted the public would ever learn their methods. But she'd know her part—their part—in righting a cosmic wrong.

Clarice had picked up the dress and draped it over a chair. "We're disconcerted to watch and not know if you're suffering in some way. But I understand your willingness to go on. In your place, I'd do the same."

"Any new clues?" Trey asked.

She closed her eyes to clarify the memories. "With the white pieces, I saw her trying them on, relishing her mama's disapproval. These outfits were so sheer they were called pneumonia dresses." She opened her eyes and grinned. "Phoebe was no shrinking violet. She wore the red velvet at the Valentine's Day party she described in the diary. Edward's stepbrother, Stephen, caught and kissed her. She enjoyed it until her guilty conscience led her to break off and flee to Edward."

"Stephen's passion was inflamed." Trey said. "That could give him motive."

"Yes. He seemed truly enamored of her. She was flattered but wouldn't let herself fully reciprocate. She ran away to dance with Edward. Then his stepfather, Victor, claimed her. She didn't trust him at all."

"She must have showed you the scene for a reason," Esther said. "Did you see their faces? Could you identify one of them as the man in the room with Phoebe on the night she was killed?" Her hands were clasped tightly under her chin.

After several moments, Tess shook her head in frustration. "I saw them clearly during the vision. Now I can't differentiate their specific features. I have an impression Victor and Stephen shared a resemblance, but I think something's missing. Something we need to literally complete the picture."

"Speaking of pictures, maybe there are some photos of Stephen and his father somewhere, and Nick. They're not here in this house that I'm aware of. None of them lived here, and the home had only been completed a few days before the wedding."

Though it was warm in the sunny room, Tess trembled. These incidents unfolding in the diary, and in her mind, had spiraled into a young couple's violent death. She and Trey had indeed opened themselves to a murder, and she felt no closer to solving the mystery.

"Are you *sure* you don't want to stop now?" he

asked. He'd risen to his feet, yet still held her hand as if gauging her wellbeing through touch.

"Yes, I want to continue. Why don't you pull out the rest of the garments while I regroup."

"The last scene makes me consider another motive," he said slowly. "If Edward dies, who inherits the business? His mother and Victor?"

Clarice frowned. "The business closed decades ago. I'll consider some angles to see if I can help Esther track down such details, along with photos. I don't know if Trey told you, but I used to be a journalist."

"You wrote a society column," he said with a grin. "Though a very nice one."

"Still, I honed some skills. I agree, if Tess feels up to it, we should work through this trunk. She's seen a good bit so far."

Tess recalled Edward's promise of wardrobe pieces from the House of Worth once they reached Paris. Such garments would be worth a small fortune now. She'd have loved to have seen them. "I'm ready to dive in, but I think I'll stay seated." She reached inside to trail her hand through the garments. The visions swirled and merged in a dizzying array of sight and sound.

"Lace the corset tighter, my waist must be twenty inches."

"Mmm, these slippers may pinch a bit, but they're simply divine with the sky-blue taffeta."

"Won't this lavender chiffon be exquisite for tea? I do look forward to all the Parisian soirees."

"The silk nightgown will look splendid—both on and off."

The visions were enticing but didn't carry the same physical or emotional punch. "I didn't see anything special, just a blur of images tied to her anticipation of wearing them." She sat back to admire the garments, appreciating the lustrous fabrics, fancy buttons, and laces. "Thank you for indulging me today. What a treat to see and touch such exceptional clothing."

"We thank you," Esther said. "You both are very brave to open yourselves to these unnerving experiences. Even though we don't have a definitive answer, I'd like to contact my siblings. I'll let you know what date they can come so we can fill them in on what we know so far. I believe I'll aim for a Sunday afternoon tea."

They repacked the trunk and agreed to leave it in the ballroom. Trey took Tess' arm. "If you'll excuse us, I'm going to buy this lady some well-earned lunch."

His mother and Esther smiled their approval. Tess imagined the matchmaking wheels turning in their heads. They whirled in hers as well.

Chapter Seventeen

Determined to spend time with Tess under more ordinary circumstances, Trey drove to the nearby Shoreline Brewery for lunch and a craft beer. He could have invited his mother and Esther but didn't have the energy to handle their additional questions and theories, though he and Tess couldn't avoid the topic, either.

After the waiter took their order on the outdoor patio, she rested her elbows on the table. "I'm sure you don't want to be reminded, but Edward's trunk must be up in the attic, too."

He'd had the same thought up there and hoped no one else would voice it. "We'll have to ask Esther about that." The idea recalled lying beside her in the soft bed in those tight pajama bottoms. She had fallen asleep quickly while he'd lain awake and wary. He now wished he'd stayed awake all night.

The vision had pulled him under, basically *consumed* him. "You know I'm not eager to expose myself to more flashes from the past. I can't comprehend going under while fully awake as you have. At least I was sleeping, and it seemed like a dream. Or a nightmare."

"I understand. That's a good analogy."

She surprised him with the sympathy. He'd expected an argument.

"I compare it to slipping underwater," she said,

"without time to hold your breath or close your eyes. Your body's still there, but your mind disappears into a murky depth. You're not even aware of what happened until you come out of it."

"Exactly. And what if we find it harder to come out? We don't know what kind of hold this could have on us." The idea freaked him out, yet she seemed unfazed. "Aren't you at all worried about what could happen?"

She smiled at him as their food arrived, wafting with the scent of French fries. "Some. Who wouldn't be? But I'm not alone in this."

The conversation didn't ease Trey's reluctance. He focused on his plateful of spicy shrimp. He had forked up a second bite when his cell rang. Jenna Delgado's ringtone reverberated: *"Whatever Lola Wants."* He let it go to voicemail, but seconds later the phone pinged a text notification.

Tess tilted her head. "Someone really wants to get hold of you. Go ahead and check."

The interactions between the two women had been awkward, and he felt caught in his role as board chair. He couldn't think of a PC way to address it with Jenna, so he'd let it hang. He tapped the phone.

—*Council hearing. Wednesday 6 pm*—

He typed with one-finger: —*Thx. Will strategize later*—

He met Tess' eyes, understanding she'd want to know about the hearing. He shared the brief message, and she hesitated. He wondered if she was mulling about the suggestive ringtone. He'd meant it as a joke.

"Marcy and I will plan to attend," she said. "I hope the man I mentioned will hear about it and attend also."

Whew. Tess avoided any catty remarks. With her strong, competitive streak, he didn't know if Jenna would have done the same.

They finished their meal, and he signaled for the check. Though he was enjoying their time together, he was drained by the events of the past evening and the foray into the trunk. He tried to keep his head in the game as he drove the few blocks to her apartment.

At her door he leaned in for a quick kiss—just a glide of lips—keeping it brief so no emotions or visions could cloud his mind and body. He descended the stairs and pictured her heading through the tidy apartment. He regretted not following her inside.

Back in the sunlight, he halted to allow a couple to stroll past, holding hands and laughing. He was slammed with unexpected frustration. His interest in Tess was real. In fact, stronger than with any woman he'd met or dated before. But was that because they were being manipulated in some way? He still couldn't swear their feelings weren't being boosted by spirits from the past.

Right now, his feelings were his own: frustration, tension, and most annoying, vulnerability. Trey decided to head home for his trunks and his jet-ski. Nothing like a day of fast, risky maneuvering on the water to drown out the drama.

Chapter Eighteen

Tess expected to hear from Trey before Wednesday evening's council hearing. As that afternoon wound down, she acknowledged she would not. Either he was engulfed in work or he'd needed distance after the weekend. She assumed the truth was a combo of both. She bit back her disappointment, closed the shop, and connected with Marcy at Northside Deli. They walked two blocks to the sprawling complex housing the council chambers.

The crowded conference area hummed with voices. Esther waved them toward the center of the spare, institutional room. She, Clarice, and Trey had saved seats. Marcy entered first, leaving Tess next to him. The aisle seat remained open.

"Jenna asked me to save her a seat," he said. "Presenting a combined front."

He was president of the board, she reminded herself. He'd also admitted to an attraction to the director and that they'd considered dating. She stashed her purse on the floor and accepted she had no hold on him. They'd been thrown together by incredible circumstances. She pushed aside any jealousy and glanced around the room, recognizing several faces. Nearly every seat was filled. Jenna stood off to one side, speaking to a group of shopkeepers. Gustavo held court nearby, his gruff voice rising above the crowd.

Trey leaned toward her ear, sending a sizzle of awareness through her system. "We had an emergency executive board meeting to discuss the resource center strategy. I'd say the majority here support the concept, but sometimes the loudest voices get the most attention."

"I hope this doesn't get ugly."

"Me, too. And Tess, I've been thinking—"

The council members gathered at the front table rapped for attention. He halted as Jenna sat next to him, her skirt riding high on her tanned thighs. She touched his forearm and spoke to him in an urgent tone. As the politicians introduced themselves and moved straight into public comment, the chairperson referenced a sign-up list.

"I added your name," Trey whispered to Tess.

The crowd was much larger than the one at the restaurant, and this time she had advance warning to work up her nerves. She clasped her hands tight in her lap as Jenna was called and made an impassioned argument for the center. Trey followed, building on her comments.

When Tess spoke, she avoided Gustavo's gaze and echoed sentiments similar to those she'd made before. As she left the podium, the restaurant owner's name was called. She'd have to pass him in the narrow aisle. She lowered her eyes and shrank to her side, but she could sense the anger radiating from him.

She sat and grimaced as Gustavo shouted into the microphone. He added a new twist to his argument, citing the effect on potential tourism. "You think tourists will want to spend their money here? Nope. The frou-frou shops will suffer the most."

Frou-frou shops like Divine Vintage.

Tess gritted her teeth. The man was an alarmist. From her store's front-row vantage point, she could judge the scope of the issue. Why couldn't he accept that the resource center would help people and the community?

She was pleased that a handful of current and previously homeless persons spoke to make the issue relatable: a major medical bill or broken-down vehicle could leave you in financial instability, resulting in a lost job and home. The men and women shared how offering resources in an accessible location could help them turn their lives around.

The hearing seesawed between supporters and opponents. The council members asked a few questions, and some took notes. As the second hour drew near, the president intervened. "We thank all of you for your insightful comments. We've worked through the list and we need to wrap up."

"Ma'am, I'm sorry I'm late." A man's voice came from the back of the room. "I had a job interview."

Jake strode to the front of the room. His hair was trimmed, and he wore neat khakis and a collared black shirt. She smiled in encouragement, but his eyes were trained forward. As he reached the front, a gasp from Esther distracted her.

"Oh, my goodness. Jacob."

Clarice grabbed her cousin's hand and whispered under her breath. Both of them appeared stricken. Tess wondered if Esther knew the man from her time on the nonprofit board. Yet the reaction seemed extreme for such a relationship. She turned to Trey. His face was as grim as theirs. Had Jake caused them trouble in some way? Puzzled, she tuned in to his comments on successful resource centers in other communities.

"Contrary to several of the opinions you probably heard here tonight, I can tell you these centers are a great benefit for people who have hit a rough spot. As well as for the cities." He concentrated his remarks toward the council. "They help folks regain their self-respect as they get jobs and housing. They can seek help for their issues such as addiction. Instead of them being out on the streets, people now have a place to gather where they can learn skills, tap into the support they need, and clean their clothes and bodies. Some of them are veterans like me who have served their country. We'll all appreciate the hand-up a center will provide. I strongly urge you to support The Hope Center."

He stepped away as the president rose and offered final remarks. Half-way down the aisle, he caught her eye and began to grin. His lips flattened as his eyes swept down their row. He stopped mid-stride.

"Jacob. Please." Esther's voice was low and urgent as she stood to face him.

Tess watched emotions play over his face. She couldn't decipher them, but he definitely didn't look happy. Ignoring Esther's outstretched hand, he fled.

Trey stepped over Jenna to follow him into the aisle. Tess swung around, but she couldn't see Jake. He must have practically run out the door. Trey's progress was blocked by a man who rolled forward in a motorized wheelchair. After he could scoot around him, he strode out into the hallway. The director also watched him leave. She ignored Tess and stood up to talk to other supporters.

If Jake was a troublemaker, wouldn't Jenna have reacted to his presence? Now totally confused, Tess turned to Esther. Her heart sank at seeing tears in the older woman's eyes. Clarice handed her a tissue, and Marcy held her other hand. Tess' discomfort grew. She was the one who'd urged him to come to the hearing; she was to blame for everyone's distress. "Is something wrong?" she asked.

Esther blew her nose. "That man is my grandson, Jacob. I can't believe he wouldn't stop to talk with us." She crumpled the tissue in her lap. "I haven't seen him in more than two years. Suddenly, he's in town—again without a word. I can't imagine how I've offended him."

Jake was the missing relative Trey had mentioned, but not by name. Tess exchanged a silent look with Marcy. Would it only hurt his grandmother more to learn he'd been in town for at least a month?

"Trey will find him," her assistant soothed. "Maybe he was shocked to see you here after he'd acknowledged he's been homeless. He might be too embarrassed to face you all. I seriously doubt you did anything to offend him."

"Nothing he could have done would keep me from loving him." Esther sniffed and held the balled-up tissue to her reddened nose.

Fighting her own tears, Clarice patted her shoulder. Tess watched Trey reenter the room, alone and frowning. He sat next to her and shoved a hand through his hair. "I searched around the building and outside, but I couldn't find him. He was a sprinter in high school track, so I guess he's still pretty fast. I asked a couple of the homeless guys who were leaving if they were

143

familiar with him, but they didn't know where he's been staying. I'm sorry, Esther. I promise you I'll ask around, and Jenna can help make inquiries."

Tess swallowed hard. "I don't know where he's staying, but I'm the one who encouraged him to speak on the issue after we met outside the store recently. I had no idea he was related to you." She braced for harsh words at her interference, however well-meant.

Esther's head jerked up. "He's been in town, then?"

"I don't know for how long. He said he had a job interview," she ventured. "A positive indication he's planning to settle here for a while. He may have wanted to establish himself before he got in touch." She held Trey's eyes, near to tears herself. He'd probably wait to scold her in private, to avoid further upsetting the others.

His mother nodded. "Once he calms down, he'll make contact. He may show up on your doorstep tomorrow."

"I certainly pray he will," Esther said, still downcast. "I don't know how I'll bear it if he leaves without a word."

Trey waited until the others were distracted to murmur in Tess' ear. "You couldn't know who he was. Sure, it would have been best if he'd shown up at her house with a job and on his own accord. But he also could have gotten spooked and taken off again without us ever knowing he was here. Now we can try to find him. At least we know he's alive and well."

If he hasn't already run away. She didn't usually look at the dark side, but she'd recognized Jake was skittish. His life story undoubtably was complicated, with challenges that kept him on the move.

As they filed out of the emptying room, Trey and Clarice supported Esther between them. She seemed somehow smaller and more fragile than before. Tess hung behind with Marcy. "Can you check around and find out the places where the homeless guys sleep in the warm months?"

"I can try. But you are not going out looking for him alone." She adopted a fierce expression, a kitten puffing up as a lioness. "I'll go with you. Better yet, Trey should join us."

"He ran away from him. Maybe he'll talk to us if we're alone."

"I saw a friend in here tonight who's a therapist at the local mental health center. I'll bet he can give us some ideas." Marcy's oversized hoop earrings swung as they walked toward the waiting trio outside the building.

"We should go tonight, if possible." Tess whispered.

Trey waited for them to catch up. "I was just saying we should set a time to pull out Edward's trunk. Do you have some free time on Sunday?"

"Sounds good." She smiled at his willingness to throw himself under the bus to distract the ladies.

"Then I'll call you to confirm a time." They exchanged goodbyes and parted.

Marcy's eyebrows waggled as they walked out of earshot. "I bet he says you two should get together before then to *strategize*."

She cast her a side glance. "I don't know. He could have an under-the-radar thing going with Jenna Delgado. Maybe I've just been a cover, so no one suspects the head of the board is playing around with the exec. She's definitely interested in him and gives me a very cold shoulder." She crossed her arms over her chest, watching Trey open the doors of Esther's nearby sedan.

"She is hot, but she can't hold a candle to you."

"Thanks for the reminder of her hotness." She imagined him as the center of a catfight sandwich, as she and Jenna reached around him to slap each other. Some guys might enjoy the attention. He would not be pleased.

"Sorry, I meant that as a reassurance." Marcy slowed and grinned at her. "She looks to be pretty professional to me. You may be reading too much into her reactions."

"Could be she just doesn't like me." Tess acknowledged. "As for Trey, even without her in the equation, I'm the one mixing him up with these visions. I also engineered a heartbreaking encounter tonight with Esther's long-lost grandson."

"Don't beat yourself up. There was absolutely no way you could have known about their relationship." Marcy dug in her purse and pulled out her keys. "Speaking of which, we'd better get moving if we're going to try to track down the elusive Jake tonight."

Chapter Nineteen

The sun had set, enveloping them in dusky gray that would thicken into a black, starless night. Though she wasn't keen about searching in the dark, Tess would never forgive herself if Jake—or Jacob disappeared again.

Marcy called her counselor friend as they neared her parked car. She cloaked the true intent of her inquiry. She clicked off to update, "He told me from October into April, overnight pads shelters for men and women rotate between local churches. He also named a handful of locations where a few of the homeless sometimes sleep."

"You'd make a good spy."

"Never underestimate my feminine wiles." She offered one of her familiar winks. "I'll drive."

Her stomach rumbled, but Tess didn't want to delay their adventure. "Hold on. I'll run into Divine Vintage for supplies." She grabbed granola bars, apples, bottles of water, and a flashlight and rejoined her partner. They jumped into Marcy's lemon-yellow Bug, and she drove to a wooded park, tucked into a neighborhood that had seen better days. Though they'd wanted to find Jake immediately, faced with the reality of darkness and the unknown, Tess questioned the intelligence of doing so alone.

"How about we stay in the car," Marcy suggested.

"This area's small enough we can see into the corners with the headlights." The nervous catch in her voice echoed Tess' unease.

They circled the parking lot, illuminating a jungle gym, monkey bars, and forlorn swings with drooping seats. A small huddle of people stood outside the rim of the glow. Marcy stopped, but left the motor running.

Tess rolled down her window and called, "Hi. We're looking for a blond man named Jake who's fairly new in town. We're friends of his. Is he with you, or has anyone seen him tonight?"

One form detached itself and began to walk toward them. Her pulse kicked, and she glanced at Marcy, sitting with her hands tensed on the wheel. The man remained in the shadows a few feet away. His voice was polite but raspy, age indeterminate. "Nah, haven't seen him. He doesn't hang here. Not sure where he goes at night."

"Thank you. I have some apples and granola bars if anyone is hungry." She had brought along the full packages for this purpose. She pulled them out as an owl hooted, low and unseen from a distant tree, lending to the disquieting atmosphere.

"Appreciate it. There are three of us out here." The man advanced to her window, maintaining a respectful distance. Up close, she saw deep lines of exposure to the elements grooving his face.

He accepted the food and water. "Thanks. Sorry we couldn't help you. But if we see this Jake, we'll let him know some kind ladies are looking for him."

Marcy let out an audible breath as he ambled away. "I don't think I'm meant to be a spy after all. Not that I'm worried about those folks, but it's spooky out here in the dark. Should we head to that abandoned warehouse on the list or wait to search tomorrow?"

She heard the reluctance in her voice. The same dragging emotion urged her to turn tail, but she couldn't give up that easily. She was responsible for the disastrous non-reunion; she couldn't sleep if she didn't try to find Jake. "Let's try that place then call it a night. Esther will be devastated if he moves on before I can convince him to see his family. Her sadness tonight broke my heart."

"She's such a sweetheart. Anyone would be lucky to call her Grandma." Marcy put the car in gear. "We'll drag him over to see her if we have to. I mean, he's only got about four inches and twenty-five pounds on me. And you could jump on his back like a monkey."

Tess laughed as Marcy's natural spunk returned. A few minutes later they approached a warehouse toward the edge of town. The vintage car jolted over the rutted dirt drive toward the back.

"Criminy." Marcy muttered when they discovered there were no lights. To the left, a border of towering pine trees blocked the crescent moon. "I don't think I should honk the horn because it could cause people to scatter." She stared straight ahead.

"You're probably right." She again questioned their actions, especially as they were out of sight of the main road. She tamped down her anxiety. "Wait here. I'll try the door."

"No, I'm going, too. Leave the car door open to give us more light."

And a faster getaway. She gathered her courage and flipped on the flashlight. They exited and approached the door through trampled knee-high grass, evidence someone had been there in the recent past. The scarred metal door didn't seem to be locked, but it resisted when she rapped and tried the knob—as if something heavy was jammed against it. When no one responded, they exchanged a shaky glance and moved toward a broken window. It was too high for even Marcy to see into.

She raised her voice to shout, "Jake, this is Tess from Divine Vintage. If you're in there, could I please talk to you for a minute? I'd really appreciate that."

She detected faint noise, more than an animal would make. The unseen street remained quiet, emphasizing their vulnerability. "Please, Jake?" she appealed again. "We have food and water for you and your friends."

They waited silently. Her pulse danced a two-step, and she was ready to admit defeat when she heard a grating noise from inside. She trained her flashlight on the opening door and shot up a little prayer of thanks as he stepped into the illuminated circle. His eyes were hooded against the glare, his mouth a grim line. He had changed into jeans and a plaid flannel shirt covered by a sweatshirt. She tilted the light toward his knees to keep from blinding him, throwing an elongated shadow.

"Thanks for coming out." To keep his attention, she spoke quickly. "As you can see, Marcy's with me. We just wanted to talk to you about tonight."

He held the guarded expression and remained silent.

"I'm so glad you spoke at the hearing," she said. "Your first-hand testimony deflates the opposition's tactics. I also want to apologize for getting into your personal business. But I have to talk to you about your grandmother. I've grown fond of her, and I wouldn't do anything to hurt her. Or you. She was thrilled to see you again, and I know she'd love it if you'd visit."

He exhaled noisily as he stared her down. "I only went there tonight because *you* asked me to."

She was taken aback, unsure how to respond to the revelation. So, she didn't.

"Honestly, if I'd had any idea I'd see them, I wouldn't have come," he said. "I've been keeping a low profile until I was ready to connect with her again. I don't want to go into details, but I've been pretty messed up since leaving the service. I couldn't put that on her, or my mother." He kicked at a rock with his booted foot. "I suppose I could have sent a postcard or something."

Tess jumped at the sound of an approaching motor. She grasped the flashlight and swung it toward the noise. Another vehicle pulled around the building. He sprinted away as the car braked to a hard stop. The driver's door flew open.

"Jake, damn it, hold on!"

Trey bolted into the glare of his headlights. "Give me your flashlight."

She flinched at the heated gaze but didn't relinquish it.

He stared toward the dark tree line as if estimating the risk of running off into the darkness. He shook his head with one fierce jerk. "Please give me the light. I can't believe you two came out here alone."

Marcy stepped toward him. "He came out for us. Now you've scared him off."

She'd made things worse, Tess thought sadly. She handed over the flashlight and he aimed it toward the pines. She followed the arc and gasped, surprised and relieved to see Jake approach.

Trey stalked forward to meet him at the edge of the headlight beam. "Where the hell have you been all these years? Why haven't you contacted Esther?" His voice pitched low and furious. "She's been worried sick, not knowing if you're dead or alive. It shattered her tonight when you walked right past her. She's not going to judge you or anything. We all want to help."

"You have no idea, *cousin* Trey." Jake's jaw worked as he shoved a hand through his hair. "Not that it's any of your business, but I was beyond help for a couple years. I couldn't trust myself to see her, or even my mom. Shit—sorry ladies—I really don't even know how or why I ended up here last month. When the weather got warm, I followed the stupid urge to come back to Michigan City. Obviously, the issue was forced tonight."

"Nothing you've done will make Esther love you less. With your father dead, you're her only link to her son. You're family. *We're* family."

Tess stood frozen next to Marcy, afraid to look at Trey's face. She was pleased to hear his tone soften but now she saw his hands were curled into fists. Here she was again, a catalyst negatively impacting his life. Her spirits plummeted as Jake walked toward the building.

He didn't enter but braced his arms against the door, body language shouting his desire to end the conversation. "Back off. All of you. If I decide to stay around and see her, I will."

He stretched for the handle, and Trey lunged to grasp his arm. Jake stiffened and flexed to shrug him off. Worried the argument would turn physical, she shot forward to defuse the situation. "Guys, cool off. Please. I know we can reach an agreement." She wrapped a hand around Trey's restraining arm, placing the other on Jake's back. And the world went dim.

"Stephen! Edward! Stop behaving so childishly." She stepped between them, pushing her hands against each heaving chest, fearing they might well come to blows.

"My stepbrother needs to learn his boundaries." Edward forced the words through clenched teeth.

She'd never seen him so enraged; his taut control had evaporated. He'd totally misread the situation, leaping to untoward conclusions when he'd rounded the corner to find them together. The veins in his neck bulged as a fiery blush crept across his face. She lifted her hand to caress his hot cheek, trying to calm the burst of rage. "Stephen came in and found me balanced on the stepstool trying to reach the tea service. I admit it was foolish and precarious. He placed his hands around my waist, merely to steady me. To get me down safely and allow him to finish the task. The action was entirely innocent, Edward."

"I would still remind him it's most judicious to keep his hands to himself." Her fiancé stared above her head to lock eyes with his non-blood relative. Stephen glared back with equal hostility. She felt pinned in an angry vise.

As her body jerked, she clutched Trey's arm, grounding herself to rise out of the vision.

Clutching her hand, he demanded, "Tess. What's going on?"

"Stephen," she murmured.

He wrapped his arm around her waist as she sagged

against him.

Marcy bounded over. "Is she all right?"

"What the hell?" Jake demanded.

Tess opened her eyes but didn't speak. She'd let Trey reveal as much as he wanted.

"She'll be fine." He glared at his cousin. "This is too much to explain out here. I'm begging you, Jake, to connect with us again. We want to fill you in, but the story's long and convoluted. Will you trust me and consider sitting down with us? You can stay with me tonight, if you want."

His cousin's face reflected suspicion. He backed away. "No." He paused at the door. "I can only promise to think about connecting with you all. Don't push me. Don't try to find me again."

He tossed another questioning look at Tess. She tried to smile. He disappeared inside the building. A harsh grating, like metal across concrete, indicated he'd placed an interior barrier.

"I'm taking you home," Trey ground out.

She didn't argue as Marcy would have to backtrack to take her. And the eerie darkness was keeping her off-kilter. In the ballroom, she'd been able to prepare herself for the flashes. This one had slammed into her with the same force as the cousins' real-life confrontation—without the aid of vintage props. The idea was rather terrifying.

She realized Trey was speaking to her. "How do you feel? Do you want to sit down?"

"Did you see a vision?" Marcy hovered next to him, appearing torn between alarm and excitement.

"A short, powerful one." She kept her voice low in case Jake was listening near the window. "Edward jumped to the wrong conclusion when he found Stephen helping Phoebe step off a small stool. He was jealous and super angry."

Trey frowned. "If he later found the two of them in the bedroom together, he could've flown off and killed her. By accident."

She pushed out of his arms and glared up at him. Trey wouldn't discount Edward as the murderer, but she was just as determined to prove his innocence. "Or Stephen got the wrong idea about her and tried to push himself on Phoebe. I'm telling you, the blond man killed her. Not Edward."

"We aren't any closer to solving the mystery," he sounded weary. "And we shouldn't be standing around out here."

"You're right. We'll go." She reached to hug Marcy, appreciative of her easy acceptance of the surreal circumstances. "Thanks for joining me tonight. At least we found him before he took off."

"I'm not sure I'll tell my mom about our big adventure, but I was glad to help. Take care of yourself, boss, and get a good night's sleep." Marcy headed toward her car, and within seconds she drove away.

"You two do know how *idiotic* it was to go trolling around in the dark searching out homeless campsites? You could've been hurt." Trey launched his full disapproval.

Of course, she'd known it wasn't the smartest course of action. But she'd had to do *something*. "My intervention landed him there tonight. Because of *me*, Esther knows he's alive and chose not to even talk to her. Damn it, Trey. I couldn't let him run away again without trying to convince him to see her."

He crossed his arms over his chest. "Obviously, I had the same thought. If you had talked to me beforehand, you'd have known that. We might've gone out together." He held her eyes for an intense moment then stalked to the car. He didn't open her door, but he did crank the heat and hit the seat warmer button as he noticed her shivering beside him.

She shoved her hands under her legs to warm them and continued the argument. "Jake made it clear at the hearing he didn't want to talk to you. He came out to see us when we called through the window. I highly doubt he would've honored you with his presence."

He flipped her an appraising glance but held his tongue. The vortex of adrenaline, nerves, and the heated vision slammed into her, and Tess lost the energy to argue. She slumped into the seat as he drove through the quiet streets.

"Why do you think you had a flash about Stephen out there?" He finally spoke as they neared her apartment.

She sighed. "Who knows? Maybe, in another wild twist, he was drawn back to town because he's part of the solution."

"You think Jake represents Stephen." The words reflected his exasperation. Trey pulled up to her building. He shut off the car but remained facing forward. "This keeps getting more complex. But hey, why not?" He threw up his hands. "I got a jolt myself when you went under. I didn't see anything, though. Seems we don't have any control here at all."

"Apparently, we don't even need a vintage assist."

He scrubbed his hands over his face. "Great. I hadn't registered that nuance." He avoided her eyes and opened his door. "Anyway, you've had enough shocks for the night."

This time he walked around to open her door. He followed her up the stairs as usual, but the night had been as atypical as a trip to the moon. *Maybe even a breaking point*, she thought. Her hands shook when she dug out her keys. He took the ring and opened the lock. She was relieved to see his expression begin to thaw.

"To think, my life was actually kind of boring a few weeks ago. You know you're making me crazy, right?"

Tess bit her lip. "I am sorry about that." She felt fragile, as if she'd fracture at the slightest touch. Yet she wanted him to touch her. She watched his face change again, to reflect caution. His eyes narrowed, but with desire. She knew he wanted the same thing—to kiss her senseless.

He ran his hands beneath her hair, cradling her face with tender warmth. His lips brushed her forehead. She reveled in the pressure of his chest against hers, the reassuring scent of his aftershave. Her eyes drifted closed. She lifted her face toward his.

"Good night, Tess."

The warmth dissolved as he retreated down the stairs. She pushed through the door, her body and mind churning. *She* was driving *him* crazy?

Chapter Twenty

Trey Dunmore didn't seem to realize her life also had flipped topsy-turvy, Tess fumed the next afternoon. She didn't *enjoy* losing herself in visions from the past. And their push-me-pull-you attraction frustrated her. She cleaned the shop's glass counter with extra vigor, telling herself to keep her head together or she could risk her hard-won business. Nothing was worth that cost. Foot traffic had been slow today, despite the heat building outside. People must have headed for the beach in anticipation of the rainy weekend forecast. She'd best spend a few hours boosting her web presence, posting more pieces online.

She looked up when the doorbell tinkled, pleased to greet an actual visitor. Her pleasure changed to surprise when Jake stepped inside. He remained at the entrance and looked to see that they were alone. "I spent a lot of the night walking around, thinking." The shadows under his eyes confirmed the lack of sleep, but his expression was calm compared to the previous evening.

"You had a lot to think about." She wondered if he'd come to tell her he was leaving town. Though he probably would have skipped without such niceties.

He shrugged out of the ever-present backpack and leaned it against the wall, akin to letting down his guard. Without the familiar anchor, his arms hung tense at his sides. "I'm as bull-headed as Trey. Pains me to admit you two are right. I need to see my grandmother and make amends for disappearing without a word. For two years she hasn't known if I'm alive. Or in jail." He nudged the backpack with the toe of his boot.

"I'll see my mom, too. I won't ever tell them the depths of the hell I've been through, but they deserve to know I've been fighting PTSD. I got caught in a painkiller addiction after I was healing from a leg injury from an explosive device. I'm one of those great American statistics." He paused to watch her face.

Feeling certain he wouldn't want sympathy, Tess remained behind the counter so as not to interrupt his flow of words.

"It's not been easy, but I'm clean now. I'm trying to get my life back on track. Whether that means settling in the area or somewhere else."

"I'm glad to hear that." She stepped out to join him, admiring his candor and bravery. She couldn't imagine the trials he'd been through. Sometimes life derailed even the strongest of people, especially when addiction grabbed hold. "I also want to thank you for your service to our country."

"Thanks." He held up a calloused palm. "I want you to know I wasn't mad at you and Marcy last night. Caught off guard, definitely. I understand why you tracked me down. You must be pretty fond of my family."

She detected a slight emphasis on the word "family." Was he questioning her relationship with Trey? He'd seen her sitting next to him at the hearing, and their conversation after her vision hinted at a deeper involvement. Yet at this point, she wasn't sure about the state of their relationship. "They'll all be thrilled to reconnect with you again."

His gaze held hers. "I hope so."

Tess felt a blush rise to her cheeks. "Trust me in this—and them. Initially it might be awkward, but they'll give you space—and respect—to tell your story." She again noted the neat haircut complementing his attractive features. A resemblance to Stephen, she thought, though her memory of his exact features remained hazy. Her mind jumped to recall the emotions flaring between Edward, his stepbrother, and Phoebe. Emotions that nearly took her down.

She broke eye contact and walked toward the bay window to straighten a collar on a mannequin. "Do you have time for a cup of coffee?" She was being polite; she'd prefer to be alone again, to process the new information he'd shared.

She sensed him watching as he answered. "Appreciate it, but I'll pass on the caffeine. I stopped at the food pantry down the street, and they always have a pot brewing."

She turned to see his lips curve, but not with humor. "People's kindness and generosity have bolstered me for a long time. I'm ready to stand on my own feet again. With any luck that job offer will come through and I can at least bank enough money to give me breathing room to make some decisions." He retrieved the pack, his arm and leg muscles bunching at the weight. She wondered about the extent of his injury.

He straightened to face her. "Don't get me wrong, I have had jobs at times, and even housing. Then I'd hit a rough patch and mess it up. I'd be almost ready to reach out to my family, and I'd lose stability."

"You're very brave," she said, meaning it. Even without the family connections, and despite his adversities, she was drawn by his story. "I know it wasn't easy for you to speak last night. I really hope for the best for you in the future. I'd be happy to help work something out for you to visit with Esther, Trey, and Clarice. If you'd like me to."

He shouldered his pack, taking a few moments to ponder the offer. "You say I'm brave. But yeah, I would appreciate your help. I know my grandma is hurt. Trey's majorly pissed at me. Might be better if a neutral party opened the door."

"He's not especially happy with me either," Tess said, reaching a swift decision. "Trey, Clarice, and I were talking about getting together on Sunday at your grandmother's. I'm sure they'd love to have you join us. Could you make two p.m.?" If she was overstepping her bounds, she'd gladly take the hit.

"As it happens, my calendar's free that day." Jake's eyes narrowed. "Why is it when you ask me to do something, I override caution and common sense?"

Tess was struck by an *uh-oh* moment, that his interest was becoming personal. Was this how Phoebe felt, recognizing the attractions of multiple, related men? Confused, and a little exhilarated? "Well, that's great. We'll see you then."

He opened the door and walked into the street. "On Sunday, then, Divine Tess."

The nickname carried impact this time. She hadn't been trying to encourage him. Not because of the homelessness, but because of her interest in his cousin. Yet maybe she was reading too much into it. She should be focusing on Trey's reactions.

That evening, she took a deep breath and called to fill him in on Jake's visit and the tentative Sunday reconciliation. She hoped he wouldn't accuse her of sticking her nose in too deep.

He sounded pleased when he answered. Not wanting to shatter the truce, she asked about his day to delay the possible clash.

"Went to a job site. Took a call on our Paris consulting project. Yada yada. I'll fill you in on that as it progresses. How about you? You're the one with the enticing new career."

"Slow. As far as shoppers." She paused before admitting, "Jake stopped in."

He whistled, long and low. "I'm surprised he stuck around. What'd he say?"

She spilled the details in a rush, barely stopping for breath, and ended with the Sunday invitation. "Do you think Esther will approve? Or would she rather see him alone first?" Darn, she hadn't thought about the older woman's feelings at the time, just seized the opportunity.

Silence. Her stomach flipped as she mentally counted: One thousand one. One thousand two. One thousand three…

"I suppose she'll be okay with it." His cool tone sliced through, as though she'd proposed a business gathering. "He must trust you. More than his family right now. If that's what it takes to get him to visit his grandmother, I won't stand in the way. He'd better show up, though, or she'll really be crushed."

Tess grimaced. She hadn't considered that scenario, either, and couldn't bear the added guilt. "I believe he's sincere," she tried to convince herself, as well. "Maybe we shouldn't tell her. When he shows, she'll be overjoyed."

"I don't like keeping this from her. The alternative is just as bad."

"I could find him and tell him not to—"

"You are not going on the prowl again. We'll tell Esther and pray he keeps his word."

Because she felt she'd overstepped, she didn't cringe at his command. "I didn't share anything about the visions," she added. "I thought we should present a joint front. If we even tell him about them that day." Would he now suggest the reunion be limited to the family? She believed Jake wanted her there, but she couldn't horn in if they didn't want her.

"Yeah. Talking about weird visions could send him straight out of town."

Good, he hadn't disinvited her. She couldn't resist a teasing note. "We may even have time after he leaves to pull out Edward's trunk."

Trey groaned. "I was hoping you'd forget about my distraction pitch."

Her spirits lightened. "Esther won't forget, and neither will I."

They exchanged a few more comments before he offered to pick her up on Sunday. "I'll call her now. No, I'll run over there and call my mom on the way."

He didn't offer to stop by her house or touch base later to fill her in. Tess buried her disappointment by sending a text to her own parents as they were rolling around the country in their well-equipped recreational vehicle. They'd left for the extended vacation after planting the spring crops. During spring and fall, farmers buzzed from early morning to late evening with planting and harvesting. The summer and winter seasons were more laid back, and her parents liked to roam. They'd taken her on many fun-filled car trips in her youth.

She texted to touch base and assure them all was well with her life and the shop. No way could she share the out-of-this-world situation she'd been thrust into. The concept was far beyond their comfort level. She again wished she could hash it through with her grandmother. She felt sure Gram would be proud of her. Both in handling the visions and the business. Not to mention Trey. Though she'd never remarried, Gram had an eye for a good-looking man.

Her phone chirped, and she read her mother's listing of interesting locations they'd visited in the Southwest. She relaxed onto her couch and tapped back and forth for several minutes, imagining their excursions. They arranged to call over the weekend, as her father was out for a walk.

Tess ended the conversation with a trio of heart emojis. Jake's painful estrangement from his family was a reminder to cherish her own beloved parents.

Chapter Twenty-One

Tess chided herself for spending too much time choosing an outfit on Sunday. No one would judge her clothing, but she wanted to look good for Trey. Wearing a vintage dress might signal she was trying too hard. Shorts were too casual. She opted for a floral shift in muted peach and pinks, which contrasted against the light tan she'd gained walking around the city. She grabbed her sunglasses as he knocked.

He grinned. "You look great."

"Thanks. You, too."

She was glad she'd made the extra effort with both her dress and makeup. He looked very attractive in khaki slacks and a red knit shirt, his hair still damp from the shower. She resisted the urge to try to tame his cowlick. The silky texture of that thick head of hair would conjure the memory of the heated kisses at her door, and on her couch. He took her elbow to guide her into the bright sunshine, and she wondered if he also recalled the sensual moments. If so, he kept the feelings locked deep. No teasing comments or longing glances passed between them.

As they rolled toward their destination in his vehicle, he said, "Esther's excited. And hesitant, I think. She doesn't want to admit he might not come. Or the encounter might go sideways."

"He'll be there," Tess said. Though she wasn't

convinced. *Please, please, Jake, show up,* she prayed. "You don't realize what he's been through. How hard it is for him to admit he's screwed up."

His eyes, covered by his sunglasses, disguised his feelings. "At least you do," he said in a clipped tone.

She wanted to defend herself but realized it wouldn't help. She stared out her side of the car and, when he parked, she jumped out before he could help her. They didn't speak as he tapped with the brass door knocker. He didn't wait for admittance and stood back to let her enter. They found the two ladies in the parlor, hovering over a loaded tea cart. Clarice exchanged hugs and kisses and urged them to sit.

Esther seemed unable to land for long, and she popped up to return to the kitchen for teaspoons, to glance out the window toward the street, and to rearrange the peonies swimming in a crystal bowl. No one had the heart to try to make her sit still. They attempted light conversation as the grandfather clock chimed two resonant notes. The minutes ticked past, and Tess exchanged a tense glance with Trey. Had Jake fled again? She had no idea where he'd travel to next.

The knocker sounded against the door. Esther clasped her hands together and dropped to sit in a throne-like oak chair. "Would you two answer that?" Her face looked pinched as she directed the two of them with a trembling wave.

Tess stood aside as Trey swung the door open to reveal Jake dressed in the slacks and shirt he'd worn at the hearing. Her heart flooded with relief.

"Tess. Cousin." He peered beyond them down the hallway. He shot a small smile at her, easing her tension.

"Esther and Clarice are in the parlor," she said. "They're so excited to see you."

Trey added a tight-lipped, "Thanks for coming" as they stepped aside.

After he stowed his backpack on the floor, Jake followed through the arched doorway into the sunny, open room. Esther gasped and lifted a hand to her heart. As she made to rise, he took her hand and knelt beside the chair. "I'm sorry, Grandma. I should've called or something." His voice was low and unsteady. "I knew it would only hurt you to see me so messed up."

She placed a hand on his bent head. "You have always been—and always will be—welcome here, my dearest." Her face was alight. "My heart breaks for whatever pain you've endured, but I'm so very happy you've reconnected with us."

His head remained bowed. "I'm not ready to go into all the details, but I was injured when a device exploded near me. Messed up my leg when I came down on a pile of metal. Some of my buddies were less fortunate. As I told Tess, I've been wrestling with Post Traumatic Stress and addiction issues since my discharge. I'm clean now. I think I've got my head together to finally turn my life around."

His grandmother embraced him, her head tucked into his chest. Tess swiped under her eyes with a finger and felt Trey's hand press against her back. They stood nearby, not wanting to disturb the poignant reunion.

Esther lifted her head. "Jacob, we will help you in any way we can." Her voice expressed sincere determination. "I don't want to push, but I hope you'll feel welcome to stay here, in this house, as long as you want. I certainly have plenty of room."

"That's not why I came. I appreciate the offer, though." As he saw her face begin to cloud, he added, "I'll consider it." He rose and stepped away. "Hello, Clarice. I'm glad to see you again."

She took his hand. "We've all missed you. While we're happy to have you back, we're saddened to hear about your troubles. Not to pry, but could you give us some idea of the areas where you've been living since you left the service?"

He launched into sparse details. Tess saw Trey's fingers tapping on the couch beside her. She intuited he was still wary. Despite her Pollyanna hopes everything would turn out well, she couldn't help but share the sentiment. She believed in Jake's honesty and his intent. Yet those two years on the road might have changed him in ways they couldn't predict.

The conversation continued until Esther asked if Clarice would serve. Tess joined her to pass small croissant sandwiches, melon wedges, and ginger cookies.

"I sure have missed Carol's cookies," Jake said as he selected a handful. "Thank her for baking my favorites."

Tess suspected the leftovers would be sent with him, if he didn't change his mind to stay the night. She was pleased when Trey began to contribute to the conversation, hopefully indicating his apprehension might be loosening. When Jake asked about his architecture work, he grew animated, describing the long-distance partnership to assist a former co-worker who had moved back to Paris.

"Shame of it is, I might have to go over there for a few days," he said with a grin.

She sipped her iced tea as the others shared about their visits to the wondrous city. Jake recalled being there with his father as a teenager, leading Esther to tear up about her departed son.

To lighten the conversation, Clarice exclaimed over the excellent boutiques. "Have you been there, Tess? You can find some excellent vintage pieces at the flea markets."

"Unfortunately, no. Paris is definitely on my bucket list."

As the clock chimed three times, Jake surprised them by standing. "I've had a great time seeing you all again, but I need to head out." Noting his grandmother's stricken expression, he leaned to kiss her cheek. "I promise I won't disappear. In fact, I should hear soon about that job." He had filled them in on the positive interview at a local packaging plant.

"Stop by any time," she urged, smiling again. "And stay for as long as you'd like. Please come to dinner soon, as Carol would be ecstatic to feed you. Her skill is restrained in cooking for the two of us."

Clarice rose and asked if any of them would take leftovers from the tea cart as Carol had overdone the bounty. Her comment was worded carefully. Both Jake and Trey accepted the offer.

Jake made his goodbyes while Clarice gathered the food. He headed toward Tess as she and Trey rose from the settee. "I have you to thank for this reunion today. I appreciate you coming out to find me so I wouldn't turn tail again." He tossed a sly glance at Trey and added in a low aside, "You, too, asshat."

He snorted out a laugh. "Hey. Remember I used to kick your butt when we wrestled. Though to give you credit, you've picked up some muscle since then."

Jake laughed, too—the first time he'd done so since they'd met him, Tess thought. He reached to shake Trey's hand, but as their hands clasped, he frowned and jerked back. He peered toward his cousin's palm. "You got a joy buzzer in there?"

Trey showed his palms, his expression neutral. "Nope. Static, I guess. Sorry about that." Jake returned to hug his grandmother, and Trey shared a knowing look with Tess.

"Whoa," she mouthed. Her mind buzzed with excitement. If her hypothesis was correct, could he provide another piece to the mystery?

They watched Esther lead him out, locking in the details for a mealtime visit. The trio waited silently for her return. She burst into the room clapping her hands, a smile wreathing her face. "I'm too keyed up to sit. Let's head to the attic and dive into Edward's trunk."

Chapter Twenty-Two

Trey didn't try to stifle his moan. He registered the pleading, hopeful looks, and caved. If it was that important to these special ladies, he wouldn't disappoint them. With the introduction of Jake into the equation, he was—against his better judgment—becoming a grudging believer in the otherworldly connections.

"Before we go up, you should know that our handshake resembled touching a live wire," he said. "Tess and I didn't tell you about this before because it seemed one more complication. She had a vision including Stephen after we found Jake the other night. He may be tied into this, too."

His mother pushed out a noisy breath. "I certainly didn't expect that. But I suppose nothing should surprise us at this point. Does he know about…everything?"

"No. He's already skittish, and we need to be sure. If we're going to bring him into this, we should let him acclimate with us again." He avoided adding, *or it might send him running.*

Esther nodded. "That is astounding, and he likely won't accept this the way we have. Since his father's death, Jacob has been closed off. Cynical. All the more reason we should look into Edward's trunk now, to try to find additional answers." Decision made, she led them out of the room.

Resigned, Trey trailed behind. The short trek to the attic provided the chance to admire Tess' trim waist, shapely legs, and swing of dark hair—and yes, her fine posterior. She mounted the stairs in front of him, diverting his mind momentarily.

Now he faced the undesirable task of rummaging through Edward's clothing and personal belongings. Not that he was *scared*, but his flash experience in the bedroom had been in a hazy sleep phase. He didn't know if he'd be able to surrender control of his mind and body while awake.

'Fess up, he admitted as they crossed the landing. Truth was he dreaded the possibility. Tess was a strong-minded woman, and she'd had no choice but to succumb to the supernatural invasions. Neither of them had been harmed or felt any threat, but with an uncontrollable quantity, how could they be sure the interaction wouldn't hurt them? Even the toughest man would be apprehensive.

The women stood aside as he turned the old key and swung the attic door wide. Esther picked up the flashlight she'd left behind after the last visit. "I'm glad you thought of doing this, Tess." She shined the circle of light through the dusky space. "Edward's trunk is also packed full of clothing. Here it is." She narrowed the shaft of light.

Trey ducked under the eaves to discover a second case, identical to Phoebe's. The initials E.E.C. glimmered in gold leaf.

"What does the second E stand for?" Tess asked.

"Ellington," Esther said. "His mother's maiden name. She came from another well-to-do local family. I imagine those descendants also would have great interest in our discoveries."

Tess again lent an arm to help him carry the heavy trunk out to the ballroom. They set it next to Phoebe's and stood back for a few moments.

"Should we take the clothes out, like last time?" his mother asked. Her excitement translated through action as she fidgeted with her white-blond pageboy. "Or do you want to reach in and see if you get any impressions?"

He stared at the gleaming black trunk, his leg muscles tightening as if he'd pushed beyond his limits to run a marathon. A trickle of sweat snaked down his back. "May as well jump right in."

Tess reached out a steady hand to grasp his. "You're much taller. How about we pull up a chair rather than have you bend awkwardly?"

He raised one eyebrow, recognizing the underlying support. "Good idea."

"We'll all sit," Esther said.

They pulled up chairs, and Trey sat in front of the trunk while the others ringed around the sides. His heart sped up as he swung the lid open on century-old hinges. A folded cream linen suit jacket lay on top, with a starched white dress shirt tucked to the side. He willed his hand to grasp the jacket collar, to lift the tailored garment. An image rocketed into his mind with astonishing clarity.

A parlor in an upper-class home, filled with heavy, carved furniture, a plethora of knickknacks and artwork, swags of forest green velvet drapes tied with golden ropes. Clusters of young friends gathered for an informal evening entertainment. The tinkling notes of a piano, and the floating laughter as Phoebe and her friend struggled to play a popular duet.

"She's the most beautiful woman in the room," he declared, lounging against the back wall.

"She's the most beautiful woman in any room," Nick corrected, his eyes also trained on the slim back swaying on the piano bench.

"I'm going to ask her to marry me." His declaration was spoken softly, but with determination. He had no doubt she'd say yes.

"So soon?" Nick turned skeptical eyes toward him. "Are you sure this isn't a reaction to the failed romance in London?"

No, he knew she was the only woman for him. Attractive, cultured, intelligent. And, he suspected, possessing a hidden well of sensuality. He raised his glass. "The wench in London was an infatuation, my boy. This is love. When you find it, you'll immediately recognize the difference."

"I'm sure I will," Nick muttered and averted his eyes. He pushed away from the wall. "Right now, I need to find more whiskey."

Trey's shoulders slumped, and he released the jacket into the trunk. His mind swam with dizzying color, though the shapes now were indefinable. He lifted his head and registered nausea in the pit of his stomach. The sunlight refracted rainbows across the room, as if his pupils had been dilated for an eye exam. He blinked and squinted, trying to refocus on the three women stretching forward in alarm.

"What did you see?" Esther commanded.

Still disoriented, he met their worried gazes. His mind filtered through the vivid images, as if witnessing them from a greater distance. He closed his eyes to center on the details before drawing a shuddering breath. "Edward told Nick he was going to ask her to marry him. Nick questioned if it was too soon and referenced the failed romance in London. He didn't seem happy about the thought of their engagement as he took off in search of more whiskey."

"A common occurrence, apparently." Clarice cupped her hand around his knee, her eyes probing his with motherly care.

Tess, sitting on the opposite side, touched his shoulder. Her face mirrored empathy. It disturbed him to see her after the vision of Phoebe. He closed his eyes again.

Her hand squeezed his as her voice compelled to pull him back. "I know, this is disorienting. Please don't push if you're not up for it."

Tess, not Phoebe. Get yourself together, man. If she can handle these visions, so can you.

"I'm okay." He tried to reassure himself as well as them. "Don't fuss, ladies. There's no pain. You just kind of disappear into someone else's psyche. Obviously, these scenes are important, and they shed light on the relationships. I'm ready to move on."

"Only if you're sure." His mother waited for his nod and removed the suit coat from the trunk. She laid it over a chair as Trey reached for the snowy white shirt.

Combating the surprising burst of spring heat, he hung his jacket on the wicker rocker and rolled up his sleeves. The slight breeze cooled his torso as he grasped the wooden mallet and planted his feet in a studied stance.

Whack. The orange-striped croquet ball careened down the manicured lawn and smacked into the green opposition, sending it flying under a blooming peony bush.

"Unfair." Phoebe cried, but her full lips were smiling. "Now you have to help me find my ball, you competitive fiend."

She headed toward the bush, hips swaying under the filmy white ensemble. She stooped to bend in search of the wayward ball. His breath caught, and a shaft of heat coursed through his body as he tossed the mallet down and approached.

Her attention had been diverted by the fragrant, white-pink blooms drooping heavy from their stems. She cupped her hands around a flower to inhale the heady scent.

"They're my very favorite flowers." She peeked up at him with a smile. "We must plant some starts this year. We'll have rows of grand bushes at the mansion."

"Anything you wish, my love," he promised. "I can hardly sleep at night knowing we'll be married in less than three months and moving there together. Do you feel the same anticipation?"

"I do." Her eyes held his; she laughed in delight. "Which is exactly what I'll be saying to you on our wedding day."

He smiled and caught her in his arms, not caring if they were observed by inquisitive party guests or her strict parents. "I'll repeat that vow. And then, I'll repeat this…"

He kissed her and was captivated by the sweet softness. She met his urgency, and he dared to pull her closer, with a firm hand to the small of her back. The *thin materials provided little barrier between them, and for the first time he felt the weight of her breasts rising above the corset to push against his chest.*

He deepened the kiss, and her lips parted, allowing him to probe his tongue into her mouth. Her body arched, and he feared she might pull away. Instead, her tongue darted to meet his. Passions fully ignited, he called on his consummate control to ease back from her tantalizing lips. Her face mirrored his heated emotion.

"I am surely counting the days until we can be together always," he murmured, resting his forehead against his beloved's.

Trey's body hummed with awareness as he emerged from the sensual stream of vision. He was going to have to edit his public version of this flash, he thought, meeting Tess' eyes. He noted similar concern on all the watching faces; none of them took these forays into the past lightly. Thankfully, he felt more centered coming out of this one. Maybe it would get easier each time. Till they could slip back and forth between history and reality without a quiver. The thought was way too unnerving to even consider. He thrust the shirt toward Tess and gathered his wits to share the highlights.

"They were playing croquet. I got the impression the scene was at his mother's house, during the engagement party. We read about it in the diary. They seemed happy and in sync." *And impassioned.* He braced his hands on his knees and tapped a rapid tempo. "Tess will be pleased to hear this. The vision seems to cement that, while she may have flirted with others, Edward and Phoebe went into the marriage totally committed."

She nodded. "I had the same sense from her. But yes, I'm really glad you confirm the feeling."

"I think I'm done for the day. I'm sorry to disappoint you all." Though each flash had been brief, he'd pushed through layers of swirling emotion. He was surprised at the draining nature of the visions and craved time to re-center himself.

Esther stepped forward to take his hand. Her smile made his discomfort worth the while. "How could I be disappointed after such an enlightening day? I'm thrilled the two of you are willing to take such drastic measures to help solve the mystery. Please tell us if your sensations change and become more negative. We'll definitely call it off." Her lips twisted. "I have to admit, I came up here earlier to go through Phoebe's trunk again. I halfway hoped to see a vision myself. But it appears the two of you are the chosen conduits. Perhaps we'll discover Jacob is, as well. Since I've lived here for two decades, one would think it would have happened by now if I was going to be a selected vessel."

"Tess appears to be the catalyst in all this." Clarice rose from the folding chair. "Trey has been in the house too many times to count over the years. Soon after she set foot here, she started to experience visions. Then he did, as well."

"Exactly." Esther's eyes widened. "I forgot to tell you when I looked farther into Phoebe's trunk, I found jewelry in a pouch hidden in the side." She reached into her jacket pocket and drew out a small object wrapped in a white handkerchief. "Tess, I want you to have this in gratitude for all your help."

Trey noted the P.P.C. monogram on the

handkerchief as Tess unwrapped a delicate brooch. Gold tendrils entwined in a heart shape around a deep red, circular-cut stone. Her pupils dilated. His pulse leaped as he recognized she was experiencing a flash of vision.

Before he could tell the others, she drifted back. Her smile turned wistful as she looked up at them. "I saw Edward give this to her, pinning it to her dress collar. I'm sure he had it made especially for her." She rubbed her cheek, contemplating. "He told her: '*Now you may always carry my heart with you, literally as well as figuratively.*' He's so well spoken. Poetic even. I think Phoebe wants us to see this side of him, to convince us he didn't hurt her."

She didn't seem to realize she'd spoken in present tense. Tess held the brooch toward the light shining from the high windows. The stone shot sparks of crimson fire. "This is so gorgeous." She looked toward the other females. "Do you think it's a ruby? If so, I can't accept something this valuable."

"Nonsense, my dear." Esther adopted a regal tone. "It could be paste for all I know. Though I doubt that, of course. We want you to have it. As the lady of the manor, so to speak, it's my prerogative to give this gift. You'll actually be doing me a favor, as it could be quite a competition between the nieces to decide which of them merited this bauble."

"Thank you, all of you." Tess kissed Esther's finely lined cheek. "I'm so glad you came into the shop and invited me to be part of the style show. It seems like fate, kismet—God's will."

"In more ways than one," Clarice said with a fond smile. "Not to embarrass my dear son, but I'm very pleased the two of you are getting along so well."

"Thanks, Mom. And before you scare her away completely, I think we'll head out."

Yes, she was embarrassing him, but he'd get over it. He avoided their grinning expressions by standing and shutting the lid on Edward's trunk. After hugs for Esther and Clarice, he followed Tess down the stairs and out into the waning evening. His jumbled emotions began to stabilize as they left the mansion behind.

She pulled him up short when she stopped next to the decades-old lilac bush and grasped his arm. "You saw more, didn't you?"

He halted under the limbs, now bare of blooms. "How could you tell?"

She lifted one tantalizing tanned shoulder. "You came out of the second flash more disoriented. That could also be explained by jumping from one right into the other. The continuum leaves you more dizzy."

"You're right. That one was more heated. They went to find her croquet ball, and Edward kissed her." He inhaled the citrusy tang of her hair. "He'd taken off his suit jacket. She was wearing some filmy, lightweight dress. Possibly the one from her trunk. He registered them coming together for the first time without the separation of multiple layers of clothing."

The scene had been both romantic and sensual— though not as charged as the honeymoon, he thought. He could tell that his description of the croquet scene was lighting up her imagination, as well. He reached for her hands as his body relived the wave of encompassing heat. "The flash was passionate. Steamy." He whispered in her ear. "He did have a poetic way with words, but his instincts were pure male."

His thumbs danced over her knuckles as she swayed toward him, her enticing pink lips opening. Reminding himself they were in a public place—where his mother could come dashing out at any moment—Trey attempted to distract his body's growing response. He spotted a peony bush next to the iron fence, loaded with blooms. He reached around Tess to pluck a delicate white flower, maintaining a hair's breadth of distance between their bodies.

"These were Phoebe's favorites." He held it up so she could bury her nose in the fragrant petals. She inhaled, closing her eyes. The pull was magnetic, irresistible. He raised his other hand to caress her smooth cheek.

The peony fluttered to the ground as he vented the arousal swelling through his body. She cradled his head to hers, and he urged her body into the shadow of a tall, leafy oak. He pinned it with his, muscles contrasting against her softness, reveling in the melding heat.

Lips sliding, shifting, opening, and indulging, soaring beyond the point of Edward and Phoebe's shared passion. Trey embraced the fever, subconsciously aware he'd never been overwhelmed by such a torrent of raw desire. Knowing he wanted desperately to make love to this woman, even if the sentiment was heightened by unseen influences.

But not here on the street. Like Edward, he exercised supreme will to pull back and peer into her flushed face. The blood throbbed through his body.

"Obviously, we need to move on," he suggested hoarsely, "or risk being arrested for public indecency."

She smiled and closed her eyes again, resting her hands on his upper chest. "Sadly, you're right." Her lashes fluttered open over dreamy eyes.

The desire was evident on both sides, he thought. If the invitation was issued, he'd gladly join her inside the apartment and see where the night might lead. Hell, he knew damn well where it would lead. His body protested when he eased back, attempting to banish all thoughts of Edward and Phoebe.

She matched his hurried strides back to the car. He helped her in then leaped around to his side and drove over the limit toward her apartment. As he rolled through a stop sign a block from her building, his phone jangled the opening strains to *"In the Mood."* Which seemed especially apropos at the moment.

He wasn't about to answer it. "Just my mother."

"Maybe they discovered something after we left."

Afraid of dampening the mood, he answered in a clipped tone. "Hi, Mom. I'm driving Tess home."

He listened to her breathless explanation, and his heart clutched with anxiety. "Okay. Stay calm. I'll drop her off and head right there."

He clicked off, frowning, and braked as they reached her apartment building. "Esther had some sort of spell and almost fell down the stairs. My mother's driving her to the hospital since it's so close. She didn't want to go at all and refused to ride in an ambulance. I need to join them."

She looked as distressed as he felt. "I'll go with you."

He made a tight U-turn and headed toward the nearby hospital. Had the events of the day taken a toll? Jake's homecoming paired with more visions must have been a strain for her. Damn, if anything happened—

"Nothing serious, right?" Tess asked, her hair

whipping across her face as he accelerated. "Your mom said she was dizzy but didn't pass out or anything?"

"Hopefully, she's just tired or dehydrated." He didn't voice his thoughts. She was smart enough to come to the same conclusions. He didn't want her to blame herself, yet he couldn't even consider losing Esther in his life. Sure, she was in her late seventies, but she was so vibrant he couldn't imagine her succumbing to an unexpected health issue. If these vision sessions were impacting her wellbeing, he'd put a stop to them right now.

He shot around a slow-moving SUV, earning a sour look from the female driver. Really, who drove the speed limit these days? Tess glanced at him but remained quiet. He appreciated her comforting presence as he parked, and they trotted toward the sprawling multi-story complex. She took his hand, and he sighed inwardly, thinking how close they had edged to moving beyond the hand-holding stage. They stormed the emergency room to find Clarice pacing, her face contorted with worry. Though well aware of his mother's dramatic leanings, his emotions amped another notch.

She met them in the center of the room, grasping at his arm. "They've taken her for tests already because they think it could be her heart. She finally told me she'd had some pressure lately which she thought was indigestion. I pray this wasn't a serious heart attack."

****

As Tess watched Trey provide steady support to his mother's shoulders, she couldn't help being catapulted back to the small county hospital where they had awaited word of her grandmother's prognosis. The stroke had taken her life that night, so swiftly she never regained consciousness. She wasn't able to say "I love you, Gram" one last time while she was awake and functioning.

She crossed her arms over her chest and buried her fingers beneath them, chilled by the memory and the air conditioning. Her head jerked up as she remembered Esther's rediscovered grandson. "How can we let Jake know about this? I'm sure she wouldn't want to worry him, but he should be aware. He might even want to be here. Not that anything is going to happen…" her voice trailed off.

Trey's frown deepened. "You're right. He needs to know. I'll go out and see if I can find him. Hopefully, he's staying in the same location."

He charged out of the waiting room, and she took Clarice's arm and convinced her to sit. She engaged her in conversation, though she felt just as unnerved. The television program focusing on political banter set her teeth on edge, as did the shrieking toddler brought in by a harried mother fretting about his high fever.

She tried to tune them all out and kicked herself for the way she'd pushed Esther to meet with Jake. Though the gathering had been a success, the older woman undoubtedly had been anxious he wouldn't show. They should have insisted she rest after he left, rather than tramp upstairs.

Her anxiety rose as the minutes ticked by. She was getting cups of water from the nearby machine when a middle-aged woman wearing blue scrubs finally approached. She abandoned the cups as the woman introduced herself as the cardiologist.

"The tests show a blockage. Appears she had a

small heart attack. We're prepping her for stent surgery." Seeing their stricken expressions, the doctor soothed, "These surgeries are very safe and quick. The procedure itself should be about twenty minutes. After recovery, they'll take her up to a room. She's in good health otherwise and might only need to stay overnight."

As she walked away, Trey burst back into the room with Jake. Clarice hurried to share the information. The men looked anxious, even as Tess added the doctor's reassuring comments.

Jake stood silent and pondering, his brows drawn together in a sharp line. "I'm going to take her up on her offer to stay for a while. I know Carol will be there, but if it makes her happy, I want to do that. Then I'm there if she needs me." He'd changed to his jeans and sweatshirt and looked a little rough and tumbled next to his polished cousin.

Trey shot him a surprised glance. "Great idea. How about tonight you come home with me. We'll have more of a chance to catch up." His firm expression seemed to dare his cousin to argue.

"Fine, Cuz." He chose not to fight him. "I do appreciate the offer."

Tess hid her smile at the relationship dynamic. They'd alluded to being competitive while growing up. Certainly, they'd taken very different paths in life—and maybe that complicated their current interactions. Similar to the complex relationship between Edward and Stephen?

Trey turned to his mother. "Will you call Carol? I'm sure she'll appreciate staying informed. She'll probably want to come down here, and she's welcome to. But let her know the prognosis is positive."

"Good idea. I've been too worried to think about that." She walked outside to make the call, and the others settled into a semi-circle of chairs to wait for an update. Within the hour, a male nurse arrived with an upbeat report. The procedure had gone well; Esther was stable and being settled into a room. They could visit soon, two at a time for a brief period as she'd need her rest. She might be sleeping already, in fact.

The news raised their spirits, and they began to talk and joke as they made their way through the maze of halls to the unit. Trey teased that architects considered it a job well done when visitors had to wander for at least fifteen minutes before finding their way through any hospital.

In her room, Esther was groggy but awake. Jake and Clarice entered first. Esther's exclamation of joy filtered through the door at her grandson's intent to move into the mansion. When Tess and Trey exchanged places with them, they urged her to listen to the professionals so she could return home soon, and healthy.

"You bet I will," she said as her eyes began to shut. "I have to get home to welcome Jacob."

****

Knowing Esther was in good hands after her release the next day, Tess kept an appointment in a nearby town. The elderly woman practically gave her the garments to ensure they'd go to appreciative homes. With a loaded back seat and a head-full of related stories, Tess wove back through the countryside toward Michigan City. As a farmer's daughter, she appreciated the green shoots of corn and soybean crops popping up in the flat, plowed fields.

Her phone pinged, and she pulled off on a side road to open Trey's brief update on Esther's condition. She was pleased to learn her friend was not only in good spirits but seemed to be recovering well from the stent operation.

—She wants us all to do dinner Wed pm—he texted. *—Think we should talk to Jake then?—*

"Probably should," she dictated by speakerphone. "He could begin experiencing flashes. Best tell him when we're all together."

She drove on, hoping for new progress in their quest—depending on how Jake accepted their revelations.

Chapter Twenty-Three

Between a lull in customers on Wednesday morning, Tess filled Marcy in on Jake's visit and concluded with the trip to the ER. "Thankfully, those stent procedures are routine and successful. She's doing fine, and we're all relieved."

Mentally relieved, physically frustrated, she thought, remembering the hot kisses she and Trey shared outside the mansion. Without the medical issues, they might have run to her apartment and gotten better *acquainted.*

"How scary. I'm glad to hear she's recovering," Marcy said as she steamed new merchandise from the recent buying excursion. "I'm sure she's over the moon about Jake moving in."

"She is. Too bad he was motivated by the health scare. I hope this helps him ease in and get comfortable. Though I can't imagine he'll leap right in and believe in the visions and support us."

Marcy grinned. "You mean like I did?"

"Thank goodness you're such an open-minded person so I have someone to share all this with. If you weren't, you'd still be a great employee. But I'd wall off that part of my life."

"You've perked up my days, for sure. Some time, I'd like to introduce you to my best friend, Justine. She's had her own cool ghostly encounters. Right now, she and her handsome hubby are in Los Angeles. He's a screenwriter so they split the time between Indiana and California."

Still too engulfed with the shop and the mystery to link into other social networks, Tess did want to make new friends. "Hmm. What a tough compromise," she teased. "I'd love to meet her and hear the stories."

Later, after Marcy headed off for her second job, she tackled mundane tasks, including paying the dreaded mortgage. The bank balance confirmed a profit, though not a hearty one. It still woke her up at night. Marcy also had begun to post the new items on the web site, and she hoped they'd move soon, either virtually or in the shop.

At the stroke of five, she locked up and walked to the mansion carrying a box of chocolates. She wanted to remind Trey of the initial delicious plunge into Phoebe's diary at her apartment. The fragrance of blooming flowers caressed her as she strolled in the warm air: purple irises, bursting rhododendrons, and her favorite peonies. She peered beyond the plants and bushes to the houses on the side streets, featuring gingerbread trim and deep porches. Though some had gotten a little rundown over the years, she preferred to imagine them in their prime.

In comparison, Carver House loomed as a polished jewel on the huge corner lot. Clarice answered the door when she knocked, and Tess questioned why Trey's car wasn't parked outside.

"He'll be here soon. He had to finish a late conference call," his mother confirmed. "We're having a glass of wine while we wait." She lowered her voice. "Though Jake's drinking lemonade."

He stood when Tess entered the parlor. She smiled and said hello before dipping to hug his grandmother. After assurances of Esther's improved health, Clarice poured Tess a glass of chilled white wine. They'd resettled to make small talk when the sharp rap of the door knocker sounded. Trey let himself in. He headed first to Esther as his mother jumped up to pour him a glass.

He leaned over to hug his older cousin, displaying an expanse of lean, muscled back and taut butt. Tess smiled and welcomed the little hum of anticipation. She caught Jake watching her. His pointed look seemed to probe inside her head as he lifted the lemonade glass in a mock toast. Her cheeks warmed, and she wondered if Trey had shared any details about their relationship. She kept her eyes on the goblet and took a measured swallow.

At this point, their status was hazy, and she wished she knew how he'd define it. There was definite attraction and sizzling heat, but while they'd been together a few times in various circumstances, they'd actually only been on one "date." Was that enough to say they were dating? Due to his wariness of being manipulated by Phoebe and Edward, he probably preferred caution and considered her a friend. Without benefits.

Though she knew without question that had been about to change on Sunday night, intimacy would have added complication. It surely would have been way outside her usual conservative nature. She'd never let passion rule and jumped into bed quickly. But in this case, her control submerged under the currents of emotion, romance, and plain old lust.

When Trey joined her on the couch, giving a roguish wink, Tess forgot any apprehensions. The buzzing awareness of his nearness continued as the group talked for a few more minutes.

A small, rounded woman in a red apron entered with a cheery smile. Tess guessed this was Carol, Esther's housekeeper and dear friend.

"Hello everyone," the lady chirped. "I do love cooking for a group. Jacob, how wonderful to see you." She stepped to take his hand, then approached Tess. "We haven't had the joy of meeting, but I've heard great things."

"I've heard so much about you, as well. And I've tasted the proof in your excellent cooking."

"I hope you say the same after dinner. If you're all hungry, the food's ready." She shooed them into the dining room. The chandelier shimmered over the massive carved table set with Blue Willow dishes and crystal. Tess wondered if they were Phoebe's, but she didn't want to introduce her name until they'd talked to Jake. She also figured the others didn't want to have the serious conversation during the meal.

Carol carried in a platter of roast beef and followed with bowls of mashed potatoes, brown gravy, and broccoli. Tess was transported to Sunday dinners at her grandmother's, floating with the heavenly scent of homemade yeast rolls. Though Gram's farmhouse, and her own family home, had been much simpler dwellings. She'd never eaten an everyday meal in such grandeur, surrounded by burgundy walls bordered with cherry-wood wainscoting.

She accepted the bowl of broccoli from Jake. Any sense of his hesitation to rejoin the family seemed to have faded. If she didn't know better, she'd never have guessed he'd been living on the streets and dealing with hard times. He looked more relaxed and yes, attractive, as he enjoyed the meal and the conversation. His blond hair was combed back off his forehead over the pale blue eyes that echoed his grandmother's.

He lifted his fork and speared through a bite of roast beef, those eyes flashing mischief. "This is a feast fit for a prodigal grandson. Though with Carol, even simple meals are delicious."

The others laughed as the housekeeper flapped her hands at him from her seat at the end of the table. "Such a flirt. I remember you hovering in my kitchen as a boy and a teen, tossing out compliments in hopes of snagging hot cookies."

"Worked, didn't it?" He drew another round of laughter. "I do have an announcement to make," he added, scooping more potatoes onto his plate. "I learned today I got the job. I'll start orientation on Monday. You'll be happy to know a future partner of the resource center helped me polish my resume and interview skills."

Esther apparently had been told, as she beamed approval. The others offered excited congratulations. Carol gave him another piece of beef without asking.

He murmured thanks before drizzling gravy over his food. "I can save money to hopefully rent an apartment or small house," he continued. "It's starting to feel right to settle down again. I also have an appointment for outpatient therapy. I've been attending a Narcotics Anonymous group already. To tie up the loose ends, I called Mom. After she teared up, she chewed me out—rightly—for disappearing. She's planning to visit when she can arrange time off from her own work."

"Sounds like things are falling into place for you." Trey lifted his glass. "Along the theme of good news, while we wait to hear about The Hope Center, our board asked me to design a concept for a community of tiny houses to provide long-term shelter for some of the homeless."

Another round of smiles and exclamations followed. Jake joined in. "Like I said, Cuz, it seems this was the right time to land back here in Michigan City."

Trey caught Tess' eye. They could only hope he'd accept their explanations of the visions and not distance himself again. The thought caused more than a little anxiety, but she pushed it aside and concentrated on her last bites of tender beef.

The opportunity for the conversation arose after they'd eaten homemade angel food cake with strawberries picked from the backyard patch. Carol declined help with the clean-up, and the others returned to the parlor to visit. Trey stood by the fireplace, resting his arm on the mantel.

"You know, Jake, you said you felt compelled to come back here. Maybe that's a figure of speech, but we want to share something you're going to think is pretty far out. In fact, the idea has stretched my logical mind way beyond the comfort zone."

Jake stood a few feet away from him, near his grandmother's chair. He frowned and crossed his arms over his chest.

"We just ask that you hear us out," Trey continued in the professional tone he'd used at the hearing. "I'm going to start at the beginning, when Edward Carver built this house for his new wife, Phoebe."

"If I recall the family history correctly," Jake said, one blond eyebrow raised, "he murdered her here."

"That's how the story was told, but we now have strong cause to believe otherwise. With Tess' help, we've been doing some…research."

Jake's eyes darted around the room. "What kind of research can you do on a decades-old murder?"

Tess held her breath. This was where the narrative would turn tricky. Trey came to sit next to her on the couch. He trained his eyes on his cousin as the women remained silent.

"Without going into a lot of detail, Esther held a style show celebration in the ballroom last month for the mansion's centennial. Tess modeled one of Phoebe's trousseau gowns. I wore Edward's wedding tuxedo." He paused and rubbed his chin. "Here's the crazy part. During the event and at a few other times since—in the house and even outside it—Tess and I both have seen flashes of visions from their past."

They watched the expressions war across Jake's face: disbelief becoming mocking amusement. He leaned back in the chair and crossed his legs at the ankle. "You're messing with me, right?"

"He's serious as a heart attack," Esther said from her throne-chair. "We know how incredible this sounds, but they've witnessed actual scenes from Edward and Phoebe's lives, echoed straight from her diary. They saw some of these things even before they read about them. Also, look at this picture of the couple taken on their wedding day." She retrieved the photograph from the nearby table.

He examined it for a few seconds before staring at

the couple across the room. He handed it back to Esther. "Okay. I accept the strong resemblance, but you're blowing my mind here."

"Our minds are blown, too," Tess said. "In more ways than one." She leaned forward with clasped hands. "I was the first one to see a vision. I fainted at the style show and saw Phoebe in bed upstairs, waiting for Edward. Another blond man I couldn't identify came into the room and manhandled her. When I came out of the vision, I told the others 'my husband didn't kill me.' "

Trey nodded. "I've seen Edward bursting into the same bedroom to witness the man holding his new wife. I only saw the guy from the back."

Jake stood and stalked to the wall of windows facing the garden. He peered out, jamming his hands into the pockets of his slacks. "If I didn't know better, I'd think you'd been doing mushrooms. Yeah, this is beyond crazy. But there's more to it, isn't there? Why tell me now?"

"We think you might be another link in the chain," she answered softly. "When I got between you two the other night and touched you both at the same time, I channeled a vision of Edward, Phoebe, and his stepbrother, Stephen. He's one of the men mentioned in the diary. We consider him to be a strong suspect."

He turned, his eyes flashing. "You think I might be a link to him? Man, I've seen lots of things that were beyond my comprehension in war zones, but this pushes way farther." He flung up his hands. "Look, I have the greatest respect for all of you, but I don't believe in this bull—this mumbo jumbo you're trying to feed me for some reason."

Trey interjected. "Remember the shock that passed between us when we shook hands here the other day? That wasn't just static, bro."

Jake shifted to look at each face in turn. All eyes met his with solemn acknowledgement. To Tess' surprise, he dropped his head into his hands. "Even if I did believe this—and I'm trying to give you all the benefit of the doubt—what the heck do you want from me? Did you ask me to stay here so you could experiment with me?"

"Of course not." Esther sprang up to stand before him, and he let his hands fall to his sides. "We had no hidden intentions in connecting with you. Even if you don't believe and don't want to participate in any way, you are still my beloved grandson. I'll continue to welcome you with open arms." She cupped his cheeks in her own hands.

He leaned back to disengage. His grandmother's face reflected sadness as she stepped back.

"I'm sorry. That comment was out of line." He watched her retreat, his hands fisted on his thighs. "I know none of you would do that, but you understand this has been a huge surprise. I need time to think it through. You talk about 'visions.' Mine are PTSD-related from Afghanistan and the explosion. I've been fighting to rid myself of them for years."

Tess hadn't contemplated how the visions could strain his mending psyche. He couldn't afford to jeopardize his wellbeing that way. They would have to work around his involvement.

"By no means do we want to see you hurt," Clarice said, voicing similar sentiments. "We'll all understand if you don't feel you can assist. On the other hand, you being here may be a catalyst in itself."

He stared across the room at Tess and Trey. "Sounds like you two don't have control of what happens to you. Makes me question if I should stay."

"Oh, Jacob," Esther murmured. Her expression remained downcast as she sat next to Clarice.

"I don't mean stay in town. I mean live here in this house. Or with Trey, either." He slapped his palms on his thighs with a startling crack of sound. "Might not make any difference though. You all seem to think the die is cast, and it won't matter if I'm game. Look, I'm sorry to break up this nice evening, but I'm going out to clear my head." He stood and left the room with long strides.

Tess winced as the outer door slammed shut. As they looked around the silent room, the others seemed to share her sense of guilt. They'd pushed too far, too fast. At least he hadn't taken his backpack. He would return for that necessity, hopefully in a better frame of mind.

"I think, overall, that went well," Clarice ventured with her characteristic poise. "He'll calm down. He may not believe as we do, but he'll give us the benefit of the doubt." She stood to refill their wine glasses.

Trey accepted his and tossed down half the contents in one swallow. "My mother the eternal optimist."

Chapter Twenty-Four

The next evening Tess was tidying her apartment when the phone rang. She dropped the dust cloth she'd been swishing through the living room. Anticipating Trey's voice, she answered with an upbeat "Hello."

"Tess. Hi. Hope I didn't catch you at a bad time."

Brett Stenson's voice instantly cranked up a fight or flight response, and her hand began to tremble around the phone. There'd been so much going on in her life she hadn't thought about her former boyfriend in weeks. She'd welcomed the respite, using it as an opportunity to finally bury his negative comments and rebuild her self-esteem.

"I'm catching up on my cleaning. The shop's going so well I don't have much extra time. What are you up to?" *That sounds more polite than "what in hell do you want?"*

"Sadly, in case you hadn't heard, I wanted to let you know my grandmother died." His tone was solemn.

"Oh no. I'm so sorry." Truly disturbed, Tess had been quite fond of the older lady whom he credited with practically raising him in his rebellious teen years. The influence had helped keep him on a relatively straight path, rather than veering off into trouble like his older brother did after their father left the family.

"What happened?" she asked.

"Breast cancer. They caught it late, and she didn't

have much time. She's only been gone a couple of weeks." Brett paused and cleared his throat. "I still can't believe it."

She pictured him trying to maintain a strong front while his heart was breaking with grief. She blinked back the tears filling her eyes. "You know how much I liked and respected her. She was a good friend to my grandmother, too."

"Thanks for your sympathy. Means a lot. I'm also calling because she asked me to give you a few pieces of old clothing from her mother and grandmother. She thought you'd like to have them."

Tess ignored the derogatory reference to "old clothing," to focus on the gesture. "That is so sweet of her. I'll keep them in my personal collection."

"I'll be in Northwest Indiana for a meeting tomorrow. At the end of the day, I'll come to Michigan City and drop them off."

As usual, he presented his case without considering her feelings, or her schedule. She flinched at the thought of a personal, in-your-face interaction. Tonight's conversation had been cordial—a swing from the critical comments he'd slung until she gathered the backbone to boot him from her life. She wouldn't open herself to such treatment ever again.

"I'd love to see your shop," he added. "I'll plug the address into my map system, and I should be able to get there around five."

Her eyes widened at the unexpected interest in the store. "You don't need to go to all that bother. You could ship me the items."

"I said I'll be in the area." His persistence gene reared. "I want to bring these things to you. My grandmother made me promise as one of her final wishes."

The statement eliminated further excuses. Tess assured herself it would be a quick, minimal contact. She would not play the role of doormat. "All right. I guess that would work." *What else could she do?*

"I know your parents are traveling. Would you tell them about her?"

"They must not have heard, or my mother would have mentioned it. Thanks for letting me know." Eager to end the call, she rattled off the shop's address. After exchanging goodbyes, she dropped onto the couch, her hair swinging to veil her warm cheeks. Though the tone of the interaction had been positive, she did not look forward to seeing Brett Stenson again.

****

Marcy offered to stay late the next night during his visit. "For moral support. Or to kick his butt if he's obnoxious." She kicked her foot, in a three-inch platform sandal, into the air.

"I know you have plans tonight. I'll be fine. Really. He's not a threat to me." Tess was tempted to have her assistant stay as a buffer, but she could handle the encounter alone. "As I said, we parted on nasty terms. Awkward, yes, but he sounded okay on the phone. I think he's bringing the clothing as a peace offering."

"You call me, though, if you need me."

"You saw me handle Gustavo. Brett's a puppy next to him."

She'd sounded cool and prepared, but her pulse zoomed as Marcy left. Darn it, she was nervous. She didn't want to fight with him if he started dissing her efforts, but she wouldn't allow him to belittle her. She locked the door and paced back to her office. She certainly didn't want to appear eager to see him.

Ten minutes later she heard a rap on the door. She gathered her courage and walked slowly to let him in, breathing deep to calm her heartrate.

He stepped in carrying a mid-sized garbage bag. "Sorry for running late. I had to follow a stupid detour out in the middle of nowhere." He plopped the bag to the floor, looking snazzy and fit in a tailored dark suit. His wavy blond hair was carefully combed, and a confident smile warmed his handsome features. "You look great." Before she could duck, he kissed her on the cheek with a soft graze of lips.

"Thanks." She didn't return the compliment. Radar humming, she stepped away toward the safety of the counter.

He nudged the bag forward with his foot and stepped closer. "Here's the clothing. Must've been special to her to hold onto for years."

Diverted like Pavlov's dog, she reached for the bag and carried it to the counter. Anticipation soared as she pulled out a long red tube of a dress. Layers of fringe swirled from the waist downward. She beamed up a smile. "This is fabulous. Probably from the early 1920s. It might have been your great-great grandmother's."

She dated a navy dress with curling white trim to the late thirties. The "plaid and plain" dress, with panels of red and black plaid, she attributed to the following decade. She examined the last piece, a floral-patterned mini, and held it aloft in awe. "Mary Quant. Oh, this is iconic. She's credited with designing early miniskirts in London, then shipping them over here so the craze caught fire in the United States."

Brett laughed and shook his head. "You still get worked up about this stuff, don't you?"

Her spine stiffened as she draped the dress over the other garments. *Do not. Let him. Rile you.* "Yes. And now I'm excited about the products I sell translating into a successful career. We have a solid business and also ship items from our web site. As you probably saw from my file at the bank, all my loan payments have been on time."

He held up his hands in a surrender stance at the frosty change in attitude. "Yeow. I didn't mean to offend you. You've got a nice place here."

She crossed her arms over her chest. "Brett. Why exactly are you here?"

"Truthfully?" He hesitated, pursing his lips. "Okay. You know my grandmother really liked you. Before she died, she gave me a hard time about us breaking up."

Hmm, who twisted that version? She attempted to keep a straight face.

"She was crying because I was a selfish ass—her exact words. She said I'd messed things up with a woman who was just what I needed. Who could keep me in line and wouldn't tolerate my excessive ego." Grinning, he took Tess' hand. "She wanted me to be happy and was afraid I'd hook up with someone just like myself and end up miserable."

Surprised by his unexpected vulnerability, she didn't pull away.

"Tess, we had a good thing once. I know we can have it again. I admit it was partly my fault we fell apart. I came to say I'm sorry, and to beg you to give us another chance." Convinced of the power of his charm, he tugged her hand up to cover his heart and lowered his lips toward hers.

She shoved against his chest just as the doorbell tinkled. She hadn't turned the closed sign or locked up again. Expecting a female customer, she turned to meet Trey's wooden expression. The blood rushed from her head. *This looks very bad...* She pulled away from Brett.

"Trey. I didn't expect to see you tonight." Her voice sounded thin and breathy as the blood returned to pound in her ears.

"I came from the city council meeting and saw your car out front. I thought you'd want to hear that they approved the resource center, and we might go to dinner to celebrate." He reached for the door handle. "Apparently, you're still busy."

Tess feared the cozy scene had him believing she was open to Brett's kiss. He stood next to her, eyebrows raised with interest. She walked toward Trey, quivering with apprehension. She had to do damage control, fast. She laid a hand on his arm. "This is an *old friend*. Brett Stenson. His grandmother passed away recently. He contacted me to bring some of her vintage clothing. She and I were very fond of each other. She was a good friend of my own grandmother."

"Brett. The old boyfriend." Ice dripped from the words.

His tone jabbed at her heart. "Yes, we dated—"

Her unwelcome visitor approached and thrust out a hand, wearing a cocky smile. "And you are?"

She threw Brett an annoyed look and gasped as his features began to shift. The curl in his hair grew more pronounced. These lips were broader, and more sensuous, the nose slightly, charmingly, crooked.

Her hand tightened around Trey's arm. "Do you see that?" she hissed as a wave of fear rippled through her body.

"No. Tell me what you see," he urged.

Confusion spread over Brett's face. He glanced behind him into the empty shop.

"Nick…" she whispered.

"Don't go there," Trey's voice commanded.

Brett's jaw gaped, and his features resettled into his own. "What the hell is going on?"

Trey maneuvered her to a stool behind the counter. "Give us a minute, and we'll explain."

She sat, her limbs still weak. *This couldn't be happening. Not with Brett.*

"What did you see?" Trey repeated in a soft tone.

"I think it was Nick. I held onto your voice, so I didn't flash any further."

Brett stomped up next to them. "Tess, what's wrong?" Irritation carved grooves across his forehead. "You two are acting majorly weird, and you're creeping me out."

She didn't want to tell him. She wouldn't allow him into her life again. Yet if he left, he might take away another critical piece of the mystery.

Trey stood close, bracing her on the stool. He tossed him a chilly look. "I know this will sound hard to believe, but she's been experiencing some psychic flashes. They apparently were triggered by a visit to my cousin's home."

Brett's expression darkened further. "What the— Tess, you never told me about anything like this." His voice reflected growing frustration.

From her place on the stool, she glared up at him.

Her head was clearing, and she matched his annoyance. "It never happened to me before I moved here. I suppose now you think I'm nuts."

"Nooo. But I sure wonder about the influences around here." His gaze bore into Trey's—who stared back with equal intensity.

She sighed and grasped the edge of the counter. "Enough. I'm tired. I need to close up and go home."

"I came all this way to bring you my grandmother's clothes. I intended to take you out to dinner and spend some time catching up," Brett said. "I'll take you home, and you can point me to a hotel or a bed and breakfast. I'm not leaving town until I'm sure you're all right."

"Really, I'm fine. You don't need to do this." She wanted to jump off the stool, but she was hemmed in by the two men.

"I want to, and I'm going to." He grasped her forearm. "I told you my grandmother asked me to reconnect with you. I promised her I'd see you, and she wouldn't be happy if I left like this. I won't be happy either."

Caught between the two determined men, Tess struggled to find a solution. She knew Trey had made his own decision when he pulled his hands off her shoulders. "If you feel compelled to talk to this guy tonight, don't let me stand in the way." He stalked past them and headed out the door into the early evening light.

"Trey—" The bell jingled with the solid thwack of the door.

Brett held out a hand to help her up. "Ready to get out of here?"

Chapter Twenty-Five

Brett followed in his car as Tess drove back to her apartment. She spent the few minutes agonizing over Trey's storming out. She wanted to call him but doubted he was in any mood for polite conversation. He'd walked in, expecting to share good news and believed he'd witnessed her accepting a kiss from a former boyfriend. No wonder he'd been angry. Yet shouldn't he give her the benefit of the doubt?

Then there was the flash of Brett's features transposed onto a man she'd assumed to be Nick, the same way she'd seen Jake to be Stephen. It blew her mind to think her former boyfriend might be another link in the cosmic chain.

After Trey's departure, he had offered, "Sorry about that." But it was clear by his tone of voice and body language that *sorry* was the last thing he felt.

Still, she hadn't had the heart to order him to leave—especially when he'd expressed regard for her. While he had a colossal ego and control issues, at the core Tess knew he was a decent guy. She had zippo interest in reconnecting romantically, but she'd rather resolve on a level of friendship than their previous cold animosity. Plus, she wanted to honor the memory of his grandmother.

Maybe Marcy should have stayed as her bodyguard and shoved him toward home, Tess thought.

Instead, Brett pulled up behind her and followed her upstairs with the cherished clothing. He entered the living room and looked around with what she gauged to be a critical eye.

"I'm happy here," she said, displeased to feel defensive. "Plenty of space, and the original woodwork is a big selling point. I plan to clean up the second floor above the shop and either move there or rent it out."

"Good thinking. Use all of your building space and save rent money." He put the bag on the couch and sat next to it, crossing his legs atop the chest she used as a coffee table.

While she felt beaten down by the scene at the shop, he appeared cheerful. Getting his way had always perked him up. She almost expected him to start whistling a happy tune.

"The place definitely works for your eclectic style," he continued. "Your last apartment was pretty bleh. Too modern for your old-school vibe."

She ignored the backhanded compliment. "I'd better pull the clothing out, so it doesn't get more wrinkled." She opened the bag to spread the garments over the backs of furniture.

"Well, you won't have any place to sit now, but I planned to take you to dinner anyway," he teased.

She didn't want to give him false hope. "I'm kind of tapped out."

"Then you'd rather not cook. Freshen up if you need to, and we'll grab dinner. Any place you've been dying to try?"

Another hour or so for the meal, and she'd say a firm goodbye and direct him to his choice of nearby motels. She didn't think he was angling to stay with her, but there was absolutely no way *that* was happening. "Are you in the mood for Italian, seafood, Chinese?"

"Your choice, hon."

She frowned at the endearment and decided to freshen her lipstick, to brighten her still-pale complexion. Afterward, she chose the nearby Italian restaurant due to closest proximity. They headed into the warm evening, and he maneuvered his coupe the few blocks down Franklin Street. Inside the restaurant they were led down a brick entryway to a tall-backed wooden booth. As a jazz pianist warmed up, they perused the menu.

"Tess, thanks for letting me come to visit, and stay to take you to dinner. It had to be uncomfortable when that guy showed up."

"Yes, unnecessarily so. And his name is Trey."

Rather than take offense, he smiled. "You should be flattered. Doesn't every woman dream of two good-looking men sparring over her?"

"The reality isn't as titillating as reading about it in romance novels. You didn't really believe you'd sweep in and we'd reconnect and live happily ever after. I think your grandmother's death has shaken you up. You're following her desires more than your own."

His smile faded as he reached for the water glass. "Of course, her passing shook me. But I'm my own man, and you know that as well as anyone. Can't you take it on faith? My being here means I truly want to see you again." He paused and wrinkled his brow. "After tonight, I'm nervous that guy has pulled you into some psychic crap that's messing with your head."

"Trey isn't pulling anything over on me."

Frustration danced along her frazzled nerves. "Both of us have experienced strange, related flashes of vision. He's much more skeptical than I am. I don't want to go into any more detail, but rest assured he's absolutely no threat."

Her mind shifted to Brett's earlier transformation into Nick. She needed to process this with Trey before explaining more to the man sitting across from her—if she ever did so.

"Are you seriously into him?" His voice rose as he leaned toward her in the flickering candlelight.

Tess answered without hesitation. "Yes, I am. We haven't known each other very long, but the connection's pretty incredible. I want to pursue it, and so does he." *At least I hope so, after tonight.*

Disappointment etched his face. He took a moment to reply. "I can't lie and tell you I'm happy for you. But as long as you're content, I'll have to be. I had my chance, and I blew it big time. Let's work on reestablishing a friendship, because I still care about you."

Considering the ugly reaction when they originally broke up, she was surprised at his tempered response. She could tell the words were hard to deliver. Relieved, she didn't think before taking his offered hand.

And as their palms clasped, Nick's features flared in an instant...then faded.

His hand quivered under hers. "Ouch. You must have picked up static from those old clothes."

She maintained a poker face, but her mind vibrated with possibilities. She closed her menu. "I think I'll have the eggplant parmigiana."

Chapter Twenty-Six

As Saturday slid into Sunday, Tess still hadn't heard from Trey. Three times she picked up the phone, and three times she returned it to the table. On the fourth attempt, late in the afternoon, she dialed. Texting provided a sort of shield, but there was always potential for misunderstanding in such fragmented conversations.

She paced across her living room as the rings mounted, wondering if he might be staring at his phone and avoiding her. *Please don't let it have come to this*, she prayed. She was about to click off when his upbeat recorded voice instructed her to leave a message.

She stopped in the middle of the room. "Umm, Trey, this is Tess. I'd like to apologize…and talk about the uncomfortable scene at the shop Friday night. So. Catch you later, I guess."

Are we all right?

She yearned to ask but didn't want to pose the critical question in a message. Hopefully, he'd call. Wouldn't he? She groaned and trotted off to raid her chocolate stash. The roller coaster of emotion was exhausting, and she craved a little comfort.

She savored the last two pieces, thinking at least she'd be too busy to mope too much during the coming work week. She and Marcy would be overwhelmed in prepping for Divine Vintage's formal grand opening. They'd held off on the big event to ensure the "summer folks" on the lakeshore were back in force. Between dealing with real customers, online orders, and the celebration details, Tess would be in high gear to guarantee a splashy success. Yet she suspected he wouldn't be far from her mind.

On Tuesday morning she started on the outside of the building, weeding the flower box in front of the shop. When she grabbed her phone off her desk afterward, she discovered a voicemail from Trey. Whew, he hadn't ghosted her. Yet she was nervous to listen to his words.

"Tess. Sorry to miss your call. I was going to tell you Friday that the project I've been working on has heated up. I had to work all weekend, and we're pushing through days and nights this week. But yes, we need to talk. We'll connect when things slow down here."

We need to talk.

Her stomach clutched. She hoped the trite phrase wasn't as ominous as it sounded.

****

She tried to keep her spirits up through the rest of the week, reminding herself the grand opening represented a huge accomplishment. She'd followed her dream despite challenges and obstacles. After all her hard work, Divine Vintage was stable. Yet she wished she could say the same for her psyche. As the hours stretched and Trey didn't reach out, a shadow of dread pounced if she caught a moment to breathe between tasks.

When Friday night arrived, she should have been exhausted after all the physical and mental labor. Instead, she lay in bed and hugged her pillow, thinking and worrying about her future in Michigan City. She could envision a satisfying life in the friendly mid-sized town. She'd build a social life, get involved in activities and organizations, find a church. But darn it, she'd prefer to explore the possibilities with Trey. She rolled over on the soft mattress, telling herself even if he backed off on a relationship, she'd try to bring closure to the mystery. Esther would appreciate the effort.

She finally slept and awoke at dawn to a flurry of butterflies circling her stomach. She and Marcy both arrived at the shop early to finish their decorating. As final touches, they draped the doorway in lavender chiffon and placed a free-standing sign Marcy had painted on the sidewalk. Both women had canvassed the town to post flyers. Besides the lure of a discount coupon, they would offer giveaways such as costume jewelry, vintage gloves, or scarves every hour. Beginning at noon, WIMS Radio would broadcast live from Divine Vintage.

"Thanks again for sharing your artistry," Tess said as she admired the calligraphy on the sign. "You did a fabulous job with this and the special touches inside. You know, you might be able to freelance some work without moving for a while."

Marcy held the door open for her to enter. "My two jobs keep me hopping, but I could check that out, I guess. Oh, my mom said she'll stop by later."

"I've been looking forward to meeting her." They walked inside, and she popped one of the petit fours Marcy had insisted on baking. "Mmm, delicious. I'll miss your culinary skills if you go." The tiny cakes were piped with intricate flowers and arranged on silver platters. They'd determined to keep the treats small and simple to protect the clothing. For the afternoon they'd add platters of cheese, crackers, and grapes.

"This is so exciting." Her assistant practically pranced through the store, channeling a floral explosion in her '60s mini. "Are you as nervous as I am?"

Tess wore a bronze taffeta cocktail shift. She re-tucked a pin into her Audrey Hepburn updo. "Worse. The anticipation is almost as mind-blowing as the first day we opened the doors." The comment reminded her of Trey and Esther jaunting in, which brought another dart of sadness at the recent rocky connection. Did he even remember this was her big day?

She distracted herself by grabbing two plastic goblets and a bottle from behind the counter. "I did remember the champagne, though." She poured and handed a drink to her assistant. "Here's to Divine Vintage. Everything's going to be absolutely great. We've gone over every detail and worked to spread the word, even into Chicago."

"Thank goodness you can do a lot with free PR. And the cost of the radio broadcast is reasonable." Marcy clicked her glass, and they both sipped. "I predict when the summer beach folks get wind of this place we'll be swamped."

Minutes later, two familiar faces burst into the shop. Tess was delighted to greet Esther and Clarice. The two women looked stylish as usual as they exclaimed over the garments. Each of them gathered numerous pieces as other shoppers trickled in.

"These will be excellent gifts," Esther said. "The jacket with three-quarter sleeves is so Jackie O, I'll probably keep it for myself." The hot pink wool provided smashing contrast to her hair.

"All of this is for me," Clarice said with a laugh. "I covet these beaded cardigans." She offered a sly smile as she pulled out her platinum credit card. "I haven't seen or heard from my negligent son lately. I hope you've been keeping him out of trouble."

Tess' smile tightened. "Actually, we haven't touched base for a few days. Trey's working on a big project. I've been buried in this opening prep. I imagine he's juggling a ton of details, too."

She signed her receipt in swirling script. "The Paris project has been all-consuming. He's still waiting to hear if he'll be needed to fly over for a consultation."

Would he leave the country without talking to her? If he did, he'd probably come back and move on without her. Tess ducked her head to hide her distress and changed the topic. "You both look well today. Esther, I hope you've been taking care of yourself and feeling healthy."

"I have. I'm so blessed to have Jacob with me." As no other shoppers were nearby, she added, "He came back Sunday night and went straight to bed. We've touched briefly on the subject of the visions. Of course, he's still skeptical and reluctant. I certainly don't want to push."

"Hopefully, Jake will continue to come around. In the meantime, you're right to be cautious." She handed over their bags as a lady carrying an embroidered cocktail dress approached the counter. She would have to share the visit with Brett and the potential connection with Nick at another time.

After the ladies left, a steady stream of customers flowed in. Some carried their coupon flyers. Others had spotted the grand opening sign following visits to the

Farmers' Market or other shops. At noon, Ric, the jovial, high-energy owner of WIMS, set up his sound equipment. He eased in by asking Tess how her interest in vintage clothing led to opening the specialty shop.

"Divine Vintage is a perfect addition in the Uptown Arts District," she began. "I consider vintage clothing an art form. Fashion also makes a definitive statement in regard to history. Changes in society, work, and leisure are reflected in the style and choice of clothing through the years.

"For instance, in the 1850s, people thought Amelia Bloomer was a radical exhibitionist with her balloon-legged trousers for women. When the bicycling craze caught on later in the century, more women jumped at the freedom and practicality."

Ric nodded his sandy-blond head. "They were trendsetters who weren't afraid to stand up to the establishment. Kind of like you." He grinned. "I was covering the hearing at city hall when you spoke in favor of the resource center."

She paused and chose her words carefully around the charged subject. "As a business owner, I think we should stand for the good of everyone in our community. We should help others whenever we can."

"The store owners and friends I've talked to agree wholeheartedly. Though not everyone is as comfortable speaking out in public."

Marcy popped up behind them. "Tess is brave and bold. Michigan City is lucky to have her. Let's hear it for the warrior-chicks."

"You go, girl." A woman in her fifties turned with a dressing gown on her arm. She started to clap, and the handful of others in the shop joined her.

The radio host laughed with delight. "You already have a cheering section. I expect people will be coming after you soon to join boards and support other causes. We've got some great folks around here who do their best to improve the county."

She covered her flushed cheeks with her hands. "Thanks, everyone, for the support. I'm looking forward to it."

The shoppers returned to the racks, and Ric shifted back to discuss clothing highlights from other colorful eras. He maintained a steady banter as he moved on to interview Marcy and willing customers. The sales continued to mount, and several visitors made a point to congratulate Tess on her success.

As the final half hour neared, she bounced on an adrenaline buzz. She'd rung up a sale when the door opened to admit their second male visitor of the day. A shimmer of electricity frittered from her stomach to her chest.

Trey stood in the archway, tall and solemn. The corner of his mouth lifted in a half smile. She couldn't decide whether the Mona Lisa expression would lead to a reunion or a "*this isn't working out*" moment. She followed the exiting customer toward the door. In her comfortable ballet flats, she tilted her head up to meet his eyes.

"Can we talk after you close up?"

His guarded manner ratcheted her anxiety. She glanced toward Marcy. Her assistant jerked a thumb toward the street. "I can talk now. For a few minutes." Her heart pounded against her ribcage as she led the way onto the sidewalk, where small groups and individuals wandered between stores. Out of sight of her shop's bay window, she turned. "I'm so sorry."

He placed a finger against her lips. "No. I'm the one who barged in on you and acted like a heel. I'm not proud of how I handled myself. I was a jealous jerk. When I saw him lean in to kiss you, I went a little crazy."

Okay, this was a good start.

"The kiss was totally unexpected. And unwelcome." Tess held his eyes, keeping her voice low. "Brett called out of the blue the night before. He said his grandmother had died and she wanted him to give me some vintage clothing. He surprised me. Said he'd be in the area the next day and demanded to deliver it."

She didn't look away. She had to make her case. "I suppose I could have said no. I was more than tempted. But his grandmother meant a lot to me, and I knew he was seriously grieving. I caved. I had no idea he wanted to reconnect as a couple."

Trey braced an arm against the brick exterior of the building, under the shade of the overhang. She feared an invisible defense shield hovered between them— fortified on both their sides.

He looked tense and uncertain as a bus lumbered by. "Much as I don't like it, I can understand why he'd want to reconnect with you. More important, how did you resolve the issue?"

"I made it clear I wasn't at all interested in seeing him again. I'm sure it hurt his ego, but he seemed to understand. I haven't heard from or seen him since he left that night to stay in a motel." She decided to go for broke. "When he met you, he knew there was something…important…between us. I hope that's still true." Unconsciously, she reached up to cover her heart.

He thrust out a pent-up breath. "I'd say our connection goes beyond important." He tugged her closer, his hands warm at her waist. "I should've called you this week, but I really was overwhelmed with work. I also needed to get my head straight. My feelings about the evening were intensified by your flash of Nick."

"I didn't go into any detail with Brett because I wanted to talk to you first. After the flash, I can't help but wonder if he's another link to solving the mystery." In her relief, Tess wanted to pirouette down the street—with Trey. Not caring what others might think. Though he probably wasn't a pirouetting kind of guy. She held still to hear his final thoughts.

"I'd rather we never had to deal with him again. Let's think on it some more." His expression lightened. "I know you've had a really big day here, but are you up to going out for dinner? To celebrate your grand opening and move beyond Wednesday night?"

Her lips trembled. She laid her head on his chest. "I'd love to." The electric nerves gave way to a sweet rush of contentment at being enfolded again in his strong arms.

Chapter Twenty-Seven

During the following week, they made up for lost time. They talked on the phone after work or got together for fun, casual evenings. Tess anticipated the sound of his mellow voice on the phone, and especially looked forward to the date nights. Whether they saw a movie, grabbed dinner out, took a long walk, or watched TV with a pizza, the time was always enjoyable. They were compatible in food choices, political and social justice leanings, outdoor activities, and the thrill of a dark, twisty television plot. If they didn't agree, the discussion was calm. Unlike Brett, Trey didn't have to win an argument or hammer his point.

Though the attraction continued to intensify, they'd stuck to his concept of "courting." The kisses were toe-tingling, but they held themselves in check—which added to the delicious yearning. Since she hadn't experienced any signs of Phoebe's intervention since Brett's visit, she appreciated the break to make sure they were developing their own true feelings. She didn't open the subject with Trey, but she hoped he might be coming to the same conclusion.

Two weeks after the grand opening, she offered to cook a Sunday afternoon meal. She was sautéing chicken for scallopini with lemon caper sauce when he knocked. He carried a lush bouquet, including fragrant

Stargazer lilies, and a bottle of wine. After depositing the bounty on the kitchen table, he kissed her neck, sending a tremor of anticipation up her spine. "One should always reward the cook."

"Absolutely. This special recipe is from Marcy's boss at the deli. I cross-my-heart swore never to share it with anyone else." Tess inhaled the delicious scent as she turned off the stove and removed the dressed salad from the refrigerator. "I hope you don't mind if we dish up the main course from the pan. I enjoy cooking, but not the cleanup."

He agreed, and, after his second helping and a scoop of spumoni ice cream, he rose to place his bowl in the sink. He began to rinse the dishes and place them in the dishwasher.

He really is the perfect man, she thought, admiring his backside as she finished her last bite. She refrigerated the leftovers—including his doggy bag—before they carried their coffee to the couch. He had brought along the diary, and she snuggled against him as he opened it.

"I've appreciated taking a break from all this for a couple weeks," he said. "Considering your flash with Brett, though, another scene I read seems relevant. Construction at the mansion was moving along, and in late July a group of them checked on the progress. Phoebe's parents were there, along with Edward's mother, Victor, Stephen, and Nick. Plus, Phoebe's friend, Penny, who'll be her maid of honor."

"Phoebe mentioned her at the Valentine's Day dance," Tess recalled. "She was trying to convince Stephen of her friend's interest before he surprised her with that hot kiss."

He turned to a page he had bookmarked. "Indulge me with a little of the architectural detail, then we'll get to the fireworks."

On Sunday a merry group of our closest family and friends traveled to our new home. I've been so excited to watch the three stories advance, brick-by-brick, soaring into the sky. Edward has gifted me with the sweetest little catwalk. I'm so pleased I could purr. I can't wait to walk around the completed rooftop, with an unencumbered view of the sparkling lake spreading toward Michigan and Chicago. Edward has expressed some fear of heights, but I'm sure he'll join me there. These days, he can't seem to refuse me.

Inside, while the doors are not hung, the plaster walls await the paint and elegant paper patterns I've chosen. The cherry wood floors are installed, covered with protective tarps. The stove and icebox are in place in the kitchen, and half of the cabinets ring the walls.

We finally could climb the staircase to our second-floor master bedroom, and beyond to the third-floor ballroom. He assures me the work will be completed within the three weeks before we marry, so he may carry me over the threshold on our wedding night.

The only fly in the ointment is the strange tension I sense between Edward, Nick, and Stephen. Edward has shared no falling out, but the three often speak more sharply than necessary. He and Nick are lifelong pals. I'm saddened by their puzzling dissension but haven't wanted to pry. As for Stephen, they've never been close. Their parents' marriage has forced a relationship that probably would not have occurred naturally. Edward considers him rather lazy and self-indulgent. Stephen, in turn, views him as an upright prig. Indeed, Stephen is closer to me as a friend. Since Valentine's Day, we have resumed our bantering relationship and never revisited the surprising kiss. Before today, I had come to believe he must regret the rash, drunken action. Now I cannot be sure.

After our parents took their leave from viewing the ballroom, Edward opened the door into the attic and walked inside. I headed over to join him, but Penny grasped my hand and said she couldn't wait to attend our house parties. She twirled me through the room to a silent waltz, her bright copper head bobbing in time. I was giddy at the thought of living in this luxurious house, positioned as a premiere hostess in the city's top social echelon. Yet as we giggled, strong hands encircled my waist and I whirled away, peering into Stephen's grinning face. He pulled me close, and we swung in widening circles.

Penny stood still in the center of the room, wearing a small frown. Though I've tried to matchmake between them, he still shows no interest, sad to tell. I didn't want to hurt her and was about to call an end to our tomfoolery when another set of hands closed around my ribcage.

My heart sank, as I believed Edward must be displeased and cutting in. I swung a glance over my shoulder and found Nick behind me, also smiling widely. I was trapped between the men as Stephen refused to relinquish his position. The three of us increased our speed to dance madly around the room. I thought it a great jest, but soon felt overheated and rather dizzy. I gathered from the men's intense expressions that their emotions also were beginning to boil. I tried to laugh and convince them to stop.

"Enough!"

The shouted command stopped our foolish dance, and we halted, breathing heavily. The arms and hands pulled away from me, and I turned to view the hostility darkening Edward's face. Suddenly, one of my companions shoved the other. I still don't know who started it, as Edward has refused to discuss the incident further. Penny couldn't tell me as her view was blocked.

I scampered away in horror as Nick and Stephen continued to push each other. Edward waded into the fray, breaking them apart with force. He sent Stephen sprawling to the floor and Nick stumbling across the room. We all recognized the incident was not playful, but I knew I had to defuse it immediately and feign innocence.

"Boys," I called, "please show some decorum, or Penny and I will decree you all attend Miss Stein's class on manners before the wedding."

Penny was shaking, poor dear. I soothed her, whispering about the male tendency to seek domination. It elicited the intended giggle, though she trembled for minutes afterward.

As the men straightened their clothing, they attempted to lighten their fierce expressions. I took Edward's arm as we followed the others down the stairs, arching my eyebrows to indicate my disquiet. Though he patted my hand, I knew the antagonistic current underlying the incident hadn't been extinguished, for any of them.

Trey closed the diary. "Quite the revealing scene, though I can't put my money on one of them above the other, at this point."

Tess tucked her legs under her and pondered the heated interaction. "They're all acting like jealous rivals. This gives us backstory of how emotions could have pitched to the horrible finale in the bedroom." She steepled her fingers under her chin. "I'm not sure of an intent to harm on anyone's part, but it blew out of control."

"Heat of passion. We also see Edward acting just as upset and jealous as the other two. And there's still the dark horse candidate of his stepfather."

She shook her head. "Who knows, somebody else could pop out of the shadows, the way they have with Stephen and Nick."

"Personally, I hope they don't." He turned to face her. "If you don't mind shifting gears, I've saved some other momentous news."

She picked up on a nervous vibe. She hoped she was going to like this big news. "What's going on?"

"They've finally decided to send me to Paris to help wrap the final structural details."

"You said you might have to go there. Oh, Trey, how awesome. When are you going, and for how long?"

"Probably a pretty quick trip, from a Saturday through Tuesday toward the end of the month." He paused. "I was hoping you could join me."

Her mouth dropped open, and her words tumbled out. "I'd love to. If I can get Marcy to watch the shop for an extra day or two. Which I'm sure she will. As I told you all, I've never been to Europe, but I've always wanted to go. Especially to Paris. Thank goodness I have a passport already." Her smile broadened. "I'm going to shut up now, because I'm babbling like an idiot. A happy idiot." Yes, the trip was a luxury, but to go with him, she'd make it work.

He grinned back. "I'll pick up the hotel room and the food, if you get your ticket. If you'd prefer two rooms, let me know, and I'll book them." The comment was offhand, but his face grew serious.

Tess didn't even hesitate. "I think we can manage just fine with one, don't you?"

"Definitely." He leaned in to capture her lips for a prolonged, heated kiss.

Oh yes, Tess thought as his hand skimmed down her back. *One room should work out very well.*

Chapter Twenty-Eight

"I don't know if I'll be able to sleep when we get there," Tess said, halfway into the eight-hour nonstop flight. "We might be exhausted, but I don't want to waste a minute. I'm going to want to run out and start seeing everything."

He reached for her hand. "We'll make the decision according to how we feel. Jet lag may not slam us until tomorrow. We have the whole weekend. I just have to recover to report for a meeting Monday morning."

They'd left the bustling Chicago terminal soon after the estimated departure time. Snagging two first-class sleeper seats had been another lucky break, with arrival before six on Saturday morning. She had tried to watch the in-flight movie then flipped through a magazine. Now she was staring up and over the words in a mystery novel.

He worked through a newspaper. "You're so keyed up I'm wondering if you'll sleep at all while we're over there."

"I'm so excited to be going. You were super sweet to ask me."

"Sweet, hmm." He wiggled his eyebrows. "How do you know I don't have ulterior motives?"

She lowered her voice to a sultry level. "I'll be very disappointed if you don't." She squeezed his hand, tripping ahead in a normal voice. "I can't help thinking how much Phoebe and Edward were looking forward to their honeymoon trip. Of course, they were going by ship, so the journey would've been much longer."

"But luxurious. Edward had booked them on a first-class liner, and they would have wined, dined, and socialized in high style. Compared to being cramped up in a flying tin can for hours, with a semi-palatable meal and tiny bottles of liquor."

Tess had foregone the offer of alcohol, drinking caffeine-free cola. Trey added a splash of bourbon to his cola. He'd lifted it to sip when she admitted, "I brought the heart brooch. Silly, I know, but I thought they might see Paris through our eyes."

He swallowed the rest of his drink in one gulp. "I hope they're satisfied with that and don't come flashing in on us." He didn't look pleased.

She now regretted her impulsivity. The action had seemed romantic when she was packing, but she should've talked to him before carrying a possible trigger. Yet she wasn't moved to apologize for her good intentions.

He signaled the flight attendant for a refill. "If they want to join the party, I'm sure they will."

"They've been very quiet lately. Once they feel real closure, they all should settle down and disappear."

"Hold onto that thought," he murmured, as the attendant approached.

****

After a smooth landing, they entered the terminal into de Gaulle Airport. She hadn't flown internationally before and was a little apprehensive of the frenzied activity and the hubbub of unfamiliar languages. While Trey was fairly fluent in French, she'd studied two years in high school. She could handle the basics but would struggle with the fast patter of conversation.

"Not a big problem," he had told her. "Many Parisians speak English. Though some don't like to humor us." He'd coached her to recall helpful phrases and verb tenses.

She also was glad he'd flown into the airport before. He retrieved the luggage, led through customs, and hailed a taxi. He rattled off an address, and they whizzed into the roadway with a burst of speed that swayed them together in the backseat. Tess pulled away and pressed her face to the window, taking in as much of the flying scenery as possible through the early rays of sunlight wavering over the horizon. The trip into the city would take nearly an hour on the expressway, zipping through urban areas toward the capitol city. Not caring if she was pigeonholed as a "first-time *touriste*," she tossed questions at him. He answered a few and shot the others to their dark-haired driver. The man mumbled in a rapid-fire stream.

Trey translated. "*Oui, tres belle,*" he answered after a final flurry. He regarded her with a mischievous expression. "You probably caught part of that. He says you're very curious, and very beautiful. He'd be happy to drive if you require further assistance."

She returned the older gentleman's smile as his eyes met hers in the mirror. "*Merci beaucoup.*"

"I'm going to have to keep my eyes on these bold Frenchmen," Trey said. "They appreciate gorgeous women and don't hesitate to make a move. You'll probably be propositioned countless times and invited to run away with at least one randy guy."

She was caught by one descriptive word. "You

think I'm gorgeous?"

"Incredibly gorgeous." His eyes held hers as he captured her lips.

Her eyes drifted closed as the kiss intensified. She didn't care that the cab driver must be amused by their exploration. A new day was dawning in Paris.

They broke apart at the announcement "Hotel du Louvre." Tess gaped as her eyes traveled up five magnificent stories, each level rising with a bank of floor-to-ceiling windows. Two matching wings of the limestone-colored block building angled off to bookend the front.

"Each side looks out on a different famous Parisian site," Trey shared, as they exited the cab. "The Louvre Museum, the Opera Garnier, the Comédie Française, and the Place du Palais Royal. This is second empire architecture, by the way. Many of the buildings in this neighborhood are in a similar style."

She knew she was standing with a foolish smile on her face as the driver pulled out their bags. Trey paid, and she gave the man a generous tip. After an efficient check-in, they took an elevator to the top floor.

"I wanted to give us the best view," he said, opening the door with the keycard.

She barely registered the sparse furniture and the white duvet on the queen-size bed. She swept to the window to drink in the glorious sight of the city.

"That's the Louvre." He placed his hands on her shoulders, and she nestled against him. "What would you like to do first? Unpack, eat, shower, sleep, sightsee? The world is your oyster." He kneaded her neck and shoulders in a slow rhythm.

She rotated her head to work out the kinks from the

flight. "I want it all, simultaneously. I'm sure we're going to have to sleep in a few hours. For now, we probably should be practical. Hang up our clothing. Grab a bite to eat. Maybe explore until we wind down. What do you think?"

****

Though Trey was disappointed not to explore his unmentioned preference of tumbling into bed immediately, he recognized that she would probably prefer to shower and—the words were snapped back in his mind as she whirled to face him, standing close and intimate.

"To hell with practicality. We're in Paris." She fused her lips to his. Caught off guard, his body reacted with a hormonal surge that had him standing at taut attention. The intensity of the kiss zoomed past the level in the cab, toward fever pitch, and he slid his hands under her blouse. She arched backward, giving him room to freely caress.

"God, I want you so much." His breathing was ragged as he tore away long enough to pull the fabric up and over her upraised arms.

Tess dragged his mouth back down as she slid up on her toes, their bodies meeting at the most intimate of junctures. He wrestled to hold onto his sanity as her busy hands tugged his shirt out of his slacks.

He fleetingly realized they were standing fully exposed in the window. As she flicked open the buttons, he backed her in an intimate two-step toward the bed. She shoved the shirt off his shoulders. He released the clasp on her lacy black bra. They sank down onto the spread, skin to skin. Though her assertiveness was driving him to the brink, he slowed to heighten the sensations, grazing her lips with his, moving to her soft cheek, the long white curve of her throat, down to her breast.

Her moan and the upward lift of her body drove another shaft of white heat to his groin. He kissed his way to the other side of her warm flesh as his hand moved to the waist of her slacks. She pulled him against her chest as they tumbled prone onto the bed.

Their tongues twined again, sensuously mating, until his body begged for release. He shivered when she murmured against his lips, "Love me, Trey."

****

They awoke later, with vivid new memories to join those sifted from the past. True to his early prediction, the connection had been electric, and consuming—deep kisses, hungry caresses, losing oneself in mindless, gasping pleasure. A greedy antithesis to Edward and Phoebe's slow explorations.

He rolled to kiss her cheek. "Welcome to Paris, sweetheart."

She lifted one side of her well-kissed mouth. "As the natives say, Ooh la la."

Chapter Twenty-Nine

Hand-in-hand, Tess and Trey strolled out the front doors of the hotel, searching for a café that still would serve breakfast. She tried to take in the surrounding scenery while keeping up with his long legs. They passed a bakery, and the sugar-scent of pastry wafted across the sidewalk, making her stomach gurgle. "I'm really ravenous now."

"I thought you'd hardly want to eat, to maintain that trim figure." He grinned and squeezed her fingers. "Hold out for some protein to boost your energy." They proceeded down the Rue de Rivoli and selected a cozy café, where he ordered a hearty country breakfast. He shrugged at her amused smirk. "I've got a big appetite myself."

"I could tell that earlier. You'll definitely need to keep your strength up, too," she teased. "We may not get much sleep on this trip."

He took her hand and kissed the palm. "I'm counting on it."

She felt the heat rise in her body, adding a blush to her cheeks as the waitress returned.

The woman smiled and set down a halved grapefruit. "Ah, *l'amour à l'américaine. C'est adorable.*"

Tess recognized the word for "love" and didn't dare catch Trey's expression. She looked down and sipped the strong coffee. Much too soon for such bold declarations, she thought wistfully. Yet she gave herself a stern internal lecture: *For once you are not going to dwell on fears. You are going to live in the moment and enjoy it with abandon. He may not be ready for a more serious relationship, but you can both take your time. There's no rush. Be cool, and for goodness' sake, don't scare him off by appearing too needy.*

****

Trey sliced around the wedges of grapefruit and watched her gaze out toward the bustling street. He suspected she'd translated the casual statement, and was, in her analytical way, weighing the balance. He took a bite, and a sharp citrus tang kicked into his throat. He choked on it as he acknowledged his own jumbled emotions. He was flippin' crazy about this woman. Spending time together in the romantic city had only cemented his feelings. He swallowed and coughed to clear his throat.

"Are you all right?" She regarded him with concern through those amazing wide-set eyes.

"Yeah. Went down the wrong way," he croaked.

"Good. Not sure I could Heimlich you." She grinned and took a dainty bite of a croissant.

He grabbed his water glass and drank deep, watching her kiss-swollen lips open and chew. Not an especially sexy action, but today it riveted his attention. They'd spent a lot of time together over the past few weeks, he reflected. The interactions had been open, fun, and responsive—mentally, physically, and emotionally. In past relationships he'd been able to maintain distance, a defensive wall to protect his emotions. With Tess, the feelings were a full-frontal assault, cracking through the barrier.

Frankly, it scared the crap out of him. Not so much that he had such feelings. But he wasn't sure if she shared the intensity. When she had reached for him and said in that sexy, throaty voice—*love me*—he had nearly whispered "I do." Instead, he had kept his silence and plunged deep to join them as one. There was no wisp of Phoebe and Edward, just their heated, straining bodies rising to a passionate crescendo.

Then the waitress tossed the word "*amour*" into their laps. He believed Tess shared a definite level of interest, but how deep did that interest go? Were they being drawn together by the intensity of the romantic mystery? Or would their own emotions carry them forward—even if they couldn't crack Phoebe and Edward's secrets?

He didn't want to dwell on that potential. After eating, he led toward the famous art museums, heading first to the namesake of their Louvre hotel. He couldn't resist sharing details about architect I.M. Pei's crystalline pyramid entryway before leading her through selected portions of the collection. They didn't have time to do it justice—that could take days in his estimation—and he also wanted to take her to the Musee d'Orsay as Tess had expressed fondness for Impressionists.

Three hours later, inside the second, smaller museum, he was drawn to stop at Renoir's "Girls at the Piano," featuring blonde and dark-haired beauties at a pianoforte. "This reminds me of Edward watching Phoebe and her friend playing a duet."

Her expression dimmed as she stared at the canvas. "In happier days."

He should have scooted right past. He draped his arm around her shoulders. "I'm sorry. I probably shouldn't have introduced them." Now the specter would linger. "You haven't felt anything over here that seems related to them, have you?" *Like during our lovemaking?* Though if they'd intruded then, he'd rather not know.

She shook her head. "No, I haven't. Not that I'd mind. Don't feel bad about discussing the picture. They're part of our reality right now. Unreal as that may sound."

Even stranger, Trey wasn't skeptical of her answer. He seemed to have drifted toward his own wary acceptance. The idea unsettled him, and he grabbed her hand and shifted her to a landscape that didn't evoke thoughts of ghostly visitors.

Chapter Thirty

Back in their suite, Tess popped into the bathroom and changed into a satin teddy, intending to take a brief nap. She stepped through the doorway and stopped at the sight of him stripped-down, in black briefs, on his way to the bed.

A tremble of desire whispered through her body. Trey kept his eyes on hers as he advanced quickly to pull off the bedspread. She moved just as swiftly and they met in the middle, on their knees, with lips and hands seeking.

"How am I supposed to sleep when you look like that?" he whispered into her ear, as they stopped to gasp for breath.

She indulged a heady thrill of sensual power. "How am I supposed to sleep when you feel like this?" She roamed her hands over his muscled torso. "Knowing you taste so strong and masculine." He moaned as she slid her tongue down the column of his neck.

****

After finally giving in to the need for sleep, they napped then showered before getting ready for a Saturday night on the town. Tess' taste buds tingled as they enjoyed a coq au vin dinner on the patio of another charming restaurant. They people-watched while sipping their espressos, making up teasing little stories about the passersby.

Trey gestured toward a tall man who glanced furtively around the street as he walked past them with a pretty brunette. "His wife is at home with the three kids. He told the girlfriend he's separated."

"She checked him out and knows the truth, but she doesn't care. No commitment, no foul." She tilted her head, waiting for his answer. "He's got it made, eh?"

He drained his cup and grinned. "Too much risk and deception for me. I'm a one-woman man."

"Good to know. I echo the sentiment."

She kept it light, but the revelation pleased her. Throughout the day, she'd caught several women tossing interested glances, some more apparent than others. He never seemed to notice, centering all his attention on her. As a result, her confidence soared. And when he aimed that intense concentration on bringing her pleasure… *Oh my God.* Her body warmed at the mere thought of the incredible sex. Before this, she'd believed the stuff of romance novels was all hype. Now she knew those heights were possible—with the right person.

The feelings were too new and fragile to ask if he felt the same. She just hoped her thoughts weren't emblazoned on her face. She ducked her head and finished her coffee.

On the waiter's recommendation, they moved on to a nearby nightclub with a smooth jazz ensemble rather than a heavy dance beat. The place was half-full, the hour early by Parisian standards. Settling into a high-backed booth, she watched Trey observe the quartet of riffing musicians. He looked handsome and assured in his casual suit jacket. After they ordered drinks, he reached for her hand. "Let's dance."

On the floor they melded to the slinky music. She wound her arms around his neck and discovered he was a smooth, assured lead. He met her eyes then honed in on Phoebe's brooch pinned to her chest. He quickly looked away, over her head. His eyebrows had raised when he'd seen it in the hotel room, but he hadn't commented. She was glad he hadn't asked her to take it off. She was fulfilling her intent to introduce them to Paris.

The music shifted to an upbeat rhythm and he spun her, twirling out then back into his arms. "Did I tell you I like that dress?" He tightened the hand at her waist. "Red's a great color with your hair and fair skin."

"You told me once. Or twice. I appreciate it every time."

"Your hair's very nice tonight, too." He caressed the nape of her neck, raising goosebumps.

She had worn it upswept again. "*Merci beaucoup.*" She whispered. "*Vous etes très galant.*" She thanked him for his compliments and hoped she'd used the correct tenses.

His eyes gleamed as he bent to kiss her. "I struggle to be a gallant gentleman when you're so close."

She nestled against his chest and lifted her lips to his. The brooch pressed into her collarbone, and she whirled across the ocean to Carver House's ballroom.

"Stay in close to me, darling. Now turn...and pivot." Edward swung her out with a dizzying whirl then pulled her back into his arms. "Good. You must relax, Phoebe, to master the fluid lines of the tango."

Thank goodness, he appeared to have forgotten about the disturbing recent incident with their friends in this room. She certainly wouldn't remind him. She waved a hand to cool her flushed cheeks. "Edward, this new dance is all the rage in London, but likely too racy for Michigan City. We'd scandalize all the neighbors. Not that I'd particularly mind, but we're supposed to be practicing our wedding dance."

He smiled, as loose as she had ever seen him in a starched white shirt without a jacket. "You're right, of course. But we already waltz well. No need to practice. I predict even staid Michigan City will kick up her heels to the latest dances within the year. In the meantime, I suppose we can save the scandalous tango for when we're alone."

His eyes twinkled as he tilted her chin with a finger and kissed her. She responded, opening her mouth to his. Yes, the neighbors would be aghast…

Tess snapped backward from the waist, akin to a puppet whose strings had been jerked. Trey's arms tightened as she swayed toward him.

His face reflected concern. "What just happened? Was that a new dance move, or did you see something?"

She clutched his shoulders to reorient herself. "I saw them in the ballroom, practicing the tango. When he kissed her, I felt his lips, and yours, at the same time. And the same electric sensation. Did you feel it?"

He shook his head, appearing troubled. "They don't seem to sync at the same time, and I'm grateful."

She became aware of the glances as they stood still on the dance floor.

"Let's sit." He led her off, with a hand to the small of her back. "Do you want to go to the hotel?"

"Of course not. I prefer to sit down, finish the wine, and enjoy the music for a while. Then I'd love to dance again." She smiled to reassure him. Yet as the jazz spun a sultry web around them, the vision lingered, reminding her of the doomed couple who'd been robbed of such magical nights in Paris.

Chapter Thirty-One

They continued sightseeing through the remainder of the weekend. Monday morning, Tess lazed in bed as Trey rose to prepare for his day of on-site consultations.

He stooped to kiss the end of her nose. "Be careful out there today. You've got my cell and the number of the office in case you need me. I'll be back by late afternoon."

She showered and dressed then braved a Métro ride to the largest flea market, Le Marché aux Puces de Saint-Ouen—The Fleas—in search of vintage treasures. She had intentionally packed light to leave room for a few choice items, either to sell or to keep in her personal collection. She checked out displays of hand-thrown pottery, furniture, and antiques in the labyrinth of stalls before coming upon a clothing vendor. Trey had advised to approach in a continental fashion, greeting a worker and asking permission to see the goods.

The proprietor tucked her graying hair behind her ears and smiled. "*Oui*. I may practice my English with you?" She held up a finger and disappeared into the hanging racks. She emerged with a full-skirted turquoise sundress.

"Nice. Perhaps…" Tess downplayed her enthusiasm, in hopes of haggling on the price. She joined the woman to sift through her inventory. The pieces were good quality, similar to her own shop. She doubted she would find any bargains, yet the cachet of having garments direct from Paris was irresistible. She reached a compromise on the price and paid for three dresses ranging from the 1930s through the 1950s. Farther on, she bought two beaded cardigans—they sold well at Divine Vintage—from a craggy-faced gent who didn't speak English. They transacted a fair sale by writing down numbers.

Back at the hotel, she soaked in the tub, hanging the new sundress on the shower rod to steam. She'd sunk beneath the bubbles when a muffled slam indicated the suite door opening and closing.

Trey poked his head through the door. "Now that looks inviting after a long day of talking structural integrity of a skyscraper." He shrugged out of his jacket. "Is there room for two in that tub?"

"I can make room, and there're plenty of bubbles." She sat up, knowing the foam would cling to her upper body.

"Scoot over, babe." He grinned and began to shed his shirt and slacks. "Before I totally lose my train of thought, we're invited for dinner tonight at Jerome and Isabelle's. But we have plenty of time before we have to leave."

****

Three hours later she savored the last bite of beef bourguignon at Trey's former partner's boho-chic row house. Jerome had attended grad school in Chicago before landing a job at the New Buffalo firm. They'd stayed in touch when he'd moved back to France, including consulting on buildings such as the new skyscraper on the edge of the city. He was a suave, assured man, with high cheekbones and a full mouth.

His wife, Isabelle, animated the evening with stories about the city. Despite her dramatic appearance, with long, blue-black hair and wide dark eyes, Tess found her to be as warm and welcoming as her traditional beef stew.

They were gathered close around a table in the couple's combined dining / living area, accented by colorful dishes and candlelight. Rather than clean up, Isabelle pushed aside their empty bowls and continued the conversation. "I'm pleased you found vintage bargains at our flea market. What else is on your sightseeing agenda?"

"We're going to the Eiffel Tower tomorrow night." Tess caught her slight smile, probably amusement at the tourist agenda. "Do you recommend any other must see—"

She halted as a scream sounded from deeper in the house. Running footsteps pounded down the hallway. Her pulse zoomed as Isabelle lurched to her feet. A youngster in a short nightgown burst into the room. "*Maman.*" She threw her arms around Isabelle's waist and launched into muttered French that Tess couldn't interpret.

During the evening, she'd enjoyed hearing tales about the couple's five-year-old. The girl was supposed to be in bed, sleeping soundly. Her mother stroked the tousled dark head and murmured in a calming tone.

Trey leaned toward Tess. "Vivienne must have had a nightmare. She says she saw a ghost."

A ghost? Tess stared toward the child as Isabelle shrugged. "I'm so sorry. Sometimes she sees the ghosts in the apartment. She's used to this, so I'm surprised at the reaction. We apologize for the disturbance."

The girl's head popped up. Her eyes were still round, but her face had composed. Isabelle continued, "Vivienne, you've met Monsieur Trey before. This is his friend, Mademoiselle Tess."

The child pointed at her and shot out another stream of French. The other adults frowned. *Have I broken an etiquette rule they've been too polite to reinforce?* Tess wondered. She gripped her napkin, her cheeks warming at the scrutiny.

Trey appeared bemused. "She asked why you were in her room."

Her mouth fell open. She had been with the adults all evening, not even seeking out the bathroom.

Jerome corrected his daughter. "She has not been in your room, *ma cherie.*"

The girl's lips jutted in a pout. "I saw her," she said in English.

Trey rubbed his forehead. "Tess, did you wear or carry something with you tonight?"

"Yes. A monogrammed handkerchief. I took it with me today. I'm so sorry. I didn't think to leave it at the hotel." She offered a tight, apologetic smile. She hoped he—and their hosts—wouldn't be upset. Would he tell his friends the truth now, or evade?

"This is not something I intended to discuss with you all." He scanned the adults' puzzled faces. "But Tess and I are involved in a very interesting…situation. With supernatural overtones."

She was relieved at his decision. Though she'd have played along with either outcome, she thought it best to 'fess up.

"Isabelle, would you prefer to take Vivienne back

to bed before I continue?" he asked.

"Will this scare her more? Or might you explain so she can be comfortable back in her room?"

"I can do that."

She hoisted her daughter into her lap. "Then please proceed."

He rested his forearms on his thighs to address the girl at her level. "Vivienne, since you're obviously a brave and smart girl, I'm going to share a very special story with you."

"Like a fairy tale?"

"Kind of. Since we met, Tess and I have been seeing people, too. One of them was my cousin, who lived many, many years ago. From his picture, we know he looked a lot like me. He was married to a beautiful lady who looked like her. Her name was Phoebe. We think you might have seen her in your room, because Tess has been sitting with us all night."

"*Oui*." The girl's expression remained clear and alert as she kept her eyes on Trey.

"We want to apologize if she scared you because Phoebe is a nice and friendly spirit. She loves little girls and probably thought you'd be more fun than the adults."

Vivienne chewed on her finger. "The others are nice, too. Maybe she wanted to say hello to them."

"That's possible." He matched her serious demeanor. "You can go back to sleep now, and know Phoebe was just here to visit for a little while."

"And to tell us the message," the girl agreed.

Tess stared at her and crumpled her napkin in her lap. Jerome moved to crouch next to his daughter.

"A message? What did she say, sweetheart?"

Sandra L. Young

The girl bit her finger again, in concentration. "She said, 'Edward is a man of peace.' I did not meet him, though." The youngster's eyes closed as she yawned. "Can I go back to bed now?"

"Of course, my darling." He lifted his daughter into his arms. "As Trey said, you were very brave to come and tell us about your fascinating visit." He regarded the adults with a small smile. "I'll re-settle her. Please don't finish the story until I'm back."

"She knew his name," Tess murmured as his footsteps echoed down the hall. "This is as unreal as our flashes of vision. Phoebe reinforced her husband's innocence, reaching out through an accepting child."

"Innocence?" Isabelle questioned. "I hope he hurries so you can finish this story." She grabbed the wine bottle to top off their glasses. "Please don't be afraid we'll judge. We're French, we're open, and we believe in spirits and supernatural possibilities. Vivi has talked about ghostly figures since she was very young. Though she has never relayed a message before."

Jerome returned and smiled. "She's fine. Went right back to sleep. Don't hold back, friends. What've you been dealing with?"

Trey squeezed her hand. She took the lead and relayed her early flashes at the mansion through waking up after the fashion show. He interjected to detail the diary entries and their additional visions.

"*Sacré Bleu*, what an amazing story." Their host appeared unruffled. "Frankly, Trey, if I had not heard this from your own lips, I would doubt you believe in such things."

"If you had asked me two months ago if I believed in ghosts, I would've scoffed. But I've lived through

246

these flashes more than once. Unfortunately, now I'm a believer. Vivi's connection only reinforces that direction."

"Do you think you are a reincarnation of Edward, and Tess is Phoebe?" Isabelle's expression was eager in the flickering candlelight.

He caught Tess' eye, and they shook their heads. "No," he said. "The resemblance is uncanny, but after all, I'm related to Edward. We consider ourselves vessels for these visions. The clothing and accessories seem to be a catalyst sometimes. The handkerchief likely triggered tonight's visit."

Tess drew the fine linen square from her purse and smoothed it on the table. The P.P.C. initials curled in delicate stitchwork, perhaps done by Phoebe's own hand. "In hindsight, I shouldn't have brought any of their articles along. Call me silly and romantic, but they never made it to Paris. I hoped they might somehow experience your lovely city while this link exists."

A sheen of tears lit Isabelle's eyes. "Such a tragic, yet romantic story. You were very thoughtful to carry them with you." She held her glass aloft. "With your help, let us toast that the mystery will be resolved, and Edward and Phoebe may soon rest easier in the afterlife."

"Thank you for your understanding. I know Trey wants to bring an end to the flashes. Personally, I'm open to whatever will bring them justice." She drank, recognizing Phoebe's message had cemented her own conviction. Edward was a man of peace. An innocent man, bearing an unfair stain against his reputation.

Chapter Thirty-Two

Tess occupied herself shopping for additional gifts while Trey wrapped his Tuesday morning meetings. She browsed through postcards at a store near the hotel and pondered his acceptance of the previous night's events. She'd been thrilled when he'd shared the story and said he believed in the ghostly visitations.

He'd been so good with the child, as well. Tender and caring. He was a special man who'd make an excellent father. They'd make lovely children together, she thought with a smile. Her smile faded, and she dropped the postcards she'd chosen. She drew a quick breath. Trey Dunmore had moved far beyond "special" to her. Over the past whirlwind weeks, she'd gone and fallen in love with him.

He made her laugh. He respected her opinion. He boosted her confidence, both as a woman and as a business professional, opening her to trust again. She couldn't wait to see him, to spend romantic moments together.

She loved him. The realization made her giddy, yet vulnerable. Elated, but a bit scared. The seesaw of emotion carried through the afternoon as they visited the Palais Garnier—the Paris Opéra. She savored the warmth of his hand covering hers but caught herself holding back as they strolled up the sweeping staircase and through the exquisite, golden interior. Viewing their relationship through this new lens left her trying to dissect his responses. Did he feel the same? Or was he still on guard, protecting himself after the painful failure of his previous relationship?

She watched him examine the gleaming viewing boxes floating high above the theater rows. Maybe he viewed their trip as a fun flirtation in a magical city. Would their relationship cool back in the States? What if he tired of the mental and physical demands of the visions and decided he'd need to distance himself—from them and from her?

****

She tried to put her misgivings behind her that evening as she put on a sassy crimson dress from the flea market. Trey gave her an appreciative smile, until he saw the brooch in the mirror.

"You're wearing that again?"

"Our last night in Paris. It just feels right." She fingered the gold filigree. "I'll take it off if you prefer."

He groaned. "No. The pin's perfect with your new-old dress. You know I can't refuse you anything."

"Exactly what I like to hear." She twirled for his approval and giggled with relief. The ruby sparkled until he muffled her laughter with a kiss that left her head spinning. Her heartrate calmed as they headed out of the hotel toward a bistro. After another multi-course dinner, with daylight beginning to fade, they took the Métro to the Eiffel Tower for a nighttime view of the City of Light. She was struck by the immensity and grandeur of the structure as they walked the last block.

They purchased tickets, intending to take the lift to the top rather than tackle hundreds of stairs. Numerous visitors milled about, conversing in multiple languages.

Eventually, with two other couples, they boarded an elevator. They huddled and flirted in low tones as dusk retreated into darkness, stepping out to a panorama of Paris glittering like a sequined gown.

Tess touched the brooch at her neck. Phoebe would have seen significantly fewer lights a century prior. "Magnificent," she murmured. She turned to catch Trey watching her, rather than the view. "Am I overplaying the uber-tourist? Everywhere I look I see something new and fascinating. I can't thank you enough for giving me the opportunity to tag along."

"Tag along?" He smiled, his eyes intent on hers. "Paris is an exciting city, but the trip's been even more special reliving the beauty through your eyes. I've loved making memories with you. Truth is, I've had a hard time concentrating on work because all I can think about is how you're waiting for me." He reached for her hands.

"I wouldn't want to affect your project, but I'm happy to hear that." She stiffened as his face changed to reflect a tinge of nerves. She gripped his hands, intuiting his next words would decide the future direction of their relationship.

He looked earnest and maybe a tad unsure. "I've discovered I don't want to lose this feeling. I want to go through life knowing at the end of the day, we're there for each other. I love you, Tess, and I want you in my life, in my heart, in my bed."

Her heart took wing at the poetic yet sexy declaration. The words that danced around the edge of her consciousness burst through: "I love you, too, Trey. Very much."

He smiled wide and pulled his right hand away to

dig into his inside jacket pocket. She gasped when he held up a small velvet box. She didn't dare to hope.

He flipped the top, revealing a square-cut ruby in a gold setting, flanked by rectangular diamonds. "I saw this in an antique store window today and knew I had to buy it. Tess, will you wear this ring and be my wife?"

"I'd be so honored to marry you." Tears welled in her eyes as he slid the ring onto her finger. A perfect fit.

"I love you," he said against her lips, before deepening the kiss.

She reveled in the heat of his mouth and of his hands spanning her back. A growing warmth spread over her heart, and she welcomed the change in her equilibrium.

"Paris. At last. Thank you, darling. I will treasure this moment forever."

****

Trey heard the words through a fog of joy and desire. He tried to resist, but gave in to the subconscious persuasion from Tess, Phoebe, and Edward.

'My dearest Phoebe, know that I will love you for all eternity.'

The image was gone; Tess remained in his arms. He blinked back into the shadowy night. "They were here together. That's what you wanted."

She looked up to meet his eyes, a little sheepish. "I didn't know what was possible. After all, how is any of this possible? I'm glad we could do this for them. I really believe we're near to bringing them closure. I hope you're not upset."

"No. I suppose the flash was fitting. They helped bring us together."

"Are you convinced of his innocence now? If Edward was the murderer, she wouldn't be so forgiving and charitable in the afterlife."

Trey didn't want to break the mood by debating. "Good point. If that's the case, we may not see them again." He'd rather have definitive proof, yet they'd probably have to settle for a cobbled-together version of the truth.

She rested her head on his chest, and he relished the moment of complete and utter happiness. He could envision a long and happy life together. Hopefully minus their ghostly companions.

Chapter Thirty-Three

Despite the beginnings of jet lag, the couple headed to Carver House the next afternoon. They didn't want Esther to hear their big news secondhand. They had called their parents on the drive back from the airport.

Clarice's eyes sparkled as she wrapped Tess in an affectionate embrace in the hallway. "What a glamorous vintage stone. My son has great taste." She also hugged him and led them into the parlor.

After they'd greeted Esther, Tess said, "We had a wonderful trip and picked up a few things in Paris."

"Gifts. Jewelry," he added.

She held up the bag containing the trinkets they'd purchased. She rocked her fist gently. The ruby caught fire in the beam of sunlight streaming through the tall windows.

Esther's eyes widened. "My goodness, you're engaged. How marvelous."

Footsteps sounded on the staircase. Jake entered the room with slow steps. Tess thought his manner seemed guarded, but perhaps he'd adopted a wary approach as protection during his struggles.

His grandmother waved him forward. "Jacob, look." She pointed to Tess' uplifted hand.

He reached them, and his brows drew together. He stared at her before smoothing his expression. "Cousin, you done good," he drawled. He clapped Trey on the shoulder and reached for her hand.

His warm fingers tightened on hers. She watched his eyes glaze, as Trey's had done more than once.

****

He stood in the stuffy third floor ballroom watching Phoebe twirl past in the arms of Penny Cooper. The two giggled as if they'd never left the schoolyard, but Phoebe's womanly figure erased any notion of girlish innocence. He smirked as her partner stumbled. The duo recovered and kept whirling.

Certainly, life would be easier if he had any interest in the freckle-faced redhead. Despite Phoebe's persistent efforts to push the two of them together, he couldn't conjure interest in the woman. Not that she wasn't attractive. She just wasn't Phoebe.

He ground his teeth, reminded that the beautiful woman before him was engaged to his stepbrother. They would marry in under a month. Yet his heart couldn't bear to believe she'd go through with it. The lovesick organ overruled his logical side once more, and he found himself trotting toward the dancers. With a courteous but firm gesture, he maneuvered Penny out and away, leaving her standing in the center of the room. Phoebe seemed taken aback, but soon she was smiling again.

That gorgeous, inviting smile. Soft lips, white teeth. Yes, she surely shared his attraction. He'd recognized it beneath the jests and flirtation, intensifying after the staggering Valentine's Day kiss. He drank her in, reveling in the sensuality of her swaying waist under his hands as he swung her in wider circles.

He should speak, though he wasn't sure what he could say that wouldn't upset her in this public setting, with his prig of a stepbrother lumbering nearby. He could plant a seed though—

As if reading his traitorous thoughts, Nick, the ever-loyal friend, rushed up to cut in. He read the unspoken challenge in the fool's eyes and spun to try to shake him off. The cad clung to them, encasing Phoebe's waist from behind. His broad, calloused hands sought dominance as the three of them swept around the floor in an ungainly, raucous dance. Behind Phoebe's back, Nick's teeth bared in a snarl.

His temper arced, and he matched the fierce frown.

"Enough!" Edward's voice rang over them, echoing through the vast, empty space.

He could see his face, cold and angry. At him, of course. He'd never judge Nick so harshly. Chastised, he stepped back. Nick did the same. Phoebe pressed her hands against her heart, her chest heaving from exertion.

He was out of breath himself, panting, aching, and suddenly furious. Ensuring she was clear of them, he shoved Nick back with a mighty blow…

****

"Jacob. Are you all right?" Esther's eyes darted between the three young people.

His drooping head and posture had put her on alert. Tess empathized with his struggle to refocus, but she was eager to hear his words.

He rubbed a hand over his eyes and stumbled away. "What the…" His jaw tightened in his reddened face.

"What did you see?" Trey asked, in a calm voice.

"Nothing." He stared him down.

Her heart sank. He was trying to preserve his tough

image by stonewalling them. "Please tell us if something strange happened. We won't judge you. As we told you before, we have our own stories to share." She was fortunate that her previous mini-visions and her grandmother's influence had opened her to easier acceptance. Yet the initial experiences still rocked her.

Jake hesitated. He shook his head hard, as if to clear it. "I dunno. Like a crazy dream or something. Reminded me of a post-traumatic stress episode. I saw the ballroom here. A bunch of people in old costumes dancing. Actually, I was dancing with a woman who looked a lot like you." His face softened as he looked to her. "I suppose y'all think that was Phoebe. A guy named Nick tried to cut in. Trey's look-alike got fed up with them and yelled 'Enough.' " He stalked toward the window and turned his back.

"The last man was Edward Carver." She tamped down her excitement. She wanted to pull him in, not spook him. "I've seen the same vision. You've described a scene from Phoebe's diary. The details match exactly."

He faced her again, his cheeks still flushed. "Why would I see that?"

Esther walked toward him. "You're here for a reason, my dear. Beyond my happiness to reconnect with you." She placed a hand on his arm and drew him to sit next to her.

Trey stood beside Tess, his posture tense. "You must be channeling through Stephen. Another link to the mystery."

"If I didn't know better, I'd say you all are trying to gaslight me." Jake's fists clenched in his lap. "But I don't know what the hell you'd gain."

She feared he might storm out. "Please. Would you at least listen to this?" They'd been intending to return the diary to Esther. She retrieved the booklet from her purse and began to read the ballroom confrontation aloud. After several sentences, he walked over and took it from her. He paced away, skimming the pages. His face reflected confusion and denial.

"Yeah, the last thing I saw was this Stephen guy shoving the other one. Nick." He handed the diary to her as if he couldn't stand to hold it.

Clarice stood to join them. "Thank you for sharing with us. These visions don't seem to hurt Tess or Trey, but of course they're disorienting."

He shrugged. "I know you told me about this stuff, and I refused to believe you. The reality's mind-blowing. With my PTSD and painkiller addiction I'm familiar with mind-altered states. Nothing compared to this though. I sort of…disappeared." He pushed out a heavy sigh. "Everybody, sit. I'm feeling claustrophobic enough."

"Sorry." Trey settled next to Tess on the settee. "Seems you're another unwilling catalyst for solving the mystery. After seeing several of these visions, I became a grudging believer myself."

"I don't want to see any more," he muttered.

"You might not." She tried to reassure him. She knew he'd never welcome the images, but he could at least accept them. "Maybe your purpose is to reinforce this one particular scenario. I've seen several, and they do get easier. I took Phoebe's brooch and handkerchief to Paris and even experienced a few flashes there. We had the same joint one of her and Edward when we were at the Eiffel Tower."

Esther nodded. "Perhaps you're all meant to see the same scene, which will reveal the truth behind the murder."

Trey's fingers drummed against his knee—the usual pressure-release reaction. "I've been thinking the same thing. Much as I dislike the idea, there's another player we might need in the mix." He shared brief details about Brett's visit. "I think he could be critical, too."

Tess wrinkled her nose. "I don't know how we'll convince him to join us. I told him I didn't want to get back together. If he hears we're engaged, he knows he doesn't have a chance, and he'll keep his distance. I don't want to hide the truth or trick him into coming here."

Jake flung up a hand. "You're assuming I'm open to trying this, too. I haven't even wrapped my head around it yet."

His grandmother appeared torn. "We would never force you to do anything you don't feel comfortable with. Though Edward and Phoebe's wills may be so strong you'll all have these experiences until the mystery's solved."

"Just when I'm regaining control of my life, it spirals away again. Figures." He sagged in the chair.

Tess suspected Esther was correct: Edward and Phoebe wouldn't fade away. She had to push their agenda forward. "If we're all agreed, I'll call Brett tomorrow to see if I can convince him to visit again. I'll want him to believe he can be a hero and rescue me— but not drive him to contact the police or my parents. He did mention Trey's influence after hearing about my visions. He may feel the engagement's a ploy to take advantage of me and come back to check it out."

Trey groaned beside her. "I'm not crazy about the setup, but I'll go along with whatever will put this behind us. I'll be the fall guy if necessary. How about you say you'd like him to get to know me so he's at ease?"

****

When she called him to report in the next night, her news was discouraging. Brett had been friendly and welcoming till she discussed having more visions. When she shared about the engagement, his mood and tone darkened. "He basically hung up on me when I asked if he'd visit to get to know you better."

"We'll have to try this without him," Trey said. "Maybe the three of us will be able to pull it off, if my cousin will open up to the idea."

In the coming days they had further friendly contact with Jake—not aiming to coerce, just to put him at ease in his new hometown. They took him to dinner at a downtown restaurant on Sunday night, where Marcy joined them. They sat under an umbrella on an outdoor patio surrounded by a noisy, hip, young crowd drawn to the Uptown Arts District.

Tess told herself she wasn't matchmaking, but why not include her friend in having some fun together. She had to smile, though, when she thought of Penny Cooper pining after a reluctant Stephen. While Marcy and Jake seemed to enjoy each other's company, she hadn't detected sparks between them, either. She was a little surprised because they both were attractive, intelligent people with likeable personalities.

She watched her friend offer half of her fries to Jake. He took them without hesitation, and when he reached for the ketchup, he caught Tess' eye with a lazy grin.

Unless Jake was interested in someone else.

She smiled back as her mind raced. She'd picked up on potential interest before, but surely that had disappeared with her engagement. She dropped her eyes to her plate and began to box her leftover fettucine. He'd given her a probing look when he'd first seen the ring, but since his own vision, he'd treated her with reserved friendliness. She shouldn't let her imagination run amok during this challenging time. She'd only create an uncomfortable atmosphere between them.

Marcy nudged her shoulder and pointed to the skyline. "What a sunset."

Welcoming the distraction, she joined her in admiring the streams of pink and gold. "We should walk over to the beach to catch the last rays. Are you guys up for a trot to work off some of these calories?"

The men agreed and, after paying the bill, they set a good pace to reach the nearby public beach. Jake and Marcy led the way with their longer stride. Trey held back with her, and they swung their hands between them. The scent of the lake reached her, and she felt blissfully happy, and lucky to have found love, passion, and friendship in her adopted city. Lake Michigan was another major perk of the area. As they joined the remaining clusters of people on the beach, the colors melded into the murky canvas of rippling water, mirroring an impressionist scene. The horizon illuminated the vague outline of the Chicago skyline.

Jake reclined beside Marcy on the sand and kicked off his sandals. "Tess, has anyone told you this is the yellow brick road that L. Frank Baum wrote about in

The Wizard of Oz? Locals say he saw the golden ribbon of sunlight connecting the Lake Michigan shoreline to the horizon and immortalized the scene."

"That's lovely. One of my favorite childhood books. I'm enjoying learning about the rich history of the area, including the Victorian female lighthouse keeper. She had to run down a slippery dock in a long skirt to light the lamp, even when the waves were crashing."

He sat up to face the others, wrapping his arms around his legs. "Speaking of history, thanks for not giving me a hard time about the visions. I've thought about this a ton, and I've finally reconciled to giving it a shot. Whatever it is you think we need to do."

She smiled her approval rather than shout in triumph. With his help, the resolution could be near.

Trey kept a straight face and shooed away a curious gull. "I'm glad you're in. I know the decision was tough. From my angle, we try to draw a conclusion about the murder and move on with our lives. As soon as possible. What say we get together at Carver House next weekend and see what we can do together?"

Marcy grabbed her arm. "Not to butt in, but do you think I can come and watch?"

Jake snorted. "I'd sure rather you took my place. I don't know about you all, but I'm starting to get a Scooby Doo vibe. Maybe we need to bring a talking dog."

"Poor baby. The warrior-chicks will protect you." She flicked sand onto his bare feet, and they all joined in the laughter.

As he retaliated, Tess grinned. Maybe a spark would ignite between the two of them after all.

Chapter Thirty-Four

Tess nearly fumbled the phone when Brett called a few days later to apologize for how he'd ended their call. "I still worry about you, you know," he said smoothly. "Without your folks around, yeah, I do want to get to know this guy. My grandmother would have wanted me to ensure you're in good hands."

She hid her excitement and invited him to the Sunday get-together at Carver House. She pumped her fist in the air afterward and dialed Trey, rationalizing she hadn't lied to Brett. She couldn't say with certainty the gathering would be out-of-the-ordinary. They might sit for an hour of stilted conversation, then he'd go his merry way.

****

Her former boyfriend arrived a few minutes early on Sunday afternoon. Her stomach rolled with uncertainty as she and Esther greeted him at the door. He appeared confident and at ease, every blond hair in place above his striped polo and white slacks. She allowed him to kiss her on the cheek and made brief introductions. He charmed Esther with compliments about the house as he followed her into the parlor. Tess tuned out, worried about how the time would unfold. Would they achieve their aim to bring closure to the mystery? Unlike Trey, she feared if they didn't uncover the clues soon, the visions might fade, leaving Edward under a permanent cloud of condemnation.

In the parlor, Brett headed straight to Trey. "Congratulations on the engagement. I know better than anyone you've found yourself a fine woman." He stopped an arms-length from him and crossed his arms over his chest. "Even though I'm a few hours away, I'll jump in to help her if she ever needs it."

"Nice to know she can count on her old friends." He held out his hand to shake. She bit back a grin as Brett slowly uncrossed his arms. Yet her heartbeat stuttered as the two men clasped hands. They pulled apart, and she thought they both appeared tense, but there was no indication of anything unusual. She wasn't sure if she was relieved or frustrated. She walked up to introduce their visitor to Jake, Marcy, and Clarice. He greeted each of them and shook hands without apparent incident.

She caught Trey's eye, interpreting his tight jaw as frustration. He was a man who appreciated immediate results. She squeezed his hand and tried to communicate a *be patient* reminder.

Esther began the planned approach. "My apologies for boasting, but the mansion is celebrating a centennial this year. I'm always pleased to show newcomers a few of the highlights. Brett and Marcy, would you be interested in a tour before we have refreshments?"

"I would. They sure don't build 'em like this anymore," he stood and stretched. "The exercise will be good for me. I'm still stiff after the drive."

Clarice clapped her hands. "We'll all go. Work up our appetites."

"Please do," Marcy agreed. "I grew up in the area, and I've been dying to see inside."

They had plotted before he arrived and decided the ballroom might trigger the shared dancing vision. If not, the master bedroom would provide the chilling scene of the crime. He didn't seem put off by the group tour, and he chatted with Esther as she led to the third floor.

Inside the grand, wood-paneled space, sunlight streamed through the floating dust motes. Jake stayed near the entrance, his hands dug deep in his pockets, while Marcy twirled to admire the crystal chandeliers. Brett walked around her to look out the wall of windows.

Esther drew his attention to Edward's trunk in the corner. "This is from the original owner of the house. Still filled with his clothing." She leaned to open it.

"I bet Tess got excited about that." He joined her and skimmed a finger across the edge of the lid. He paused for a long moment but moved on without changing expression.

"Vintage clothing is my livelihood *and* my passion now." Tess reinforced her newfound success as she took his arm at the grand piano, to jumpstart a flash.

"If the economy holds, eventually you could make a decent living." He tinkled his fingers over the keys and glanced at his watch.

She released his arm and stepped away. Same old know-it-all attitude. He couldn't resist a jab of judgment. She simmered a bit, and Trey offered an empathetic grin.

He leaned to whisper in her ear. "Don't let the creep rattle you."

Esther stepped toward the door. "We'll continue on to the master bedroom, where the house's notoriety began." She and Clarice shared brief history, building a sense of anticipation, as they descended to the second floor. After everyone had assembled inside, she said, "Sadly, this is the room that's tainted our family history. The bedroom where Edward Carver supposedly murdered his new bride, Phoebe."

Though she was very aware of the tale, an icy shiver skimmed along Tess' spine. She rubbed her arms, catching Marcy's wide-eyed excitement as she took in the elaborate antique headboard.

Brett glanced around the room. "I sure didn't expect that kind of story from this house." He touched a brass pull on the matching tallboy chest and frowned in confusion. His head swayed forward, and his eyes fluttered closed.

She took his arm. Trey linked with hers, and Jake clapped a hand onto his back. Marcy snuck her palm onto Trey's shoulder.

"What in blazes are you doing here?"

Edward jerked hard on his shoulder, and he spun, loosening his hands around Phoebe's throat. She slid, motionless, to the floor. He knew how he must appear: wild-eyed, disheveled, stinking of whiskey. For a brief floating moment, he stared down his friend and rival. With a wordless cry, Edward tried to shove past him to reach Phoebe.

There was no going back. He leapt forward, feral and intense, and propelled him into the wall. An insane barrage of emotions coursed through his veins as he threw and dodged punches. Regret was tempered with self-preservation. He was determined to emerge the victor.

They were well-matched in size and strength. Similarly fueled by love for the silent woman crumpled on the floor. A love bordering on obsession. He ducked a punch that would have crushed his jaw, wondering why Phoebe hadn't awoken. Surely, she had only fainted. She couldn't be… No, he wouldn't allow himself to consider it.

He was torn with fear, but he couldn't withdraw to check on her. He was here to win this woman; he wouldn't leave without her. Perhaps she was feigning to avoid alerting Edward to her complicity.

He'd let down his guard. He grunted in pain as his opponent delivered a stunning flurry of blows. Shocked and winded, he broke away, clutching his ribs. He must recover and fight back. Through his red haze, he now realized only one of them would leave the room alive.

He ignored the searing heat in his chest to thrust a punch into Edward's stomach. He watched him bend under the solid impact and hoped it would take him down. Instead, he stumbled back into the dresser and wrenched open a drawer.

He watched the handgun emerge with shock and horror. He hadn't come here armed. Hadn't planned for violence. He'd been certain Phoebe would welcome him, and they'd slip away quietly. Either this very evening or the next day. He raised his hands in a surrender gesture.

Edward panted with loud gasps; his arms trembled as he raised the gun to center on his heart. Strange, how he suddenly felt composed and clear-headed. Did his friend have the courage to kill him? Or did he just want to drive him away? And turn him in to law enforcement.

He'd face ruin. Phoebe would despise him.

Edward hesitated, his finger slack against the

trigger. With animal instinct, he crouched and lunged, pushing the gun up and under his opponent's chin.

"What the hell was that?" Brett wrenched away from their human chain. His face flushed, and his legs seemed to give out. He sat on the far end of the bed. "Tess, what's going on?" He stared around the room with a panicked expression.

Though her own heart pounded from the terrible scene, she sought to reassure him. "Please stay calm and listen to me." She grasped his forearms and spoke in a low, soothing voice. "If you saw what I did, you were watching a man murder his friends in a jealous rage. I know you thought we were crazy for talking about visions from the past, but you saw for yourself we weren't lying." She turned to the others' stunned faces. "Did you see the fight?"

The trio nodded, including a pale-faced Marcy. Clarice and Esther stood to the side, looking anxious.

"You set me up," he growled. His hands clenched into fists on the duvet.

She had hoped never to see the harsh expression on his face again, but this time she wouldn't let him bully her. Trey put his arm around her waist as she held her ground. "That was never our intent. After you visited, we thought we might need you here to complete the visions and end the cycle. We didn't know if you'd be the final connector. Apparently, that's the case."

Trey tightened his grip on her. "We didn't want to trick or harm you. We wanted to finally get to the bottom of the story and know the truth. If all of us saw that Edward didn't murder his wife and commit suicide, the knowledge clears his name, at least within our family."

Brett jerked away and moved toward the door. "Well, it was a crappy way to approach it."

"Would you have come if I asked you to join us in channeling a century-old murder?" she tossed after him. Her eyes appealed for understanding as he paused at the doorway. "I'm really sorry this has been uncomfortable for you. Trey and I have experienced several of these flashes. All we want is peace, for ourselves but also for Phoebe and Edward as well."

She held up her hand to halt his anticipated angry comments. "We do plan to tell Esther's immediate family, but we won't bring you into it in any way. I won't share all the details with my parents. I think you'd agree this is hard to wrap your head around."

"That's an understatement," he sneered. "And to clarify, the vision ended before the gunshot. You can rationalize the who-dunnit ending all you want, 'cause I'm not your guinea pig. Have a good life, Tess." He stalked through the door, and his steps pounded down the stairs.

No one spoke. Her heart pounding, she followed him out at a fast pace, trailed by the others. She neared the bottom landing, assuming he'd veer off and run out the front door. "Wait. Please."

He suddenly halted by the arched doorway into the library. The hair stood up on the back of her arms when he didn't move, just continued to stand frozen in place. She swung around to the others with a finger to her lips. Trey stepped around her to cup Brett's left shoulder. She closed her eyes and placed her hand over his.

The front parlor was hot and damp, crowded with mourners in dark finery. Their whispers and tears spilled into every corner. The furniture had been moved to accommodate the mahogany coffin. The top was closed, draped with a swag of fringed black velvet. Sharing in the grief and condolences, he kept his glass refilled from the ready hip flask of Jameson's whiskey. Mercifully, his vision was as blurred as his mind. But no matter how much he drank, he couldn't erase the hideous memory of how he had betrayed his best friends.

Consumed with drink, lust, and rage, he had allowed his most depraved instincts to rule. He fervently wished Edward had shot him first, relieving him from living in this miserable hell on earth. Yet a harsh preservation instinct kept him from confessing the sin and accepting his rightful punishment. Instead, he moved among the crowd, embraced as one of them by his friends, neighbors—even Edward's grieving family.

Enraged by their dear daughter's supposed murder at Edward's hands, the Pattersons were holding their own service a few blocks away. He didn't know if he could bring himself to attend. Conversely, he didn't know if he could prevent himself from barging in and throwing himself on the coffin. Beautiful Phoebe's final resting place.

The guilt was far too much to bear. He hung his head and stumbled out of the room. He reeled down the dark hall, opening the first door, escaping inside Edward's library-office. The tears flowed, hot and painful, and he buried his face in his hands, slumping at the desk. Contrition tore at his heart, an unimaginable, wrenching agony. He swiped his arm across his wet eyes and rummaged for a scrap of paper. His shaking fingers scrabbled for a fountain pen.

He blotted the end of the pen and wrote in jerking script. "I am sorry, my dear friends. I am an animal. A coward. Yet I cannot openly confess and bear the consequences I deserve. Please forgive me. I never meant to hurt either of you. Your precious blood is now a stain, un-washable from my hands. Edward, I do regret the unfair burden of murder I've placed on your innocent soul. I pray you are together in eternity."

He swirled his initials, N.S.J., and pulled out the small secret compartment Edward had revealed after purchasing the masterful desk. At the time, they had joked about what might be hidden there someday. Ironically, he himself was entrusting his purged confession to the dark confines, attempting to somehow ease the consuming guilt. He folded the paper in half, stuffed it inside, and slammed the compartment shut. He readjusted the concealing drawer.

Confession did not bring relief. He bowed his head to the desk, praying for oblivion to a God who surely must have turned his back on such a treacherous soul.

As Brett's shoulders jerked, Tess swam up out of the vision. He refocused and shook his head hard before stomping across the foyer and out the door. Trey's hand remained warm on her shoulder.

"What did you see, my dears?" Esther called down to them.

Trey held Tess' eyes. "Hopefully, the final revelation. Follow me."

They all filed into the library. Esther pressed a hand to her heart, and Marcy urged her toward a chair. "I'm fine," she murmured. "Please proceed."

The others circled around her as Trey stood before the desk. He opened the middle drawer and bent to search inside. "There's a hidden compartment, if I can find it." After a few moments he dipped his fingers deeper inside.

He withdrew with a triumphant smile, holding a piece of thin, folded paper. "If the vision holds true, we're about to hear Nick Judson's confession."

Chapter Thirty-Five

Marcy waggled a neon-polished fingertip at Jake and her best friend Justine's husband, Jackson. "I know a couple of you are skeptics. Please keep an open mind and behave yourselves."

She and Justine had pleaded with them to participate in the "haunting tour" in an old theater on Chicago's near north side. Marcy had been especially thrilled to land tickets on August 16, the century wedding anniversary for Edward and Phoebe. The theater connection, and the promise of the French dinner they'd eaten, had led Jackson to relent and join the crew.

Tess linked arms with Marcy, teasing, "Jackson's had to develop a skeptical skin to survive in the world of screenwriting. Maybe today he'll get his own spooky little nudge at Tangier Hall. Whoooo."

She trilled her version of a ghost voice, glad her assistant had introduced them to the fun-loving couple when they returned from their latest stint in California. Justine emitted Midwest positivity while her hubby viewed the world through a cynical lens behind hip, dark-framed glasses. Her former work at the local historical society museum had led to a quick bonding with Tess over vintage clothing. The composed strawberry-blonde also had revealed her own otherworldly encounters. Tess and Trey had felt comfortable sharing their experiences with them prior to holding a press conference in late July.

As they approached the crumbling brick façade of the Tangier, she recalled how he had focused on the basic facts. He'd emphasized Edward's innocence and Nick's guilt without discussing the visions. The handful of regional newspaper, radio, and television reporters accepted the proof of Nick's age-authenticated confession note, bolstered by matching his initials to a Carver Shipping log Esther found in rummaging further through the attic. The deal was sealed with excerpts from Phoebe's diary and a headline article Trey dug out of news archives. The sensationalized account speculated a drunk, despondent Nick, grieving his best friends' deaths, intentionally stepped in front of a train a month after the murder-suicide.

The story went viral after Chicago news outlets picked it up. At Esther's urging, Tess and Trey supported her in a few on-air and print interviews before he called a halt, saying he'd had enough notoriety. Jake had flatly refused to take part. In the meantime, Marcy discovered the ghost tour. The session promised a paranormal "circle" with a husband and wife regarded as renowned psychic ghostbusters. They'd written books, lectured, and conducted tours and individual sessions over the years. Tess and Justine had jumped at the idea. The men complained but finally gave in.

Through all the hubbub, Phoebe and Edward stayed off the radar. She hoped they were pleased and finally at rest, but she wasn't persuaded. She thought this evening could provide them with a few laughs at an amateur effort to fool them. Or they might discover kindred souls who could help them communicate with their departed visitors. She squeezed Trey's hand, doubting he shared her nerves or her anticipation.

They walked up the cracked concrete steps and entered a compact lobby, where strands of burgundy and gold wool had frayed into a muted pattern under countless tramping feet. Dusty red velvet curtains drooped across the two inner doorways. The center box office was sealed behind a plywood panel.

A tall, thin woman glided between the curtains, enveloped in a gown of multi-hued, gauzy material. "Welcome." She held out her arms as if she might take flight. Her graying hair was long and curling, tumbling halfway down her back. Tess stifled a smile at her dramatic appearance.

"I'm Marcy Alexander, and these are my friends: Tess, Trey, Jackson, Justine, and Jake." As the instigator of the trip, Marcy moved forward.

"How very alliteral. Except for you, my dear. I appreciate an obvious free spirit." The woman winked. "How wonderful to meet you all. I'm Dorinda Castalane. My husband, Richaud, and I are your hosts for the evening. Please, come join the rest of the group. We keep these sessions small and personable. Only sixteen tonight."

She led them through the curtains into the theater, where strips of patterned wallpaper skewed down from the walls. The rows of faded upholstered chairs remained anchored in place, flanking two aisles. Tess supposed they'd left the place intact to build the eerie atmosphere; and it worked. The cool, dim room evoked decay and sadness. A slight musty smell tickled her nose as Dorinda instructed them to settle into the semi-circle of chairs onstage. They crossed the scuffed pine floors to join the other chattering guests. Beyond loomed the dark recesses of the wings of the theater.

A side door flew open, and several people jumped in their seats as a white-haired gentleman with a mustache burst through. "Good evening. I'm Richaud Castalane," he greeted in a stage voice with a hint of a French accent. He wore a scarlet cravat, a pop of color against the somber dark suit. "First, I'll assure you the establishment is structurally sound," he said, waving a hand around the room.

"Though, as you can see, the years have not been kind to the old girl. The Tangier was a premiere theater in the 1920s through the forties. Ownership changed numerous times, and the building wasn't attended to in the following decades." He walked toward the edge of the stage. "About thirty years ago, the management went bankrupt. The doors were shuttered and didn't reopen until we achieved permission to begin our tours here last year. That provided a period for the resident spirits to become entrenched."

Dorinda glided to his side. "We've found this a fertile location for our sessions. We're sure you look forward to the possibility of encountering the inhabitants tonight. If you'll please follow us—"

"Wait." Her husband lifted his chin and stared up at the ceiling. "Someone has carried a spirit with them."

Tess stifled a gasp. The room seemed to buzz with tension as their host scanned the group. He stopped at her and Trey. "Have you experienced psychic interactions?"

"We have," her voice quavered. She didn't dare look at Trey.

"Pray, tell us."

She hadn't expected to be put on the spot immediately. Rather, she had hoped to catch the couple for a private discussion. She peeked at Trey, and he nodded with a resigned expression. "Actually, four of us have seen visions that helped solve a century-old murder mystery."

Dorinda smiled. "Fascinating. I sense a woman." She stepped forward till their knees brushed. "She's similar to you in appearance."

"Yes. I'm wearing her brooch." She raised her hand to the V-neckline of her dress, not wanting to give away details. A true psychic would discover them herself.

Dorinda's eyes fluttered closed. "She's fond of you. She follows you, even though you've pleased her by solving the mystery of her untimely murder." Her lips quirked up. "She's 'living vicariously' through your romance since hers was cut short tragically." Her eyes flew open, and she grasped her hand with cool fingers. "Would you prefer she leave you?"

What did she prefer? Did she have a choice?

"I'm not threatened by her. I understand she means us no harm." Tess drew a deep breath. "Still, I very much want her to be at peace. She and her husband—who was wrongfully accused—should be able to be together now. Happily. We'd prefer all of the spirits leave us, including the other key players, Nick and Stephen." Oops, the names had slipped out.

She glanced at Jake for confirmation, but he stared straight ahead, hands fisted in his lap. "We'll always be thankful to be able to help them," she added. "We especially cherish that this situation brought Trey and me together, and it connected the rest of us."

Dorinda's eyes closed again, and she swayed in a gentle rhythm. Tess caught Marcy's open-mouthed expression. Justine sat forward in rapt attention, while even Jackson appeared to be caught up in the mystical moment. Trey edged closer to her and took her hands.

"Phoebe. Edward. You need to leave this dear couple," Dorinda commanded as her husband placed a supporting arm around her waist. "They have done you a great service, but you must find your peace in the light, together for eternity. Nick. Stephen. You are released, as well." She shuddered, her shoulders and arms quaking.

A stream of white mist curled up from the floor and hovered in front of them. Tess had a brief vision of Phoebe's smiling face. Warmth spread through her body as the haze dissipated up toward the lights. Excited comments erupted around the room.

"Did you see that?" Marcy whispered to their group. "I didn't imagine it?" She squeezed Jake's hand so hard he winced.

"I…think so," he muttered.

Justine's fair complexion had paled another degree. "Incredible."

Jackson sat frowning beside her. "Quite a parlor trick. Remember, folks, your story was all over the newspapers."

Marcy interrupted. "I only gave them my name when I made the reservation, Mr. Cynic."

Their musings were cut short when Richaud approached with a satisfied smile. "We'd like to debrief with you all after the tour. We keep meticulous notes on our cases." He turned to the rest of the participants.

"The remainder of the evening may prove anticlimactic after that interlude. Then again, perhaps the channel is clear and other resident spirits will be inspired to make an appearance. Follow us, and we'll tell you about them." He and Dorinda moved to the side door where he'd entered.

Jackson stood and stretched. "I'm not sure I want to meet any ghost actors. Live ones are challenging enough. But whether the exorcism was real or not, this added a great ending for your supernatural story. Would you guys be willing to sell me the film rights?" He grinned as Justine sent him a narrowed look from her cat-like green eyes.

Trey snorted. "On the condition a Hollywood hunk plays me."

The others tossed out names of actors to portray their own characters as they rejoined the tour group. Tess hung back with Trey. "Wasn't that wild? I think they're really gone. Time will tell I suppose." She rubbed her hand over the sharp facets of the brooch.

"Don't tell me you'll miss them," he teased.

"I might. Did you see anything? When the fog rose?"

He stared at her. "Yeah. A flash of Edward's face. He looked happy."

"She did, too." She rose on her tiptoes to kiss his cheek. "Love you."

"Love you more. And I'll gladly go the rest of our lives together without any more ghosts or visions."

They followed behind their friends, listening to the hosts' intriguing stories as they led through the dressing rooms and other dilapidated backstage areas. Yet no mysterious entities met the eager visitors. As they wrapped the tour in the lobby, Tess and Trey were surrounded by fellow participants asking about their encounters. They offered sparse details.

After the others filtered away, Dorinda stepped up. Her previous animation had drained away; she appeared wan and tired. "I'm sure you're anxious to leave and process what happened here. I need to do the same. Would you be open to speaking to us further about your experiences? We are enriched when we understand the full backstories."

"I imagine you also want to check back to see if they're really gone," Tess said. She shared her phone number as Trey stood with a tight smile. They walked out into the dark evening, and she took his hand. "You will talk to them, won't you?"

"If you promise to cook your homemade spaghetti sauce. Plus, a couple other yet-to-be-named favors." He chuckled and steered her toward their waiting friends.

She decided to let Jake process his own feelings before asking if she could share his piece of their story. She would never jeopardize his trust, or his stability. He'd already advanced into supervision at his job, and he had saved enough money to search for an apartment in Michigan City. He attended outpatient therapy to cope with the post-traumatic stress and assisted with a Narcotics Anonymous group at the thriving new Hope Resource Center.

After they'd all buckled into Jackson's vehicle, Marcy addressed Jake. "Now aren't you glad I convinced you to come? Their spirits are finally at peace, and you shouldn't see any more visions. Too bad we didn't do this at the press conference."

Jackson smirked at her in the rearview mirror. "I

doubt the reporters would have been as believing and gullible."

"Gullible." Justine swatted at his shoulder from the passenger seat. "Are you going to sit there and say you didn't see the cloud of steam, smoke, ectoplasm—whatever—waft up after Dorinda asked Phoebe and Edward to leave?"

"How do we know it wasn't a smoke pot planted under the stage, triggered at the perfect suspenseful moment?"

Tess spoke up from the back. "How do you explain the vapor floating right in front of us? Were they taking a stab in the dark that someone in the crowd was there because of their own psychic interactions? Plus, she said the apparition looked like me. And I didn't mention their names."

He sighed and pulled onto the street. "Too many questions without rational answers. This mumbo jumbo stretches my boundaries. You all seem to be sane individuals. Though there is the power of suggestion to consider, even with joint visions." He laughed. "To dig myself out of this hole, I'll just reinforce the story would make a heck of a screenplay."

Epilogue
June 2014

Tess shifted on one high heel to the other, waiting outside the ballroom for the pianist to begin the processional.

She clutched her father's arm and marveled how the months had flown in growing the business and planning for this big day. After a year in her new hometown, Divine Vintage remained in the black, her friendships with Marcy and Justine had flourished, and her love for Trey continued to deepen. He was her greatest supporter, the person she couldn't wait to share the rest of her life with. Phoebe, Edward, and their companions had disappeared after the theater outing. She missed the intrigue of pursuing the mystery, but she was thrilled their efforts had paid off. Her senses seemed to have heightened from the experience, as her flashes with clothing increased and intensified. Thankfully, they'd all been agreeable moments.

When she'd discovered her 1940s satin wedding gown at the local Goodwill store, she'd smelled a sugary-vanilla scent and seen a radiant brunette cutting the cake with her beaming groom. Tess had searched for the perfect dress for months, and the vision confirmed her decision. She loved the appliquéd roses decorating the sheer net overlay, and the full skirt sweeping out to a long train. Under her long veil, her updo featured interwoven strands of seed pearls. She carried a bouquet of peonies, clipped that morning from the bushes outside. The jazzy notes of *"At Last"* floated toward them. Her father appeared nervous but happy in his rented tux. "That's our cue, sweetheart."

She lifted the heavy skirt, accompanied by a rush of nerves. The good kind, driven by anticipation. *Don't cry*, she told herself and stepped through the doorway. Tess proceeded down the white runner and smiled at the dozens of well-wishers standing in her honor. The females had embraced her suggestion to dress in vintage finery, and some even wore hats. In the first row, her mother dabbed away tears, and she blew her a kiss. On the other side, Clarice and Esther beamed. Marcy and Justine waited before her in 1940s lace bridesmaid dresses. As rehearsed, her father kissed her on the cheek and sat with her mother. He was not "giving her away." She had freely, completely, given her heart.

And then there was only Trey, tall and handsome, in an immaculate black tuxedo. His probing gaze reminded her of locking eyes before the style show, when he was still a mysterious, compelling stranger. Their lives had meshed so suddenly and profoundly she had no doubt the hand of fate had intervened—with ghostly assistance. She continued the few steps alone as he smiled, just for her. Their fingers crept out to each other, the touch generating a faint sizzle of electricity. A little reminder from Edward and Phoebe? If so, she knew it represented support and blessing. She sent them a tiny prayer of thanks and wellbeing, inhaling the scent of the peonies as she handed them off to Marcy.

A word about the author…

Sandra L. Young's appreciation for vintage clothing inspired her to write her debut novel, Divine Vintage. She's gathered an impressive collection, wearing pieces onstage through years of performing in community theater. She also wears it out on the town for special occasions. To round out her love of the arts, Sandra sings with a trio, a praise band, and at karaoke nights. She draws from these experiences in her writing, as well as her work focus in communications and nonprofit management.

Questions for book club discussion:

After Tess's vision at the end of the style show, the ladies immediately believe her, while Trey is a skeptic. If this happened to you in "real life," what court would you fall into, and why?

If you had "empathetic" reactions to something, similar to Tess with vintage clothing, what would be your trigger and what would you envision?

Phoebe's diary depicts her as a rather mischievous, forthright person in an era when many women were demure. Did you question her choice to pursue a relationship with the more-solemn Edward rather than Stephen or Nick?

Tess displays a social justice leaning when she champions the homeless resource center. Do you admire her for taking a stand, or do you feel as a new business owner she should have kept quiet?

Do you understand why Jake didn't contact his family for two years? Did this color your impression of his character?

Marcy is a creative, free spirit, yet she hasn't chased her own dreams in order to help her mother. What do you think of that decision?

Tess states early on that her former boyfriend's demeaning comments damaged her confidence. How did you see that playing out through the course of the story?

After Trey apologized and he and Tess reconnected, were you surprised that he proposed in Paris?

How did you feel when Tess lured Brett to join them at the mansion without being upfront about the reason?

After the "exorcism" at the theater, did you believe the psychic link would disappear?

Thank you for purchasing
this publication of The Wild Rose Press, Inc.

For questions or more information
contact us at
info@thewildrosepress.com.

The Wild Rose Press, Inc.
www.thewildrosepress.com